Until
The Death
Of Me

BRICKHOUSE

DEDICATION

To my mama, Debra Fisher, thank you so much for being my biggest supporter. It means the world to me that you go so hard for me since I've started this journey. Love you forever. I hope to make you proud!

ACKNOWLEDGMENTS

Father God, I thank you for this gift. My prayer is the same for each book; you strengthen me to write. Blow on my talent and transform it into what you desire it to be.

To my children. I believe Gabriel's exact words were, "Make sure they know this was all possible because of my love and support." LOL! Erika, I can't wait until you finish your book, baby girl! Quan can't wait until the world sees you shine!

ASHA

I was exhausted as I dragged through the front door of my apartment.

Chipped cabinet doors, rust-stained sinks, and a good for nothing baby daddy greeted me at the door like sour garbage.

Fairgrounds Valley, or the F.G.'s, was what most people called our projects. Others referred to them merely as "The Grounds."

Brian was sitting at the kitchen table, drinking a Steel Reserve 211 beer.

My stomach dropped because he was like a lunatic who couldn't control his temper when he drank.

Brian had a problem with his hands, and I wasn't in the mood to fight today. I've been arguing with racist white people and ghetto black people at Target.

"Hey," I said emptily as I made my way upstairs.

"Why you ain't leave the money I told you I needed?" He asked, hounding me upstairs to our bedroom.

"Brian, I told you that I didn't have it when you asked me for it the other day," I explained, taking off of my red Target shirt.

"What I tell you about trying to hide money from me? You ain't gone do nothing but eat it up. Look at you, just let yourself go after the kids," he spat in disgust.

WAP!

WAP!

WAP!

"Brian, I wasn't trying to hide money. I need to give Shanti gas money for a ride to work!"

My palms were wrapped around my bloody nose.

I could feel my lip swelling to match.

Smack!

The slap to my face burned my full cheeks. The hot tears stung as they poured out of my eyes. I never knew from day to day when Brian would unleash his fury on me.

He was riddled with insecurities that plagued him and caused him to terrorize me.

Clothes were tossed everywhere until he found the money that I hid inside my dresser drawer. I'm shocked he didn't do this while I was at work. I'm sure he wanted the pleasure of humiliating me.

My rent was reasonable, so I only had to worry about my gas and light bill.

In Illinois, they couldn't cut your gas or

electricity off during the Winter.

You better believe that they send out disconnection notices and cut people off as soon as the weather break. The LIHEAP line be super long with people trying to get their bill paid.

I didn't have time for that type of foolery so I just paid my little bills on time.

Brian stole most of the money when he wasn't straight up taking it.

He complained that no one would hire him because of his felony record, but he was just lazy as all get out in all actuality.

"Lying tramp," he mumbled as he slammed the door on his way out.

Brian had a weed habit, although he acted like a crack head. My mom was on crack for years, and he displayed the same signs she did when she was tweaking.

The conversation my homegirl Uneek and I had a week ago replayed in my head.

"He smoking more than some weed. Think about it. He disappears for days at a time, he's losing weight, and he rarely eats. You cook them big ass meals, and he can't even eat them most days. He a hype. Straight up," she presented her case.

"Girl, that boy just doing weed. I would know if he was doing something more than that," I attempted to sound confident.

"Chile, I guess," was Uneek's only response to what I said.

I curled up in the fetal position in bed on my worn, dented mattress. The rusty springs were popping through, cutting my side.

Brian had broken me down over the years, both mentally and physically.

I cried and cried as I prayed for the courage to put his triflin' butt out.

Brian was the father of my daughter Amor and my son Romello. We met in the club one night, smashed, and the next thing I knew, he was leaving clothes at my apartment.

It was an efficiency apartment, but it was mine.

Once Justin, my brother, left for the military, I was finally able to work on myself. I got a job at McDonald's and got me a place to stay.

Before that, I was staying wherever I could.

With Brian not working when I got pregnant with Amor, I ended up moving back to the same projects I clawed my way out of. I was stuck there raising yet another generation of my family.

With each child, I seemed to gain more and more weight. Trying to work and take care of them caused me to let myself go slightly.

I carried it nicely though, despite how Brian nagged.

Brian was continually drilling into my head that, "Nobody wants your sloppy self but me. Everybody wants them a bad chick built like girls off Love and Hip Hop or some. Yo' ass lucky I'm still here, real talk!"

I couldn't believe he was comparing me to one of them low-budget chicks off of reality T.V.

The more he sprayed his poisonous words like acid, the more I believed him. The more I believed him, the more I ate. It was my go-to in order to feel better.

I scrambled to pull myself together before my mom dropped my kids off. I had just got off work so it took all the strength I had.

I didn't have it in me to keep fighting him every other day.

I took off my khakis and draped them across the chair in the corner of my room. I was glad I had taken my shirt off before Brian bust my nose.

I was tired of hiding my bruises with concealer from my family and co-workers. Every time I put him out, he would wait until he knew I was lonely and come back.

My feet scuffled against the peeling linoleum floors as I made my way to the bathroom. I jumped in the shower to wash this day off of me. I prayed that I would dissolve into the water like a Lush bath bomb to escape my reality.

I was shaken from my hidden pain and desires by my back-door opening.

"Who's that?" I yelled, peeking from behind the shower curtain.

"It's me, mama!" Amor yelled from the bottom of the stairs.

"Okay, love bug. I will be out in a second," I called back to her.

Amor was only seven, but that girl was so smart. She had proven to be so responsible that I gave her a house key on a purple neck chain. It was her favorite color.

Amor made all my bad days fade away with her smile.

I hurried out of the shower, dried off, and got dressed.

I pulled my B.H. Cosmetics concealer pallet from under the cabinet. I quickly blended it into my skin and prayed my mama wouldn't notice.

My mom had now been clean for ten years and I was so proud of her.

I had to raise my brother Justin who was now serving in the Marine Corps. As soon as he turned eighteen, I got him up out of here. I would not allow the streets of Rockford to take my brother like I've watched them take so many other young lives. I was sick and tired of it.

I now needed to figure out how to get my kids and me up out of these projects.

"Hey, mama," I said, trying to sound upbeat.

My mom was a praying woman and she managed to always see through me without saying much.

"Hey, baby. How was work?" She asked, leaning in for a hug.

"Same ole' same," I said, grabbing Romello from his car seat.

"You okay, baby?" She asked. "You seem sad. You and that boy been fighting again?"

"His name Brian mama. You know his name," I said, rolling my eyes.

"Girl, don't be rolling your eyes at me. Life too short to be this miserable baby. You need to be present mind, body, and soul for your kids."

"I am. It was just a long day at work. Please don't start lecturing me, mama. I don't have it in me to defend myself today," I slumped as sorrow closed up my throat.

"Sit down, baby," she motioned me to join her at the kitchen table. She pushed Brian's almost empty beer can to the side.

"Amor, take Mello and put him in his swing, baby. Grab your *Mega Mind* DVD so y'all can watch it until I'm done talking to granny," I instructed her.

"Okay, mama," she replied, taking her brother from me and holding him with both arms while she made her way into the living room.

"Yes, mama?" I said, turning to her.

"I appreciate how you took care of Justin when I was out here in these streets doing God knows what. It was unfair of me to put that type of pressure on you at such a young age. I'm thankful that you bore the weight that wasn't yours when I needed you. When your brother needed you. Now it's my turn to be there for you. Anything you need, baby. Anything! You let me know. I can't tell you how to live your life and who to love, but you gotta love yourself first baby girl. You can't love anybody if you don't love yourself first. You will let a person put you through hell because you don't know your worth. Now, I'm here to help you find your way. Be it going back to school or getting a better job; mama got your back! Okay?"

Tears ran down my eyes as my heart dropped to the pit of my stomach. My throat clenched with despair at the thought of changing my life. I wanted more, but I was scared to fail. Scared to let my kids down. All in all… I was terrified of hope.

"Thank you, mama. I'm gone get it together," I leaned in to plant a kiss on her cheek.

I prayed she didn't see the bruises that were possibly revealed by my tears. If she did, she didn't say anything as she gathered her purse and keys to head out.

"Bye, Granny babies!" She yelled as I walked her

outside to her car.

Lately, there had been some new faces in our section of the projects. They would back in with their trucks and cars blasting their music until the Metro's would come around and make them turn it down.

Metro's were rent-a-cops who had the authority to detain you until the cops came. They did too much not to have actual guns.

One of the new faces, in particular, caught my eye because he always stared at me. He had a weird mohawk tapered fade he wore. Other than that, I paid them no mind.

None of them were disrespectful, but you never know when something would jump off around here.

"Alright mama, call me when you make it home safe," I told her closing her door.

I made my way back inside with my kids.

I doubt that Brian would be home anytime soon. He has been cheating for a minute but I didn't care. I hated sleeping with him. I was just something to do when his side chicks acted up on him.

He made me so self-conscious I never could enjoy myself when we were intimate.

Romello was asleep when I made it back in. I carefully removed him from the swing and took him to his crib upstairs. His room was decorated in all Ninja Turtles themed décor.

I took pride in taking care of my children. I went without if I had to so they could have what they needed and most of what they wanted.

My mom always bathed them before she brought them home. He smelled of Baby Magic lotion as I nestled my face into his neck.

I laid Romello down and kissed his chunky face over and over until he fought me off in his sleep. He was almost one, and I wanted him to stay my baby forever.

My mom said, "Enjoy him at this age because right now, he rests in your lap, but when he gets older, he will rest on your heart."

I closed the door behind me as I headed back downstairs.

I curled up on the couch with Amor, and we finished her favorite movie until we both drifted off to sleep.

We both were abruptly awakened by Brian's, who was drunk stumbling through the door. He slammed that heavy metal door all of these apartments were equipped with. The sound startled Amor, so she woke up crying out of fear more so than the noise.

"Shut up with that damn hollerin'!" He yelled to Amor, who only cried more.

He went to grab her and mama bear came out.

I grabbed the candle holder near the T.V. stand

and bashed him upside his head. Before he could recover, I grabbed my phone and called 9-1-1.

"You snitching trick! You really called the police on me?" He yelled, staggering to his feet.

I watched the blood seep from the gash in his head down his forehead.

"Sure, the fuck did! I told you, you can come for me but don't come for my kids! Ever! I suggest you get yo' black ass out of here before the Metro's come and hold your ass until the police get here. You know ya' banned from over here anyway nigga," I yelled.

He staggered out of the front door and I locked the top lock on him. I peeked out of the crooked blinds to make sure he was gone.

I hurried over to Amor and cradled her in my arms to calm her.

Once she had calmed down, I took her upstairs to her room. Her room was draped in purple and gold. It looked like that of a princess back during the early Medieval times. You would think it was a young adult's room by the looks of it. I tucked her in and turned on her nightlight. On the nights when Brian and I fought, she liked it on.

As I was walking out, Amor called out to me.

"Mommy."

"Yes, baby," I turned around to face her.

"Can daddy live somewhere else?"

"Yes, baby. I think that is a good idea just for a little while. Is that okay with you, love bug?"

"Yes, mommy," she said, turning over.

She was so mature for her age. I refused to put her through what I went through growing up.

I watched different niggas in and out of our house. Some of them dared to put their hands on my mom.

Justin and I got tired of trying to pull them off of her, but we did. We loved our mom to the death of us.

Pretty soon, she stopped coming home for weeks at a time.

I made sure to hold on to the Link card to make sure we were able to eat.

I hated supporting her habit, but I sold some from time to time so she would have cash. I just hated the thought of what my mama was out there doing to get a fix.

I tossed and turned all night. I finally went downstairs to sleep on the couch. The last thing I wanted was Brian coming in while I was sleep trying to jump on me.

* * *

I awoke Saturday morning to some kids running around outside.

These bad kids were up at the crack of dawn running around the projects. I know they mama's let them just to get some peace of mind. I couldn't really blame them.

I rubbed my neck, trying to massage out the stiffness from sleeping on this lumpy couch all week.

I made my way upstairs to wash my face and brush my teeth. I needed to get myself together so I could fix the kids breakfast.

I tried to be as quiet as possible so that I wouldn't wake the kids prematurely.

I tiptoed back down the stairs to start the bacon, eggs, oatmeal, and fresh fruit. I popped the bacon in the oven because I hated how the grease pops when you fry it. I simultaneously stirred the oatmeal and scrambled the eggs. I placed everything on the kiddie plates and smiled.

I took pride in everything I did for my children. They were my everything. I set the table for them.

The way it looked, you would've thought we were vacationing at a resort instead of living in the projects.

I went upstairs to wake my babies. I enjoyed the weekends because most times I was off. It allowed me time to be in full mommy duty. I loved everything about being a mother.

"Amor...Romello...," I called out to them softly.

I could see Romello pop his head up when he heard my voice through the crack in his bedroom door. I could tell from his energy level that he had been awake but was just lying there. Romello has always been a laid-back baby. He was jolly and didn't mind playing with himself if Amor was at school.

"Heyyyyy mama Lil' man," I sang to him.

He pulled himself up on the crib and started jumping up and down, slinging spit while he laughed and danced.

I picked him up and went over to Amor, who had pulled her blanket over her head. She was not a morning person, and it was always a fight with her to get up. God forbid I woke her up the wrong way. Her lil' butt would have an attitude all day.

"Amor, my love…get up. I cooked your favorite foods for breakfast," I bribed her.

"You cooked bacon for me?" She asked, peeking from under the covers.

"I sure did," I replied.

"What about my fruit, mommy?" She quizzed.

"I got you, boo. All that is waiting downstairs," I told her.

With the confirmation, she leaped from under the covers and bolted down the wooden stairs.

I was relieved as I checked her bed. The constant abuse from Brian caused Amor to wet the bed sometimes. It was taking a toll on my princess. My heart crumbled at the assessment of my daughter's distress.

"Yes!" I heard her yell, pulling her chair out, shaking me from my thoughts.

I placed Romello in his high chair and we all sat down to enjoy breakfast.

Breakfast was amusing as always. Romello played with his food, and Amor and I recited her sight words for the week.

Amor attended school, but I implemented homeschool tools and methods for additional learning.

The classes are so packed now that teachers spend more time disciplining the student than they have time to teach.

I commend them. Not only do they have to deal with bad kids, but also, they had to wonder if one had a gun in their backpack. Many of them pay out of pocket for any incentives or learning tools for the kids with no reimbursement on the back end.

I am a mother that has chosen to be fully involved in my children's education.

I needed to come up with a plan soon to get us up out of here. I needed to face my fears of failure head-on.

After breakfast, I washed the kids up and did

Amor's hair. She wore it natural. I was teaching her to embrace her authentic beauty. I taught her that her kinks and full lips were beautiful and coveted in this world we live in. I taught Amor to be unapologetically her.

While Amor read, Romello beat on his keyboard.

I stood at my bedroom door and exhaled. All the horrible memories between Brian and I played before my eyes like a Tyler Perry movie. I was tired and I was done.

My feet shuffled across the bedroom floor as I made my way over to the closet.

I began to toss all of Brian's stuff in a basket as fast as I could. A bittersweet smile spread across my face. I was glad that I had finally ushered up the strength to put his sorry butt out.

"*Sorry son of a bi-,*" I mumbled to myself as I gathered the rest of his things. I forced down a sick feeling when I thought about the way I allowed Brian to treat me.

I made a promise to myself on this day to never allow a man to treat me less than what I deserve.

Hope percolated in my heart as I envisioned myself in the future.

I see myself happy and loving life. I see my kids and me thriving.

Happiness flowed through me like a B-12 injection giving me the boost I so desperately needed.

As I closed the door on this chapter of my life, I had made up my mind that I would make every challenge I faced bow down!

I moved all of Brian's things to the downstairs closet under the stairs. I hadn't heard from him in over a week and I wasn't complaining in the least.

It was Saturday and the kids and I did our routine. I decided to switch it up a bit and walk them across the bridge to the park.

Romello could walk but not as fast, so I just carried him. We made our way across the raggedy bridge that led to the park.

While the kids played, I sat on the park bench on my tablet, looking into the CNA program at Rock Valley College.

I glanced back and forth between the kids and the screen as I took notes.

"I needed to get a physical, a T.B. 2-Step, and a flu shot. That's it?" I thought to myself.

I reviewed the upcoming schedule. It was summertime so I could do the certification in 8-weeks. The more I researched, the more excited I got.

It would be my first try at completing something outside of my high school diploma.

I didn't notice I was jittering my foot against the

dried-up grass until my tablet slid a bit. I was so geeked!

"You got this, Asha! Do it for you and your kids," I coached myself.

I was so caught up in planning for my new future I didn't notice the sun was going down. I didn't want to be walking across that bridge after dark with my kids.

I gathered them up and we headed across the bridge.

Once we arrived at our apartment parking lot, I noticed the group of guys out again. The one with the mohawk watched me as I passed with my kids.

I just mugged him and kept walking. I wasn't in the mood for any more hood ninjas.

Amor ran ahead of me, clutching her house key around her neck. She loved being the one to open the door with her key; having responsibilities made her feel extra important.

As she approached the doors, I saw the door yank open, and Brian standing in the doorway.

My nails clawed into my palms at that sight of him in my door. I knew it would only be a matter of time before he showed back up.

I pushed past him as he tried to apologize. I took the kids upstairs to their rooms because I was anticipating everything escalating. I wasn't backing down this time.

"Amor, no matter what you hear, don't come out of the room. Okay?" She nodded her head as tears filled her eyes. She was terrified.

"Amor, this won't happen again. I promise. Daddy is going to live with someone else after today," I assured her.

I picked up her headphones and put them on her so she could listen to her YouTube videos.

Romello was pretty much exhausted from the park and was already drifting off to sleep in his crib.

I shut their doors. As I stepped on the other side of their door, I leaned against their door and exhaled.

"Lord, help me," I prayed silently.

So much rage was bottled up inside me that it caused my blood to boil.

I marched downstairs to pull Brian's things out.

"Get your stuff and get out of my damn house," I yelled, holding the door open for him to get out.

I felt like Bernice on *Waiting to Exhale*.

"So, you done? Just tell me you done!" He spat.

"I'm done! Get out of my apartment!"

"I saw you trying to put on a show walking by all them niggas outside too. Just thirsty for attention," he said, balling up his fist.

"Why you worried? I thought nobody wanted my fat self anyway. Ain't that's what you always tell me?" I shot back, propping my hands on my hips.

"Oh, you want to put on a show, huh?" He charged at me.

We exchanged blows before I finally ended up bent over with him fisting a hand full of my hair.

I grappled with him as he dragged me outside. It was dusk and Saturday, so everyone was out kicking it.

Someone's car was blasting Yo Gotti's *Rake It Up* through their sound system.

I could hear people yelling, "What the hell?" As we wrestled.

I wore my hair natural and he had a death grip on it.

Boiling with fury, I ground my teeth and clenched my jaw so tight, it hurt.

I noticed through my tears that people had pulled out their camera phones and started yelling, "World Star! World Star!"

Anger flushed through my cheeks as my stomach rolled into knots.

I was winded from trying to fight Brian back and break free.

It was discouraging that we now lived in a world where people would rather film your demise and destruction instead of helping you.

My face burned with humiliation as he dragged me out of the parking lot.

I just wanted to disappear.

Suddenly, I heard someone yell, "Hey, nigga let her go!"

"This ain't got nothing to do with you, Prod!" Brian yelled back.

I was still struggling to break free.

"Aye, y'all put them cameras away. Right now!" He commanded.

"Nigga, I ain't gone say it no more," the man whose name I just learned to be Prod was laying down the law.

Brian reluctantly freed me.

Smack!

My right hand landed on the left side of Brian's face.

I attempted to regain some of my dignity out in the project parking lot.

Brian pulled back to punch me but Prod moved closer, raising the front of his shirt, revealing two Nina's (9-millimeter handguns) tucked inside his pants.

Brian raised his hands in surrender as he backed away from me.

"Aye man, it's cool. Let me just get my stuff and I'll leave," Brian pleaded.

I've never in all my years of knowing Brian seen him back down from a fight.

It was one of the things in my childish years that attracted me to him. The fact that he had hands and feared no one.

I guess there was a first time for everything.

Brian made his way to the apartment as Prod and I followed behind him.

I stood by the stove as Brian dragged his garbage bag and basket full of clothes.

"Aye, Izaak. Come here for a sec," Prod yelled out to one of the guys who wasn't too far from my door.

I noticed he had moved closer to my apartment when Prod came in.

I'm not sure if he was his security guard or friend. Whatever he was to Prod, you could tell he was loyal.

"Wassup, bro?" He said, peeking inside my door.

I really couldn't say anything because Brian had

made this a damn public matter.

"Help this nigga get his stuff up out of here," he told him.

"Aight," was his only response as he grabbed one of Brian's baskets.

"I need my house key," I told Brian holding out my hands.

A tiny twitch in his lips revealed that I had hit the mark.

Brian pulled out his keys and slammed them in my hand. I could see him quivering from indignation as he brushed by me.

I was thankful for Prods help, but I wanted everyone out of my house so I could check on my babies.

I could hear Brian speed out of the parking lot. He wouldn't even bother to take me to work in that raggedy Buick.

Prod watched him through my screen door until Brian was out of the parking lot.

Turning to me, he said, "That's the father of your kids?"

Father of my kids. I thought to myself.

"Yes," I finally responded.

I wasn't in the mood to talk. Since he had been

nice enough to intervene when Brian was beating me, I decided the least I could do is be polite.

"Are you going to be okay? I'm going to make sure he doesn't come back anytime soon. You're not going to let him come back, are you?" He questioned.

"Look, I appreciate your help out there. Thank you for real, for real, but you are doing a lot right now," I snapped.

"Ms. Lady, I'm not trying to be in your business. I just want you and your kids safe. Can I at least know your name?" He asked politely.

"Asha," I told him, clearly irritated.

"Do you know the origin of your name?" He asked.

"Look, I really need to check on my kids. Again, thank you for your help tonight."

"Alright, Ms. Asha. I will see you around," Prod said. "Make sure you lock up," he left like he was leaving for work and wanted to make sure the kids and I were safe while he was away.

"Goodnight Prod," I said.

"It's Prodigy. People who are familiar with me call me Prod. You don't know me...yet," he swaggered out the door.

I exhaled and was just glad it was over. I bolted upstairs to check on my babies.

Romello was still knocked out but Amor was still staring at her tablet.

She was acting like she was still watching but I saw the tears falling from her eyes.

I sat next to her and took the tablet from her gently. I placed it on her nightstand and picked her up. I cradled her in her arms as she attempted to wipe her tears away.

My heart was breaking as I held my baby.

"Mommy is okay, baby. Are you okay?"

I smothered her face with soft kisses on her forehead.

"I thought daddy was going to kill you!" She yelled, bursting into tears.

Sorrow closed up my throat as my baby confessed her fears to me.

I rocked her back and forth as we both cried. "Daddy will never hurt us ever again. Okay?" I promised her.

"Okay, mommy," she whimpered.

"You know what? Let's go downstairs and watch a movie, eat snacks and cuddle!" I tried to sound upbeat.

"Yes!" She said, smiling through her tears that were slowly drying up.

I picked her up and carried her downstairs.

Keeping to my promise, I laid out a smorgasbord of snacks for us both. I pulled our favorite throw blanket from behind the couch after I popped in the movie.

It seemed as if Amor's fears had instantly faded away. I prayed that the emotional scars would disappear just as quickly.

PRODIGY

I was chopping it up with Izaak when I noticed that nigga Brian dragging his girl out the house. We turned the music down so we could hear what was going on.

His ole' lady stayed in the house most of the time. She wasn't like all these other chicks out there trying to get attention and what have you.

She caught my eye because of the way she carried herself. She didn't have hair all weaved down her back but she wore her own. Not everybody can do that trend but she was pulling it off.

I low-key loved the fact that she wasn't skin and bones. Nah, she had curves in all the right places. To be honest, she reminded me of a curvy Taraji P. Henson down to that pretty smile she rarely showed. You wouldn't be able to tell by her face that she was stacked like a brick house.

I ran the streets of Rockford for the most part, so it was my job to notice everything and everybody.

I wouldn't have customarily injected myself into some domestic type situation, but it was something about shawty that caught my eye.

I'm not your typical street nigga in any sense of the stereotype. My government name is Prodigy Le Savage.

People around the hood call me Prod or P for short. You know black folks always got to cut your name short.

My father named me Prodigy because I was endowed with exceptional qualities from the time I exited my mother's womb.

None of which mesmerized my mother long enough to stick around and raise her only son.

I attended Northern Illinois University (NIU), majoring in Business Management. Halfway through my bachelor's program, my father went to the penitentiary.

He had the respect of the streets so there was little resistance when I returned to oversee my father's legacy.

My father never had any more kids that I was aware of but the streets talked.

You would think being abandoned by my mother would make me this hard-core nigga who disrespected women.

I was actually the opposite. I treated women as queens for the most part. Some of them are out of line though. They can't take a nigga respecting them.

It blew me away at the number of females I came across that thought because a nigga beat her that he loved her! I leave them types alone.

I'm not exchanging my freedom for a chick that doesn't know how to love herself.

Once I made sure Asha was straight, Izaak and I headed to Larry's to grab some Patron.

"Look at this nigga," Izaak said as we pulled up. I looked over to my right and Brian was standing up there talking with some niggas from Lap Court.

"Yea, if Prod wasn't with all them niggas I would've beat him down!" I heard him saying.

I'm usually not a confrontational person for the most part, but I needed to maintain my honor in the streets. If any of these niggas smelt weakness, they would go in for the kill.

I didn't like this Brian so I planned on beating him like a Mexican piñata.

"Nigga, I don't need my squad to handle you my nigga!" I spat at Brian. "I guarantee you won't try and do me like you did yo' ole' lady," I walked up on him.

"Prod, I ain't mean-"

Before he could get his words out, my right fist ran into his mouth quicker than a thot running into the club for the free before eleven.

31

"Nigga forget all of that talkin'."

WAP!

WAP!

Brian got him two in after he recovered from the stumble from the effect of my blow to his mouth. A smile spread across my face. I loved to fight even though I wasn't out here starting fights, but I was known for finishing them…and quick!

I punished his body and face with blow after blow.

I noticed Izaak from the corner of my eye standing with his finger on the trigger of his burner just in case these niggas got any ideas.

My hands stung from Brian's teeth cutting my knuckles from the initial hit that jumped this off.

Brian finally collapsed to the ground, barely coherent to his surroundings or to what was going on.

"Nigga, I bet not catch you back at Asha's house either or I'm going to break you down again, but the next time I ain't having no mercy on ya'."

Brian had hatred in his eyes and fury in his veins but that nigga had enough. He nodded his head in understanding, and the same clowns he was kicking it with now was laughing at him.

"And keep my name out of yo' mouth! As a matter of fact, if anybody tells me you spoke on me, I don't care if they are lyin' it's a wrap for you."

I stepped over him and went into the store. I wasn't worried about the cops because people knew better than to snitch.

"My friend, why you beating him up in front of my store?" The Arab that ran the store asked.

Abdul swore he was black. I mess with him the long way though.

"Man, my bad, but you know how these niggas are," I laughed while shaking it up with him.

"What you drinking today?"

"You know I only drink one thing, Abdul."

He nodded in understanding and headed to the refrigerator to retrieve me a cold fifth of Patron.

He rang me up and I paid for our stuff.

"Abdul, you still be freakin' those girls in the back?" I asked, taking my bag from the countertop laughing.

"Friend, I don't know what you are talking about," his face was just as twisted as his lies.

"I bet you don't," I said, walking out of the store.

Brian had disappeared by the time we came out of the store. He knew better than to try me.

"So, what's the move for the night?" Izaak asked.

"I'm going to the crib and play my PS4. What's good?"

"Nigga, you act like a senior citizen. Let's go to Central Tap and play some pool."

"Might as well," I told him.

Izaak and I were more like brothers than best friends. My father practically brought up together in Fairgrounds. He looked out for his mom too.

Once Izaak started hustling, he bought his mom a house and moved her out of the projects. He still lived down there because that was all that nigga knew. I wasn't sure if he would ever move regardless of how much money he made.

Izaak's baby mama was just as hood as he was. She stayed firing him up with her ghetto self. That girl stayed clowning him like that nigga wasn't going to do him regardless.

It was downright comical. She was stressing him out too. He has one son and it's with her.

"You let Camille know you were leaving out the projects nigga?" I teased.

"I'm a grown man. I do what I want to d-"

Before his lies could roll off his lips good, Camille started calling his phone. I couldn't hold my laugh in.

"Put her on speaker bro," I told him.

I just wanted to laugh some more.

"Man," he mumbled, smacking his lips.

He still did it.

"So, you just gone leave and not say anything? I walked down there and y'all were gone. Where we do that at? You just up and leave without saying anything, huh? I guess that's what we doing now, right?" She snapped.

"Man, chill out Camille! I'm coming right back. I just ran to Larry's."

"Nigga, y'all been gone forty-five minutes! Stop lying!" She yelled.

"Cam, chill out before you make me choke you out when I get back. A nigga just going to Central Tap to play pool and coming back."

"Don't bother coming back nigga. Stay out with one of them raggedy, dirty tramps you love pickin' up and bustin' down!"

She hung up on him so quickly he didn't have time to respond. Camille always did that. I didn't understand why she was trippin'; they both were whoremongering.

"Man, this why I can't stop smoking bro," he yelled, flaming up his blunt to calm his nerves.

"Well, you're the one who got her pregnant. I told you not to do that, but you kept talking about how good the coochie was and that you were gone put a baby in her sooo...," I teased.

"Man, nigga shut up. It's fire," he laughed.

We pulled into Central Tap and it was a pretty nice crowd. Izaak and I made our way to the pool table after we ordered a few shots and beers. We took turns on the table and chopped it up with some of our people in the back.

A group of girls came and sat at the table near us. They were dancing and laughing, putting on a show to get our attention.

We stood out so this wasn't unexpected.

A slim, thick chocolate girl with a thirty-inch weave down her back was the ringleader. She had her eyes set on Izaak and I was relieved.

I wasn't one to randomly slang pipe all around Rockford so I stayed curving females. They see the car and jewelry and immediately thought I was a come up.

"I got next," the ringleader said, placing her quarter on the pool table.

"You probably can't even play shawty," Izaak said, flirting with her.

"You wanna bet something?" She asked.

"What do you have that I want miss lady?" He asked her.

She seductively walked over to him and whispered in his ear. Even though the music was playing, I could hear her proposal. She wasn't much of a whisperer; I guess we could blame it on the liquor.

"If you win, you can take me in the bathroom and do what you want to me," is what she said to him.

"And if you win?" He laughed.

"You still get to take me in the bathroom and do what you want to do to me," she moaned.

"Well, why waste time playing games? We grown so let's get this cracking love," he proposed.

I just stood back, minding my business. Camille could run-up in here at any given moment.

She tried to laugh it off because her girls were now listening.

"Unless you are just selling dreams," Izaak taunted her.

I kept playing my pool game, ignoring them now that I got the just of what was going on.

Izaak and the young lady retreated to a table in a dark corner where they made small talk.

It wasn't even ten minutes before I noticed Izaak with his hands under shawty skirt. She had her head slightly tilted, trying to hide her pleasure, but her face didn't lie.

Izaak got up, straightening his pants, and headed to the bathroom. The girl who so freely given her body to him followed shortly after.

I don't know what he was doing to ole' girl, but you could hear her over the music.

I saw one of her girl's race to the small, outdated bathroom near where we were located.

I didn't know how they were able to get down back there in the first place. Both the men's and women's bathrooms had two small stalls with dim lighting and doors that didn't lock.

"Girl, you loud! Shut up before the manager come in here," we could hear her scolding her friend.

As she walked out of the bathroom, I nearly choked on my beer.

"*Shoot!*" I cursed to myself.

Camille walked into the bar as soon as the other girl came out of the bathroom. There was no way I could make it in time to warn Izaak because Camille had already seen me.

"Where he at P?" She demanded, securing her hand on her hips and shifting her weight to one side.

"Man, I ain't that nigga keeper," I retorted, hitting my solid green ball in the corner pocket.

"Y'all be glued to each other hip, now all of a sudden you don't know where he at? He left with some skank, didn't he?" She quizzed me, slamming her hand on the side of the pool table.

"That man grown-"

"Bump all that!" She interrupted.

I noticed her eyes cut to the left of me and tighten. I had no idea what she was looking at, so I turned around to see.

This nigga left his Versace glasses on the table. I don't even know why he wore those things because it was dark outside. These were no plain glasses either. They were one of a kind with all that gold trimming and a big Versace logo on each side.

Camille scanned the room and didn't see him. Before I could stop her, she headed toward the bathroom.

I noticed the squad of girls stand and make their way towards the bathroom. I stood in their way.

"Ain't gone be no jumpin'."

They smacked their lips and attempted to walk past me until I flashed my banger.

Before I could get my shirt down I heard multiple screams. The whole bar got quiet.

"Aaarrggghhh!" I heard the girl yell.

Camille had clearly gotten a hold of her.

This was confirmed when I saw Camille dragging the half-naked girl from the bathroom by the thirty inches of hair she was just slanging moments prior.

Izaak came stumbling out, fixing his pants with scratches on his face.

Apparently, Camille got to him first.

Camille was sitting on top of the girl pounding the side of her face.

"Trick, what I do to my baby daddy ain't got

nothin' to do with you! If I want to beat him up buzzard, you move to the side and pray you don't catch this fade. Now I gotta teach you a lesson about freakin' in nasty bathrooms with random niggas."

The girl's friends attempted to run up and snatch Camille off of their friend.

Izaak and I stepped to them. I didn't hit females, but Izaak will beat a female up without hesitation. His hands were bi-sexual. Men and women were allowed to get them equally.

WAP!

WAP!

WAP!

Camille exploded blows into the girl's skull. From earlier, the beautiful chocolate girl looked totally different with patches of her weave and edges pulled out by Camille.

Her face was decorated with blood, scratches, and gouges from Camille's engagement ring.

"Get off me! I can't breathe!"

"If you screaming, you breathing dummy!"

WAP!

WAP!

WAP!

Izaak finally dragged Camille off of the battered girl.

I noticed her friends coming to her rescue out of the corner of my eyes. I made my way to the bar to drop the owner a wad of cash for the inconvenience. It was also a thank you for not calling the cops.

By the time I got outside, Izaak and Camille were still arguing.

"I should've left you when you screwed that bald-headed bust down on a dirty mattress that sat on the floor. She and her baby were dirty as hell, and you were dropping off beefcake in that filthy apartment," Cam yelled at the top of her lungs.

People had gathered outside to finish watching the show she put on.

Everyone on the West knew Cam wasn't leaving Izaak.

Izaak managed to wrestle her in the car. I walked up to the driver's side and handed him his glasses.

"Aight, bro. Hit me tomorrow," I told him, shaking up with him before heading to my truck.

My Range Rover Sport was my baby. I jumped inside to head home to do what I initially wanted to do…play my game and chill.

I learned a long time ago there was nothing in these streets but a bunch of hating niggas and desperate females. Both were looking for a come up.

Just because I and my father's name rang bells in the streets didn't mean niggas wasn't looking to take our throne and end our legacy.

I hated constantly looking over my shoulders, which was why I was slowly shifting everything over to Izaak. He loved this street chaos.

My dad was locked up, but we still kept him in the loop on what was going on with the business.

I personally just wanted to operate the barbershop I owned on North Main. The shop was my baby and was how I put my business degree to work. I provided the full experience in my shop.

It was respectable and the atmosphere was comfortable enough for mothers who brought their sons in not to be harassed by men while they waited.

My staff and I offered back to school haircuts to underprivileged boys and college students in our area. We also provide free haircuts to veterans and the homeless.

I've always loved to help those in the hood understand there was something better than slanging dope. I was actually tired of feeling like a hypocrite.

Pumping drugs into the same community I helped.

I was drafted into this when my dad was locked up for a triple homicide. He found out three of his associates were informants so he executed them. One was wearing a wire at the time. That was enough evidence to put him away for three life sentences.

My father, Francois Le Savage, was not to be played with. He was Dominican and Black with a ruthless temper. To be honest, Izaak acted more like my father than I did.

I was built differently than the street mentality I grew up in.

I wanted to love the same woman for the rest of my life in a different way every day. I wanted a family, a house, and a successful business. I wanted to go on vacation to Disney Land and spend wedding anniversaries in Bora Bora. I tried to rebuild my community and provide an escape for the kids out here.

I was no saint; I mean, it had to be known in the streets that I would not be tried on any level. I did some things that I wasn't proud of but was very necessary.

My nostrils burned as I walked into my apartment that overlooked the Rock River. It was a beautiful sight since the reconstruction.

"Man!" I cursed to myself.

I forgot to take the trash out so now my house reeked. I was not too fond of any foul smell, whether it was a person, place, or thing.

I settled into my couch and pulled my vibrating phone out of my pocket. The caller I.D. read "Sable". She and I were nothing more than cuddy buddies. Sable was a freak who was fluffy and fabulous. She was flexible and always maintained enough discretion to leave without being asked.

"Hey Ms. Sable, how are you?"

"I'm good. Are you up for company tonight?"

"Sure. I just got in. I'm going to jump in the shower. Hit my phone when you get up to the door."

"Alright, will do," she said ending the call.

To look at me, one would think I would be into those model type plastic chicks.

That was nothing further from the truth. I loved my women with a lot of meat on their bones and the darker, the better. I didn't care if they wore a weave or not, but I loved to see a black woman rocking her natural hair.

My mind instantly went to Asha. She was what I think I need in my life. She was all of those things— my exact type.

You can tell Brian damaged her esteem, but I

knew I could be the one to show her she could walk on water. She didn't know it yet, but she would soon be mine.

I pushed Asha to the back of my mind as I headed to the shower. I hit the spots that needed to be hit and slipped into my grey joggers and a white t-shirt.

"Shoot!" I cursed myself when the foul fish smelled hit my nose again.

I dashed out the front door to throw it out. As I was headed back in, Sable had arrived.

She drove a red Mercedes and was all about her business.

"Hey you," I said as I held the door open for her to come in. I watched her full, ample rear end as she made her way up to my apartment.

My building was pretty safe so I left the door unlocked.

Sable wasted no time removing her trench coat. She was as naked as the day she came into this world underneath.

A small breathless whisper escaped her lips as I covered them with mine.

Sable sucked on my lip as she undressed me. My manhood was at full attention as it protruded from the thin sweatpants I wore.

Sable traced my hard six-pack with her neatly manicured fingers. Small bumps formed under her touch. I laid her on the floor so we would have more room to work.

Her thick curvy body turned me on in every way. I pinched her nipples gently between my teeth as I flicked them with my tongue.

Sable moaned out in pleasure, spreading her legs even wider. I'm confident that other men are sleeping on the flexibility of thicker women.

I leaned in to gently bite her neck, which was now glistening with sweat. Even though she was sweating, she still smelled of pears, which made me want to lick her more.

The object of this night was complete and utter gratification. I desired to please my lovers anytime they blessed me with their bodies.

"Umm-hmm," I moaned as I felt my turn coming to relieve myself of any stress that was lingering.

Sable pulled me into her so that I wouldn't try to back for yet another round.

As she held the back of my head, she licked my earlobe, which skyrocketed my orgasm.

Before I could finish, I flipped Sable over on her stomach.

"It's break time, P!" She begged.

"Ain't no breaks tonight, love. This is only half-time," I coaxed her.

"I really need a bre-"

Before she could finish, I already had another on a journey to the next climax.

I think she finally understood that a break was not an option at this point.

I wrapped one arm around her waist as I trailed kisses along her spinal cord up to the back of her neck.

I pulled her by her hair forcefully but not enough to cause her to be uncomfortable.

"Still need that break?" I taunted her.

"Not at all," she panted.

I could feel her body tremble underneath as we progressed.

I pressed my hands in the center of her back to keep her from running.

I loved the way Sable's body responded to me;

unrelenting and untamed.

We continued going in on each other bodies for a few more hours until we called it quits.

Sable never stayed over, even though she was more than welcome.

She said she never wanted to be in a position that she would be asked to leave, and I understood that.

I walked her out and made my way back upstairs. I was sure that I would sleep like a baby...thank you, Sable.

ASHA

Other than the janky Facebook messages here and there, I hadn't seen or heard from Brian. Usually, he would've tried to maneuver his way back in by now.

To be honest, I was just glad to have his bad energy out of my space. I didn't realize how much he dragged me down until he was no longer in my presence.

I thought my kids would miss him but even they were okay with him gone. That nigga was stressing all of us the fuck out.

The next man would have to ignite a flame in my soul that he fanned with his love every day of the week until his dying day. Until then, I planned on staying out of the way of men suffering from unresolved childhood trauma. It's destroying this thing we call love.

I've used this time to learn to love myself again and I even got the courage to take my CNA class. I was almost finished. I just had to take what I learned and do it in front of one of the state representatives. I hope I didn't get one of those older people with diarrhea or something. I was nervous and thinking about the worst-case scenarios at this point.

"Asha Wilde," the tall dark chocolate woman

called my name.

I was up next to show what I've learned. This was a make or break for me. If I didn't pass this portion, I don't know if I would have the nerve to try again.

My anxiety of failure wrapped itself around my throat, making me feel as if I couldn't breathe.

I walked into the room and my patient's name was Ms. Betty. She was a small Caucasian lady that weighed no more than a hundred and twenty pounds or so.

As soon as I hit the door, the smell of dookie hit my nose. My stomach immediately started to churn.

My hands were clammy because I wasn't sure if I could hold down the contents of my stomach.

Every nerve in my body was crying, "Please don't let this woman have crap up her back!"

As I made my way closer to her I secured my gloves. Once I made sure she was secure in the bed I proceeded to change her. Low and behold, dookie was not only filling her adult diaper but up her back.

The lady from the state looked at me with sympathy in her eyes, but we both know if I wanted to pass my test, I had to chop it up and make it happen.

My heart seemed to turn over in my chest as I

cleaned the woman up. My eyes misted with tears and I wondered if I was cut for this at all.

I prayed as I turned her over that it had not spilled to the front, and I be damned…it did. Screw my life.

"I'm almost done, Ms. Betty. This should make you feel so much better. Okay?" I soothed her.

"Okay," she responded feebly.

I could imagine how humiliating this had to be for her as well.

I loved caring for older people who could no longer do for themselves.

The other CNA's where I did my clinical told me that many of their families never visited them. It was like they dumped them there and forgot about them.

Once I was done I made my way out of the room. The lady grading my performance followed behind me.

"Your results will be posted online once they are complete. Unofficially, you did great, girl! That was a difficult task to complete as a newbie. I also loved how you consoled the patient," she congratulated me.

I danced my way down the hall and out the door. I rode home feeling so accomplished. I had slowly built myself back up, and it felt good loving me again!

Twenty minutes later I was pulling up to my apartment. My mom should be dropping the kids off soon.

With Brian no longer taking my money, I could buy myself a little cash car with my school check. It was a beater, but it got me from point A to point B.

I was proud of myself for the accomplishments I was making, and being honest, I was excited about setting more personal goals.

Next on the list was to find me another job. I wanted to keep my job at Target and get a third shift at a nursing home, but my babies were still little so I had to go with a CNA job.

As soon as I got inside I pulled out my tablet so I could search for jobs.

River Bluff Nursing Home. I read to myself as I search the Indeed database of jobs that were hiring.

I pulled out my Obama phone and decided to take a chance.

I figured I could apply for the housekeeping job until I got my final grades for my certification.

"River Bluff Nursing Home, this is Tarshae," the girl on the other end said.

"Yes, I wanted to speak with someone in H.R. about the housekeeping position," I replied.

"Housekeeping? Chile, the real money is being a CNA. You can pick up as many hours as you want. Most of these lazy tramps don't come to work on the weekends or on payday Friday. If you trying to check a bag ma' that's the position you need to apply for. They need people bad as hell too," he said.

The girl on the other end was ghetto and unprofessional! She was giving me Ronnie from Player's Club teas, spitting hoeology.

'Well, I'm waiting on my final grades for my certification before I apply for that position," I said, ignoring all the other stuff she said.

"Girl, long as they know you took the state test and you sure you passed, they will hire you on a probationary period until they get can pull you up online. Just come apply. I'm Tarshae so let them know you spoke with me so I can be your reference. I don't know you, but if you were willing to start in housekeeping, you have to be about your schmoney," she said.

"Thanks, girl! I am," I replied excitedly.

Although I wasn't sure if I wanted to use her name, I was grateful for the information.

"Heeeyyyy girl!" Uneek yelled as she walked into my house without knocking.

Uneek was the only person I talked to in the projects. In fact, she was one of the few females I dealt with.

"So did we pass our test?" She yelled as if we both took the CNA certification today.

"We? Uneek you is stupid," I laughed. "Yes, the lady said I did good and I passed. I just have to wait for it to post online," I told her.

"I knew you were going to pass! Guess what?"

"What?" I responded with my forehead wrinkled. I had no idea what Uneek was up to.

"I called Ms. Elisha and told her I wanted to surprise you and take you out because I knew you were going to pass. Anyways, I asked her to keep the kids tonight so I can take you out tonight to Oscar's."

"Uneek, I don't really feel like going out," I whined.

"Girl, you haven't been anywhere since Brian sorry butt got put out. You been doing the damn thing, girl! You deserve some you time!"

"Forger it. Might as well," I gave in.

"Cool, come down to the house because I made you some greens, baked chicken, and homemade macaroni and cheese."

"Awweee, you the best boo! You know I love your greens!

"I know. So come on so we can put something on our stomach before we get this Remy Martin in a rotation," he laughed.

I grabbed my keys and followed her back down to her house.

Uneek wasn't like a lot of these women down here in the projects. She stayed to herself unless she was kicking it with her family. If she wasn't messing with her baby daddy, her ass was celibate. She rarely went out so for her to take me out was a big deal.

I had no idea how she was taking me out with her non-driving self. I had been on her to get her L's but she was too nervous about learning.

Uneek and I chopped it up as we ate before heading out. We fussed over what to wear out for the night.

I was a big girl, but I believed in keeping it sexy with a bit of class.

Most of the stores catered to those small girls so I made most of my clothes.

I was pretty dope on the sewing machine too. Curvy women always complimented me and asked where I got my clothes from. When I responded I made it, they just acted like I was lying.

We stepped into Oscar's Pub & Grill, and it was a lituation. It was packed with various ethnicities represented.

It was refreshing with all the racist tension to see that it had not penetrated the bar's walls.

Uneek and I found a table near the dance floor and ordered a round of drinks for our table. A couple of our other girls came in later and joined us.

Wobble blared through the speakers and we made our way to the dance floor.

> *I got em' shakin their boobies like congos,*
> *Man I'm shaking the city like quakes.*
> *The haters blue the face like gonzo,*
> *Cause I'm rakin a cake so lets bake.*
> *I'm taking the game, the games mine.*
> *Y'all witness a change it's my time.*
> *Yea I'm new to the game but y'all might wanna save ya*
> *whack raps daylight saving time*
> *I could dance homie, I don't 2-step,*
> *Y'all looking...*

I had some curves but I could move these damn hips. I was on the dance floor throwing all these hips and ass.

I was having a ball with my girls when I noticed someone staring at me from the sidelines.

As I focused my eyes in the dark bar, I soon realized it was Prod. He had a big grin on his face watching me dance.

No lie, I danced harder when I noticed he was watching me. He started licking his lips as I worked it.

When the song ended, we made our way back over to our table.

"Excuse me ladies, these are for you. Compliments of the gentleman right over there," the waitress said pointing to Prod.

She laid out another round of Remy and some bottled waters.

"He finer than baby hair chile," Uneek said.

"Yeah, his name Prod I think. I met him that day Brian and I got into it," I explained.

Everyone looked at me crazy with their mouths open.

"What?" I said.

I didn't see what the big deal was.

"Girl, Prod is THAT nigga in these Rockford streets. He about that life, but I hear the nigga got a whole degree or something. He quiet but the streets know not to try him," my other homegirl Tori explained.

"Girl, ain't nobody checkin' for him. I'm just trying

to get my stuff together now that I got Brian out of my life," I assured them.

"Hey, Ms. Asha. Can I get a minute of your time? Hello ladies," Prod smoothly interrupted us.

"Heeeyy," they all replied in unison.

"I'm really just here to have a good time with my girls. I appreciate the drinks you sent over. That was a nice gesture," I told him.

"It was no problem. Enjoy the rest of your night. We keep bumping into each other Ms. Asha, so I have no doubt we will meet again."

He walked off, returning to his entourage at the bar.

My girls were looking at me crazy for curving Prod, but the last thing I needed or wanted in my life was a dope boy.

I was adamant about protecting my peace and self-esteem these days.

Prod was so fine I was sure he was out to ruin my entire life and leave me high and dry like a crackhead. No, thank you!

We enjoyed the rest of our night.

Uneek and I headed home. Since my mom agreed to keep my kids, I could get some rest and use the bathroom without a little person invading my privacy.

"Alright, girl. I'll see you in the morning," I told Uneek.

"Okay, boo. Talk to ya' later. Let me know when you get in safe," she said before slamming my car door.

I lived in the next parking lot over. That girl acted like someone was going to First 48 me from here to there. I loved how protective she was over me. Uneek has been a real friend to me.

I staggered out of the car and made my way up my sidewalk. The projects were quiet for it be three in the morning, but I wasn't complaining. At least people weren't out here shooting and doing some other stupid stuff.

"What the-," I yelled when my eyes fell on my apartment.

I slowly walked into my living room, where my air conditioner had been pushed in. My blinds were broken and torn; some were even hanging literally by a thread.

I was so angry my muscles were quivering internally, causing my body to shake externally.

My place was trashed. My television, along with all of my electronics, was gone.

I raced upstairs to my kid's rooms to see if anything was missing. Sure enough, their televisions along with Amor's tablet.

My nostrils flared as I made my way to the place where I hid my cash.

If it were missing, I would know for sure it was Brian that robbed me.

I reached my hand under my bed for the pink pencil case. I couldn't feel it so I felt around under the bed. Low and behold, I found it on the floor under the bed. I pulled it out only to find it was empty.

All of the money I had left from school and the money I saved from my paychecks at work was gone!

The entire house was trashed. Every room was unrecognizable. A roach scurrying across the floor further irritated my soul.

I need to get out of here. I thought to myself.

I wanted to call Uneek but I didn't want to wake her. I know one thing for sure... I'm getting a damn gun!

I took my cell phone out to call Brian.

He didn't answer so I left him a voicemail.

"I know you broke into my house, you roach, crumb scavenging nigga! How you steal from your own kids with you triflin' waste of skin ingrate! If I catch you around my crib, I will kill you, my nigga!" I screamed through the phone.

I missed the theatrics that the flip phone provided from back in the day. I would've slammed that joint shut hard as heck.

It would've made me feel better.

I was panting hard after running up the stairs and going from room to room. I sat on the bed so I could catch my breath.

My throat tightened as the tears poured out of my eyes. I just couldn't get a break. Every time I took one step, I was gut-punched back.

I pulled myself off of my raggedy bed and made my way downstairs.

The creaky stairs annoyed me as they reminded me of the weight I had been working on losing. This time I was doing it for me. Not because Brian was constantly dogging me out.

The very thought of him made my skin crawl.

I stood at the bottom of the stairs. My buzz was now gone. I had a long night. There was no way I would have my babies come home to this chaos.

These past couple of months have been great for us. Despite my mini-breakdown upstairs, I had to remind myself of that.

I didn't bother putting the air conditioning unit back in. Fall was almost on us anyway. I was just lazy about taking it out, but this was just the right amount of motivation that I needed.

I secured my windows and started cleaning my apartment.

"Damn roaches!" I screamed to myself.

I stamped over the kitchen cabinet where I kept the Raid and took some of my anger on these nasty roaches.

My next-door neighbor had a nasty ass house so these bastards migrated over here.

My assassination on my roaches was interrupted by my phone ringing. I was hoping Brian had the nerve to call me back.

"Hello, wassup Uneek?"

"You didn't let me know you made it in heffa!" She scolded me.

"Girl, Brian broke into my damn house!"

"How do you know it was him?"

"The place I had my cash hidden, only he and I knew about it. He took all our electronics, including

Amor's tablet girl."

"His ain't worth a hill of beans! My sister here with the kids and everybody is sleeping. I'm gonna head down there to help you clean up, so stick your head out the screen door and watch me. You know one of these niggas may try and take some caluche around here," she laughed.

"Girrrlll, it's coochie, not caluche," I laughed.

"Nah, this cat organic. It's caluche. Sound expensive, don't it?"

"Byyee!"

I did as Uneek asked. I watched her make her way down to my place, and all I could think was that I was grateful to have her in my life. Uneek was truly irreplaceable.

IZAAK

Camille's was pissed! She was pacing back and forth across the floor throwing stuff. I was trying to roll up. If I had to deal with this, I would have to do it high. Camille had a reckless ass mouth, and she low-key got off on talking to a nigga crazy.

"Izaak, you love tryin' my life, don't you? You like it when I drag these basic cum guzzling, mouth full of dead baby tricks over you! Keep on you gone start catchin' me out here bustin' it open for a real nigga in these screets," she threatened.

"First of all, lower your voice before you wake my son up. Second, I wish I would catch you out here smashing one of these bum niggas," I checked her while licking my blunt as I secured my weed in it.

"Your son? The son you too busy to raise because you tryin' to be some local kingpin! So, you can be out here screwing having me lookin' stupid but I can't return the favor?"

"You can do what you want, but if I catch you, you and that nigga getting beat up! On my mama Cam," I reiterated to her.

"Nigga I wish you would put yo' hands on me!"

"Uhh-hmm. Keep talking out the side of yo'

neck but you know better," I told her, lighting up my blunt. "Take yo' clothes off, Cam. I know what you need."

"You think I want to sleep with you after I just caught you with yet another bust down at The Tap?" She said,

She was trying more to convince herself than me.

It was a known fact that she took it as a personal challenge when I cheated to become a demon in the bedroom.

"So you don't want me to stick my tongue in that cat?" I eyed her body as the words rolled from my lips.

Cam shifted nervously in place. She was judging herself for wanting me.

I made another pull on my blunt as she wrestled with her emotions.

Women threw the cat at me all the time. Everything I wore was a designer and the streets knew I was papered up. I loved Cam and she was my son's mother, but I had no intention of marrying her.

Cam brought out the worst in me sometimes. To top it all off, she was childish sometimes.

Cam finally started to undress.

"Cam...get a chair from the kitchen table," I said.

"A chair?"

"Do you want some head or not?"

Without a word, she went to the kitchen and did what I asked. I stood up to get the ropes Cam used to tie the curtains back.

We have been living in Fairgrounds for years. I could've been moved us out but I love the hood.

Cam was starting to complain because she was three generations deep in living in the projects. She was ready for a house and a change of atmosphere.

She placed the chair in the center of the floor. Putting my blunt out, I made my way towards her.

"Take it all off. Now," I demanded.

Cam didn't have all that mouth now that head was on the table. She was compliant as hell. Once she was naked, I had her sit in the chair. She looked at me crazy as I tied each of her ankles to a chair leg so that she was completely spread eagle.

Cam's was completely shaven with only a patch of hair in the shape of a heart. I could see her wetness starting to spill onto the chair.

Cam's chest was heaving up and down and a hint

of fear was in her eyes. I had to switch stuff up now and again to let her know wassup.

I removed my shirt and kneeled in front of her. I trailed my hands up her silky legs until they reached her thighs. I gripped them tight enough to leave red finger imprints on her.

"You play too much. Don't try to mess over me because I'm tied up either."

I reached over and picked up her panties from the floor and stuff them in her mouth.

"Shut that up and just enjoy this ride."

Cam always talked; she never could just trust a nigga.

I was going to leave her hands free, but since she showed resistance, I might as well tie them up.

I took her shirt and tied her hands behind her so she couldn't fight me off once I hit that spot. At first, I wanted her to be able to grab my head why I ate that box but never mind. She could just take this the best way she knew how.

I lowered my head between her legs, allowing her juices to wet my pallet. I could feel her body vibrating to the beat of her heart, and I could tell she was nervous and turned on all at the same time.

I gripped her by her waist as I went in. I made

love with my mouth to the place that had her acting crazy.

"Mmmhhh…," was all that Cam could push out.

I was going in on her like I didn't already get my rocks off earlier.

I slipped my tongue in and out of her slit, pausing only to allow her clit to slither across my tongue. I could feel Cam's walls tighten around my tongue, and I knew she was almost ready. It never really took Cam long to cum, which is why I never mind sucking the soul out of her.

Cam was off the chain. She was so turned on she ripped herself free of her t-shirt I tied her up with.

She arched her back as she grabbed the back of my head with both hands. She started winding on my tongue like one of these Island girls from Trinidad.

That liquor was coming out of my pores so I was perspiring like I had on a sweatsuit.

"Yo Cam, if you wake the baby up, that's gone mess up our night, and I ain't done with you by a long shot."

"Okay. Okay. I'm gone be quiet."

"Oh, now you gone be quiet, huh? You just had a whole lot to say a few minutes ago."

I untied her legs so I could get in them guts.

I stood her up and turned around so I could bend her over.

I slid inside Cam with slow strokes. My mans glistened with her wetness, letting me know she was ready for the punishment I was about to release on her.

I grabbed a handful of her hair and gripped her by her waist to brace her for a reckoning that was soon to follow.

I gave Cam the business for hours. I was rolling off that X and doing my best to break her back. By the time we were done, we both were lying on the floor trying to catch our breath. Cam was exhausted and weak. When I looked over at her, she was asleep.

I relit my blunt and let my thoughts take me away. I ended up thinking about the business Prod and I was running. He was slowly turning things over to me, which is what I wanted. To be honest, that nigga was never built for this. His dad only left him in charge because it was his son, but we both knew I was the one that would take this business to another level.

I'm glad Prod decided to turn things over to me because I was low-key planning to have him popped off. This empire was mine, and I was the one getting my hands dirty most of the time. I made it my business to strip this nigga down piece by piece and he had no clue.

A sinister grin crossed my face as I went over my flawless plan in my head. Good things came to those who plot and plan.

Buzz.

Buzz.

Buzz.

"Tell them sluts don't be calling you're phone this late nigga," Cam spat, still half-sleep.

"Man, shut up before I stick something down yo' throat. Take yo' butt back to sleep."

"Hey Prod, wassup?" I said answering my phone.

"Yeah, I need you to meet me at the spot. Something just went down that we need to handle tonight."

"Tonight?"

"Yes. Tonight my nigga. Get to the spot," he demanded.

I pulled my head from my phone. Who did this Downy soft nigga think he was talking to? I let it ride because I knew his time was limited. If he kept trying me, I would kill him just for the fun of it.

"Aight. I'm on my way."

* * *

I arrived at the warehouse to see Prod had called the whole squad out. He called me with the rest of these simps like we on the same level. We both should've been here as everyone else showed up. He keeps puttin' me on these niggas levels and then wondered why I had to kill them for disrespecting me.

I made my way through the squad and took my place next to Prod. It was cold. Up north, it would snow without warning, and it wasn't uncommon for us to slip into early winter.

"Now that we are all here, we got something we need to address. We got a snitch that's willing to take food out of our mouths. Ain't that right, Slim?"

My eyes trailed over to Slim, who was sweating in this cold warehouse. Slim looked like a reject Bizzy Bone from Bone Thugs and Harmony. I never trusted him anyway so it was no surprise that he was talking to the Detects.

"Man, I ain't said nothing so I wouldn't know personally."

His voice quivered as he spoke.

"Oh, you wouldn't know? From what I hear, you

know firsthand," Prod retorted.

Prod's dad was locked up for killing three niggas that were working with the Feds.

One of the niggas happened to have his phone on with his contact from the Feds on the other end.

He heard the whole thing go down so when the bodies turned up, they came at Prod's dad with guns blazing.

They didn't find any of the work. They picked him up from his crib, not even a full twenty-four hours later.

Francois was a crazy Cuban with a bad temper. He didn't care about anything and dared someone to cross him. Taking him off the streets was seen as a public service because he terrorized the streets of Rockford.

Personally, I idolized the man. Francois was everything I aspired to become.

So the only time you would see Prod's father in him is when it came to a snitch. To him, a snitch caused his father to get locked up and was the reason he was dragged into this drug game.

"Bossman, I ain't no snitch," Slim fired back.

"Hmmm," was all Prod said while circling him.

Without warning, Prod took his pistol and brought it down across the back of his head.

The circle widened to get out of Prod's way while he pistol-whipped Slim.

He bashed his head in repeatedly with the gun with such force brain matter splattered on the other people standing around.

Slims bright red blood stained the dirty, cold, cemented warehouse floor. Slim went into a seizure and started foaming at the mouth.

I stood there smoking my Black & Mild watching the events unfold.

Pretty soon, Slim was lifeless on the ground.

POP!

POP!

Without warning, Prod turned his gun to his right about ninety degrees and put two bullets in Raymond. He and Slim were friends since the West Middle School days. I'm not sure if the nigga was a snitch or guilty by association.

"Man Prod, what's good? I ain't have nothing to do with what that nigga was doin'. I ain't know!" He cried rolling on the floor.

"Nah, my nigga, you got a different infraction.

The tips in Concord have been coming up short. You oversee that, so it's your job to make sure not one damn dollar is short!" Prod spat leaning in Raymond's face. Spit flew on him as he cursed him out.

POP!

Concord was another set of projects on the far West End of Rockford. Nobody messed around out there because it was one way in and one way out. It was secured by a gate that wrapped around it.

I'm not sure how Prod got those wild Waco's on board, but he did. A lot them were lil' niggas but they stayed on straight gorilla mode in the streets. They were about stayin' laced with that paper so they toned down a lil' bit.

"Anyone else feels the need to trifle with my hard work and dedication I put into building this empire so that we can all eat?" Prod asked while kneeling, cleaning his pistol with Slim's hoodie.

"No," everyone present replied in unison.

"Jigga, select a few people to help you grab these niggas and put them each in one of the barrels over there."

We kept about fifteen metal barrels filled with acid. We stuffed the bodies in there and let the acid do the rest. We had a transport truck that took them to a place near the plant in Byron that had all kinds of toxic stuff floating around already. The bodies would blend right in.

"Yo…you good man?" I asked Prod making my way over to him.

"Yeah, man. You know I can't stand that snitchin' for more reasons than one," he said checking his phone.

"Well, we good here?"

I needed to get back to the crib. I hope Cam was rested because we are about to go some more rounds.

"Yea…we good," Prod responded shaking up with me.

I took one look back as they dragged the bodies to the barrels. My lips curled slowly in a smile at the very thought of running everything.

Soon….soon.

PRODIGY

3 MONTHS LATER

The city of Rockford was bracing for a blizzard. I was so busy with the business that I didn't make sure I was stocked up on food and snacks.

The snow had already started to come down and the wind made visibility horrible.

I was making my way from Highlander grocery store on Riverside and it was a mess out. I had to drive for myself and everybody else on the road.

Skkrrrrr….Boom!

"What th-"

That's why I started not to come out this damn late! Folks could barely drive when the weather was good, so you could imagine how they operated in bad weather conditions.

Whoever ran into the back of my truck would have hell to pay! I loved my Range!

I put my truck into park and turned my hazard

77

lights on. As I made my way to examine the damages to my vehicle, I looked up at the old beater that hit me. I could tell by the way it looked that it wasn't insured.

I had a few scuffs but nothing major appeared to be wrong. I still wasn't about to let this ride, though. I may get down the street and my bumper comes apart.

The windows were fogged up so I couldn't tell who was driving. I put my hands on my waist to grasp the handle of my gun just in case this was a set up to rob me.

I tapped on the window and I couldn't believe my eyes.

"Ms. Asha. You hit my car," I told her.

"Prod is it? I'm sorry. I couldn't see your truck and when I hit my brakes, I slid into you. I called the police but they said it was so many accidents that we have to exchange information and file a report later."

Asha was looking fine in her scrubs. I wondered if she was a nurse or something?

I was thankful in any event that God had allowed us to run into each other again. Literally.

Asha now had her hair in braids that were pulled up into a bun.

Her skin was glowing but you could tell she was tired by her eyes.

"Oh, you have insurance?" I laughed.

"Umm…yes. What, do you think because I ain't in no new Range Rover that I didn't insure my car? Typical."

"I didn't mean it like that. Look, it's cold out here and this weather is getting worse. I will call a tow truck for our cars and have them taken to my mechanic. I can have one of my other trucks brought to us and I can take you home. No funny business."

Asha sat there for a moment, considering my offer. She tapped her fingers on the steering wheel as she thought.

"Why would you do all of that for me? You don't even know me like that."

"And who's fault is that? I've been trying to get to know you but you kept spinning me. I know you've been through something foul and most likely needed to get your head straight, so I gave you space. I'm doing all this because you are worth it. This really ain't nothing compared to what I want to do for you."

"I don't need you to do anything for me," she said popping her neck with all that attitude.

"Look, it's cold and it doesn't feel like your heat work. Will you please come sit in my car until the tow truck gets here?"

I was jogging in place by this time to get my blood flowing to stay warm.

She sighed but agreed to what I asked her to do. I watched as she grabbed her work badge, lunch bag, and purse.

When she got out, she opened the back door to grab the car seats.

"I got it. Don't ever grab anything heavy when I'm around," I scolded her.

I grabbed the car seats and we headed to my truck. There was little damage to it but I refused to drive it.

"Jigga, I need you to have my other truck brought to me on North Main Street? Call Rico and tell him I need to have two vehicles towed. Aight. One," I said disconnecting the call.

"So you just call people and they come out in this blizzard to do what you say? Interesting."

"There is a lot about me that is interesting," I told her.

We sat there in silence while the music played. I rarely listened to rap, so my satellite radio stayed set to the Old School R & B station.

Lenny Williams played softly in the background.

Girl, you know I love you
No matter what you do
And I hope you understand me
Every word I say is true
Cause I love you
Baby, I?m thinkin? of you
Tryin? to be more of a man for you
And I don?t have much riches
But we gonna see it through
Cause I love you
Ho...ho...ho...

Asha just played solitary on her phone.

"Asha, do you know the origin of your name?"

"That's random. No, I don't. My mom said it was the name of her best friend that passed away a long time ago. Why do you ask?"

"Well, there is a version of Sleeping Beauty in India where the princess is named Asha because she was the king and queen's wish."

"That's really pretty. I've never heard that version before. Do you always know random facts like that?"

"It was something I ran across in college," I told her.

"College?" She repeated, her eyebrows raising showing her surprise.

I wasn't shocked by her surprise. People always assumed that I didn't have a college degree under my belt because I was in the streets.

"Yeah, college. I attended Northern Illinois University for my associates. I was supposed to stay until I received my Bachelor's degree, but my father needed me. I had to finish up at Rockford College."

"Do you regret it?"

"Sometimes. What could I do? My dad needed me, and he sacrificed a lot for me to go to college. A lot of people didn't know but I had a college fund. People think he just took a lump sum of drug money and paid for my schooling. That wasn't the case at all. Now it's my turn to ask you something personal. Asha, have you ever been with a real man?"

I genuinely wanted to know the answer. In my heart, I knew that she hadn't. I just needed confirmation directly from her lips. I needed to give her something to think about.

"What makes a real man?" She rebutted letting me know she hadn't.

"He prays for you. He weathers the storms and carries the world's weight on the broad shoulders God designed for such matters. He wakes every day with thoughts on how to please his woman and care for his family. He loves you unconditionally but does everything in his power to harness the very best in you. You are his best friend. He is a faithful lover and dream restorer. He won't let you walk over him, but your opinion matters. In essence, you are the very best part of him, and he cherishes you as such. That's what a real man is…to me, anyway." I explained.

Asha's face softened as she learned a bit more about me.

Just as I was finishing up, Jigga pulled up with my truck. He had one of the other guys trailing him so they could head back out.

Rico pulled up right behind them and the timing couldn't be more perfect.

Asha stayed in the truck until I got everything transferred over to my other vehicle.

We made random small talk about nothing in particular as we drove to her house.

I couldn't see anything so we almost had three more accidents on the way to her spot.

"Prod, I don't normally do this, but it's too bad out here for you to try and make it home. You can leave first thing in the morning."

"Are you sure? I don't want to make you or your kids uncomfortable."

"My kids are with my mom. I worked a double today at the nursing home so you good."

"Okay," I told her.

"There will be no sexing going on just so we're clear," she said pointing her finger in my direction.

"We're clear, Ms. Asha. I will be on my best behavior."

I walked into Asha's apartment and it smelled of lavender plugins.

I took in the view as I followed her into the living room. Asha's apartment was clean despite the few roaches I seen scurry across the floor. Her place was simple but tasteful to be in the projects.

Asha was turning out to be the girl I imagined her to be.

Her décor screamed, "Power to the People" with her earth tones and walls full of black art. One painting, in particular, drew me in. It was a picture of a bald black man and a woman in locs intertwined like a chocolate and caramel Twizzler stick.

"You like it?" Asha asked, interrupting my thoughts.

"I love it," I told her unable to hide be intrigue.

"It's called "Interlock" and it represents the unity I desire to experience one day with someone I can trust with my mind, body, and soul," she explained nervously.

"That's wassup."

Asha and I engaged in intense conversation in which I learned why she stayed with Brian and that she had endured his mental and physical abuse for years.

She stayed out of fear more than anything. Brian had beat her down so until she felt no one would want her, let alone her two kids as a package.

Instead of praising her curves, natural hair, and full lips, he took every opportunity to tear her down.

If she would just give me the opportunity, I know I could be the man she deserved. I just wanted to spoil her and cater to her every need.

There was strength in Asha that if you were broken, she would glue you back together. If you were down, she would pull the sun and rainbow down from the sky just for you. When the weight of the world was on your shoulder, she would pray for you and rub your head why you lay in her lap.

I could see all of this and my future in her almond-shaped eyes.

My heart leaped when she spoke—her words were like hope in darkness laced with a peace that could calm the craziest of storms.

Asha didn't know it yet, but now that I have gotten a look inside at the woman she is, I wasn't letting her go. I don't care how stubborn she tried to act; Asha would be mine. Eternally.

ASHA

Prod and I had been inseparable since the storm. I couldn't believe this fine man treated me like the queen that I am.

Everything with him was so easy that I sometimes questioned had I ever loved before him.

He was amazing with my kids and we wanted for nothing.

Prodigy wanted me to move in with him but I refused. I insisted we get a new place on the East Side of town with both of our names on the lease.

I knew soon I would have it all; the ring, house, and complete family.

We were only a year in but we both are feeling each other and our bond was so clutch we knew what each other was thinking most times.

Prodigy and I pulled up to the repass of our homeboy Dre. We had yet another fallen soldier in the streets.

These Rockford streets were taking no prisoners, and it was as if anybody could be touched.

Prodigy tried not to involve me with the business, but I insisted. He got some side-eyes, especially from Izaak.

He felt like I was trying to take his place instead of reinforcing Prod's decision to fall back in this drug game.

I couldn't help it though. It gave me a thrill to have that much power, even if it was through association with Prod.

I was changing somewhat. I was still me, but I was being drawn in by the streets. It was intoxicating.

I pulled down my black fitted dress. I kept my accessories to a minimum because it was a funeral.

I was a curvy girl, what the world would currently identify as a BBW.

I wasn't insecure about my body or anything for that matter anymore. Prodigy made me feel like a queen, and I now walked like diamonds fell from between my legs.

Most importantly, I treated myself like a queen. I loved me some me, baby!

No one's dirty son was going to take that from me ever again.

"Hello. Hi. Hello," we repeated over and over

making our way through the crowd of people.

Prodigy was shakin' up with people as we made our way to Justin's mother.

She was clutching Kleenex as she greeted people in the room while she grieved.

"Babe, I'm going to sign the guestbook. We didn't sign it at the funeral," I told Prodigy.

"That's fine, baby. I'll be in the back with the rest of the guys."

"Alright. I'll bring you a drink love," I said kissing him.

Prod didn't smoke and was a social drinker. I was waiting for the skeletons to fall out of the closet, but we were a year in and they never did.

The other women in the room looked me up and down.

I was accustomed to the hatin' stares.

Prodigy was a chocolate brother with a muscular build. Not one of them steroid type of men either. My baby was put together well and drippin' with sexy sauce.

He wore this weird Mohawk type hairstyle that worked well with his square jaw. His hair was a cold black and highlighted his gingerbread skin complexion. His teeth were perfectly straight and gleaming white.

Let's just say he wasn't the type of man people usually pictured with a woman like me.

Little did they know Prodigy loved his women with some meat on their bones and wasn't afraid to show it.

I made my way to the stand and signed Prodigy and my name in the little white book with gold lettering.

Once I was done I made my way over to the fully stocked table of liquor. I poured two clear plastic cups of Mango Ciroc and took Prod his.

I pushed through one guy who reeked of cigarette smoke from his clothes. We were all outside chillin' when we heard something pop off in the house.

"What are you doin' here? We all know that ain't Dre baby so you have no right being here!" Caprice yelled.

Prod and I were nudging each other being messy and laughing under our breaths.

Caprice and Nessa have been fighting and beefing for months now.

We all knew Caprice was ballsy, but no one thought she would show up at this boy mama house.

We all stood as spectators as it all played out.

Dre's mother made her way over, trying to break them up.

"Please, y'all, just stop. This is too much. I just buried my son," she pleaded.

"Nah ma' I got this!" Keisha said pushing her mom to the side. "You got my family messed up! This is not the time or the place for this. We all know both of y'all was screwin' my brother. Hell, y'all knew it. Don't get here trying to put on no show for folks!" Keisha said buckin' both of the chicks.

Everyone in the hood knew Keisha did not play. She fought niggas and most times won her hands were so cold. It was nothing for her to put someone to sleep.

WAP!

WAP!

Without warning, Caprice bust Keisha in her mouth!

Once Keisha recovered from the combo, she ate Caprice up.

"Ahhhhh!!" Caprice screamed as Keisha dragged her through the front door down the stairs into the yard.

"Don't-yell-now!" Keisha spat rendering relentless blow after blow to her face.

"Come on you dike!" Caprice yelled, pulling the blade from her bra.

"Hey, hey, hey now c'mon," the guys yelled, jumping between them finally.

People loved seeing fights jump off so it took them a minute to break it up.

Nessa digressed and was sitting down somewhere before Keisha let loose on her too.

"Babe, you ready to head out? It's been a long day," Prod said.

"Yea babe, let roll," I cooed in his ear.

We made our way back to the car once the crowd had cleared up.

Prod held opened my door while I got in and ran around the other side to get in.

"Babe, can we stop by Uncle Nick's and get some wings and fries? All that food was nasty. That dry Wal-Mart chicken was horrendous. They be frying the life out of that chicken at Wal-Mart. I swear it's like whoever fry the chicken be mad like…forget this chicken man!"

I joked, throwing my arms in the hair.

"You don't want one of them gyros with the special sauce?" He laughed.

"You know I ain't eat that since people started saying they were using semen as their special sauce. I'm good on that."

I don't know if people were lying or not but I wasn't about to test the theory.

"I got you, babe," he said.

Prod and I lived in our own little world. We lived the fast life but he was working on changing that.

Prod inherited the drug game after his dad got locked up years ago.

Since then, he has triple the income and loyal soldiers. No one dared to cross him.

It wasn't because he was so vicious he was actually the opposite.

He cared about those who rocked with them. He made sure everybody on his team ate and they loved him for that.

There were still some snakes in the tribe, but Izaak usually handled the dirty work. He ran it by Prod and just handled it for the most part.

Prod and Izaak had been best friends since elementary and they were solid.

Izaak never hit on me or came at me sideways. We were family and blood couldn't make us any closer.

We pulled into the driveway of our ranch-style house on the East Side of town. It was quiet. Our neighborhood was a mixture of all ethnicities, but we all got along.

We were new to the area and it tripped us out when one of the neighbors brought over cookies.

I think she was trying to be nosey but we played along.

I had a surprise for Prod when we got inside. I wanted to do it before my mom brought the kids home.

"Why are you bouncing your knee like that?" Prod asked.

He cut his eyes at me, bouncing them back and forth from me to the street.

"Nothing. I can't bounce my leg. Is it bothering you?"

"I can't ask a question? Normally, you do that when you're anxious about something. So what's up with it, Asha?"

"Nothing, I'm just hungry. That's all. Sorry, nothing to see here buddy," I joked.

I watched Prod take his shirt off, exposing those sexy abs that called out for you to lick every one of them.

I bit my bottom lip as I watch my King undress. It wasn't just his body that made him attractive but the fact that he didn't entertain all these women that threw themselves at him.

I walked over to the dresser drawer and pulled out a small rectangle box with a bow neatly tied on the top.

"Here babe," I said handing him the box.

"What this? It's not our anniversary," he laughed.

"I know, silly. It's just something to show you I love you."

I watched Prod open the box with a Kool-Aid smile on my face. I loved spoiling this man.

I was almost a year in my Nursing Program and that pay increase would be everything. It also provided us a nice front along with the barbershop for the amount of money we had coming in.

"Baaabbbeee!!!! Are you serious?" He yelled, jumping up from the bed and scooping me up in his arms.

Yes, my boo was strong! He lifted all this sexiness in one swoop.

"Yep, I'm pregnant. I went to the doctor after I did the home pregnancy test. I just put that in the box for dramatic effect," I laughed.

Prod was holding me so tight as the tears crept down his face. I knew he would be happy, but not this happy.

He gave me one of those kisses that made my body jump. I reciprocated all of what he wanted to give me with some sensual kisses of my own.

Ding Dong.

I swear my mama was the only one that used that annoying ass doorbell.

"Bae, I have to get that. It's mama with the kids. You just be naked when I get back in here. You are my everything Prodigy Le Savage."

I pulled the door open before my mama lost it on my doorstep. She was in church now but she still tried to go in on me every now and again in a saved way.

"Hey, mama," I greeted her opening the door.

I took Romello from her arms while Amor ran past me, heading to her room.

"Hey, Mamacita!" I called out to Amor.

"Yes, mommy?" She said.

"Can I get a hug and a kiss please, muffin?" I asked.

She ran over to me and wrapped her arms around my neck and kissed me on the lips. That girl was the absolute best part of me.

I took a seat next to my mom on the couch.

"Mom…I'm pregnant," I confessed to her.

I wasn't sure how my mom would take it because she was old school.

She was a crackhead back in the day but she had my brother and me while still married. We never took our father's last name because he wanted us to be safe if he ever got locked up.

All the hoeing she did, she never came home with any more kids by random tricks.

"How do you feel about it?" She asked.

"I'm happy, mom. Prod is good to the kids and me."

I couldn't hide my excitement as I poured out a portion of my heart.

"Then I'm happy for you. I agree Prod is a good man. I just wish y'all would get out of that life, Asha. That's no way for you, him, or the kids to live. Either one of you can become casualties of war when it comes to the streets. I was out there; I know how rough it can be."

My mother made her case and I listened without interrupting her.

"Mom, I promise I will slow down. Prod is already transitioning out of the life," I assured her.

"How does his father feel about that?"

"You know his dad?"

I'm sure the look of shock was evident across my face.

"I was on drugs, Asha; of course, I knew his dad. He was one of the most ruthless drug dealers of our time."

My mom seemed to go off in this daze as if there were memories so deep even Jesus couldn't wipe away. She didn't look disturbed, but weirdly it was like the memory was a happy one.

I didn't remember his dad so I'm sure he wasn't anything but her dealer.

"Mom, that was just a business relationship, right?"

"Asha...Francois and I were pretty serious. When I didn't come home, I was with him most of the time. He was supplying me, but he put me in rehab when he noticed it taking over my life. When I got out, I never went back. I was messed up after your daddy got locked up. I just wanted to be held and the pain to go away. Francois never knew about you and your brother. When he found out about you two, it was another reason he made me get clean."

I couldn't believe what I was hearing.

"He was the one sending you both money why I was locked up. I know they told you it was from your dad when they delivered the envelopes, but it was Francois. He promised to look out for you both until I got clean."

I couldn't believe Prod's dad was playing stepdaddy to us, and we never knew of each other. I wondered if Prod knew. I don't think I'm telling him.

I looked out for my brother growing up. I even got a job during high school to pay our bills in the projects.

I wasn't sure if the envelopes would ever stop but I wanted to have a backup plan.

"Wow."

"Well, I know first-hand what comes with the life. It's getting late so I will let you and your family get some sleep, baby girl. I'm praying for you," she said hugging me on her way out.

"Thank you, mommy. I love you!"

"I love you more," she said over her shoulder seeing herself out.

By the time I put Mello down and made it to the bedroom Prod was knocked out.

I stood over him, just watching my lover sleep. Normally, I would wake him up but I knew he was exhausted.

It has been a long day in which we celebrated death and life.

I kissed his soft lips and cuddled up to him.

PRODIGY

I took a seat near the window at Pino's on Main. It was a family-owned Italian restaurant that made the best taco pizza in the city.

I ordered one for Izaak and me with two glasses of Coke.

I wanted to talk to him about no longer taking over the business. I'm not sure how Izaak will react when I tell him.

He has been under the impression the last couple of years that he had next to take over.

The more I talked to Asha about the business, the more I realized that I owed it to my father to continue to take his vision to the next level.

This was my legacy to carry on no Izaak's.

Yes, we were raised like brothers, but at the end of the day, my father built this empire.

Asha was right; I owed it to my dad to make sure his legacy thrived.

He sacrificed his life protecting this business.

I looked up and noticed Izaak walking in covered in designer from head to toe as usual. He never gave it a rest and refused to live under the radar.

I stood up to shake up with him, "What's good, bruh?"

"I can't call it. What's good? Why are we meeting today?"

"I know we've been working to transition you to take over the business but I've had a change of heart. I need to stay on and take my father's business to the next level. That's what he would've wanted. I'm letting him know when I visit him the change of plan."

"Bro, you been dying to get out of this business. Why the sudden change of heart? Yo' new shawty is filling your head up with nonsense. You've always hated this drug game nigga. You got drafted but you ain't never had the heart to do this long term. You trippin' nigga and that's on everything," he quivered with indignation.

His face was twisted in anger and disappointment.

"This has nothing to do with Asha. I only met with you today as a courtesy. I don't owe you an explanation my nigga, but you like a brother to me so I figure I let you know wassup'," my annoyance flared.

"You got it, Prod. You got it," he laughed.

"Bro, the only thing changing is the fact that we will be running these streets together rather than you by yourself," I assured him.

"It's cool, bro. I just want to make sure you are doing this because you want to, not because of somebody in your ear. That's all."

"I feel you. Good looking. I gotta head out to meet Asha at the doctor's office," I told him standing to pay the tab and head out.

"Is everything okay?" Izaak asked genuinely concerned.

"Man, she pregnant, bro!" I said unable to hide my excitement.

Izaak knew how much I wanted to be a father. It was one of the main reasons I did the free haircuts.

I loved Asha's kids as my own, but I wanted my own child to spoil as well and add to our family.

Asha is an amazing mother and I can't wait to see her with our child.

"Congratulations, bruh! You would think the new baby would make you want to get out of the game, not stay in it. I hope you know what you doing. Sometimes when niggas don't get out when they say they are, it tends to go left."

His tone almost sounded threatening but I knew better than that. Izaak would never cross me no matter how mad he got.

* * *

I was on top of the world after today's events. Izaak took it well that I was staying on to run the business, and Asha and I could see our baby for the first time today.

It's too early to find out the sex but I was just happy that it's healthy.

Asha always glowed, but the pregnancy had her shining brighter than the stars on a clear night in the country.

She loved watching her Love and Hip Hop so after we did some running around, we picked up the kids to head home so she wouldn't miss it. I reiterated every week that the show was scripted but she just ignored me.

I low-key liked watching it too. Fake and all, it was funny. They always meet up at clubs, nail shops, or businesses that are all free. If they are out to dinner, no one ever orders, and they drink water. It's hilarious.

Ding Dong.

We weren't expecting anyone so I made my way to the door alone to see who was there.

Maybe the kids left something at Asha's mom house. She's the only one that pops up on us.

Moms was cool though. She was most welcomed. She has become the mom I never had and I adored that lady.

Looking through the peephole, I didn't recognize the scraggly man on the other side.

"Who is it?" I yelled through the locked door.

"It's Paul," he replied.

"Paul who?" I asked.

"Bug sent me," I pulled the door open. "What do you want nigga?" I yelled.

"Yeah, I was tryin' to see if you had some good," his raspy voice sounded like the dope fiend of New Jack City.

"I don't know what you are talking about and I definitely don't know who no Bug is. You got the wrong house nigga. Get out of here before I blast you down where you stand. Understand?"

My eyebrows were drawn together in a frown and my heart pounded in my chest.

I wasn't sure who this nigga was but something wasn't right. I wasn't surprised he used Izaak's street name "Bug" because everybody knew him.

It was one of the other reasons I decided to stay in command. He didn't believe in being under the radar in the hood—flashy clothes and cars in the projects.

I watched the man walk away until he disappeared out of sight. I ain't never seen him around here before.

"Is everything okay, baby?" Asha asked as I walked past her to the bedroom to grab my phone off of the charger.

"Yea babe. It's cool," I threw over my shoulder.

I paced back and forth, waiting for Izaak to pick up the phone. I know the nigga that left was lying, but I wanted to run it past Izaak anyway.

"Wassup, bruh?" He said picking up. Izaak sounded high.

"Man, you sent somebody this way?"

"Yea, that's Cam's uncle best friend or something," he replied calmly.

"Or something? You send somebody to my home where my girl and kids live, and you not sure if you can trust them? First off, we don't do business out of our homes. Well, I don't! I don't know what Cam is letting you do down there in them ran down projects. I've only been here for two months and you are sending hypes to my crib. You got me twisted, Izaak! I know ya' plexed up about me not handing you over the business, but this is why I can't! Your emotions rule you, dude! You make decisions in the moment that could cost you and everybody else around you!" I yelled through the phone.

"First of all, don't be yelling at me like I'm a kid! I ain't one of these flunky niggas that hug the block. I built this empire with you so you will handle me with some re-"

"Some what? I know ya' wasn't going to say respect? You the most disrespectful person I know! I'm gone cut this short before we both say something that we can't take back," I hung up the phone before he could agree or disagree.

One thing was for sure. I had to watch my back around Izaak now. I hope this nigga just pissed right now and I didn't have to take him out.

One thing I wasn't going to do was look over my shoulder and watch my back around someone that's supposed to be my right hand.

Brother or not, I would have his baby mama in that black dress.

ASHA

Since Izaak sent some random man to our home, Prod has made it his business these last three months teaching me the ins and outs of the business.

He and Izaak made up but it was never really the same. You can tell neither one of them trusted the other, and it started to cause a rift in the squad.

Some clung to Izaak and others to Prod. People were slowly but surely picking a side.

When the warehouse was empty, Prod would have me show up so he can explain the set-up.

He was reluctant to explain what the black barrels with acid were for. Once he told me, I didn't even flinch.

I was becoming the Bonnie to his Clyde and was down for whatever on this ride.

Prod's love consumed me and I felt as if anything was possible.

Pregnant and all, I still attended my nursing classes. I was nearing my clinicals and I didn't care if I was about to deliver. I was determined to finish my Nursing Degree Program.

Prod and I had already planned to put more things under my name once I graduated. My income would be able to explain the purchases if it ever came into question.

I still worked at the nursing home as if my man wasn't the biggest drug dealer in Rockford.

I never touched my checks. Prod finally made me get a bank account when he kept finding my checks stacked on the dresser.

"Babe, you need to sign up for direct deposit. You just let them sit here. With direct deposit, it will go right into your account and you don't have to deal with it," he would fuss.

A mask of reserve would cover his face when he tried to be serious and put his foot down.

"Okay, babe. Whatever you say," I told him nestling my body against his while wrapping my arms around his neck, planting small kisses all over it.

It was my way of getting him to stop fussing. If that didn't work, I had other tricks to get my way.

"Babe, I'm heading out early so I can stop by and see Uneek. I haven't checked on her in a while," I yelled from the bathroom while flat ironing my hair.

"You know I don't like you down there at night. Make sure you take your gun."

"Okay," I told him.

I threw on my scrubs and headed to my best friend's house.

BAM!

BAM!

BAM!

I hated when Uneek locked her screen door! You couldn't hear anything through these metal doors in the projects. Don't be upstairs with the air on; you are definitely not hearing a peep.

"Yea?" She hollered from the upstairs window.

"Girl, come down here and open this door; I got to get to work!"

"Why you ain't call first?"

"Call first? Girl, if you don't come open this door! It ain't like you got a man in there or something!"

She was starting to irritate my soul now. I was trying to be nice and check on her. We don't see each other much since I moved to the East Side and I missed her.

I heard the deadbolt unlock and Uneek pulled open the door in a black silk robe.

"Giirrrllll…what in the world?" I laughed.

"Shut up! My friend upstairs!"

"Friend? What friend?" I asked, crossing my arms and popping my neck. "What's the tea best friend

"You don't know him but call me on your break and I will fill you in," she said placing her hand on my back escorting me towards the door.

I…don't…know… but Uneek was giving me creeping teas and vibes.

"Well, alright friend. I will call you," I said making my way back to the car.

Uneek didn't even make sure I made it to my car before I heard the door slam.

I know her butt ain't had none in a while, but that was no need to let her girl get mugged out here in these streets.

I wonder who her mystery man was?

I was tearing my brain up, trying to figure out who Uneek could be messing with as I walked down the long nursing home hallways.

"Asha, you starting to wobble," Tarshae teased, snatching me from my thoughts.

"Girl, shut up. I know!" I refused to go on

maternity leave though. I hate not working.

"It ain't like you need the money with that fine man you got taking care of you the way he does."

"Dang. Mr. Williams light on T," I exhaled loudly.

"Nope, that's your side tonight. I'm not messing with that old man. He stays with diarrhea," she whined.

"T, you know he big as and I'm pregnant. His stubborn self won't use the lift, and if he slaps me, I'm slapping him back and taking my case tonight!"

"Dang Asha! You better be glad I love you," she complained as she stomped down the hallway.

Mr. Williams was paralyzed from the waist down. He pretends he forgets that he can't walk, but he's just a jerk in actuality.

Most nights when he presses that call light, it's because he can't get his butt up off the floor.

Sure enough, when T opens the door, there he was sitting in a pile of his feces.

"Oh heck, nah!" T screamed and backed out of the room. "I quit. Forget this!" She yelled, stomping down the hallway.

"T, you know you be checking a bag at this job. Get yo' petty butt back down here before they report yo' ass to the D.O.N.," I laughed.

I laughed so hard I almost pissed myself. I was just as mad because he took his diaper off, knowing someone would have to clean him up. He was just spiteful.

I dragged T back in so we could get started.

"Mr. Williams, why you do us like this man?" I asked him sincerely.

"I was trying to go to the bathroom, honey. I wanted to try to clean myself up," he tried to explain.

I believed him, but T didn't.

"Mr. Williams, stop lying; you know you can't walk. You just want to give us a hard time for this little money they pay us to clean you."

I was laughing so hard I almost couldn't get my words out.

"Mr. Williams, we have to put you in the lift so we can get you back in the bed. We can clean you up without getting hurt if we do it that way."

"No. No. No," he complained shaking his head dramatically.

"Asha, I don't have time for this; let's just lift him," she pleaded.

I agreed. We both got a good grip on Mr. Williams and lifted him from the floor.

"Owwweee!!" I yelled out in excruciating pain once we had him back in the bed.

"You okay?" T asked grabbing me.

"Yea boo. I'm okay," I said rubbing my stomach.

"I'll clean him. You need to sit down before you hurt yourself or that baby. I just need you to take his trash out once I'm done," she said.

Tarshae turned out to be cool. Despite the sideways conversation I initially had with her on the phone when I was looking to work here.

She was ghetto but she made my time go by fast. She stayed working a double. I had no idea how she even spent the money she made.

Izaak came up here one day with Prod to bring me lunch and she walked me out. Izaak was trying hard to pull her but she wasn't having it.

"Nigga I ain't messing with you. I will have to beat yo' baby mama down and I ain't trying to lose my lil' CNA license over her," she laughed.

Everyone on the West knew Cam didn't play when it came to Izaak. She would fight anyone and didn't mind going to jail over him.

I'm sure Tarshae was just playing hard to get for my benefit because she was all about her coin, and the streets knew Izaak had them.

Ever since that night, she would be on her phone cheesing and what not. I stayed out of it.

Despite Prod and Izaak being practically brothers, Cam and I didn't mess with each other at all.

We never had words; she just wasn't the type of female I wanted to associate myself with.

My mind drifted away as T rambled on about Beloit's club over the weekend while she cleaned up Mr. Williams. Something about them shooting or whatever. I was more lost in these sharp pains in my stomach more than anything.

"Are you listening?" T asked snapping me out of my prayers for Cam.

"Yea, girl. I'm going to throw this trash out back."

"Gone head employee of the month."

"Girllll..whatever," I laughed heading to the back.

T stayed behind to watch our call lights. Normally on the night shift, once we checked them, they slept through the night. We only had a couple that needed to go to the bathroom.

We normally don't do this but we were throwing

all of Mr. Williams' linens out. My nose was sensitive, and it took very little these days to make me throw up everywhere.

I kicked the brick to hold the door open.

WAP!

I stumbled backward from the sting and force of the slap across my face.

My vision was blurred and I saw stars.

"Brian? What is wrong with you?"

Brian was dirty like he had been living on the streets. I guess none of the tricks he was cheating with would let him move in and run their house.

He made his way towards me.

"Arrgghh!" He yelled.

I pulled the switchblade from my titties and cut him! He jumped back like he couldn't believe what just happened.

"I ain't that weak chick no more Brian. You put your hands on me and I will gut you like a catfish out of the Mississippi River nigga! I suggest you get out of here before I call MY NIGGA!!" I stressed.

"This ain't over. I got something for you. Trust," he threatened.

"Bring it then nigga!"

"Girl, what's taking you so long?" T asked, peeking her head out of the back door.

I pulled myself together. I was like Beyoncé with my business. I let people know what I wanted them to know when I wanted them to know it.

I was showing Brian mercy not telling T or Prod about this. If I told T, she would most definitely tell Prod.

Brian must have literally slapped the piss out of me. I thought.

I felt a wetness between my legs, which was strange. A cold tremor ran through my body like ice water on an empty stomach.

"Here I come, girl. I need to run to the bathroom," I told her waving my hand at her on my way back in.

When I pulled my scrub pants down, a lot of blood in my panties and I freaked out.

A rush of fear stormed through my body and I couldn't think straight. I was trembling as I thought about the fate of my unborn child.

I grabbed one of the pads they kept under the cabinet for use in case of unexpected emergencies. I was still feeling the cramps, but I wasn't sure if it was more mental now that I've seen the blood.

"T…I need you to page the nurse on duty tonight. Hurry up please!" I asked her, hysterical.

"Asha, what's wrong?" She asked concerned.

"I'm bleeding, T! I may be miscarrying! Just get her!" I yelled out in terror.

Without another word, T ran off to find the nurse instead of paging her. I wanted to call Prod, but I'm not sure if he will make it in time before they rush me to the hospital.

I doubled over in the seat and said a prayer for my baby and me.

"Lord, please watch over us and cover us with your hands of protection. Lord, I'm not the best, but I do the best I can, and I'm working on doing better."

T returned with the nurse not too far behind her, running full force down the hall. I explained to her what was going on, and she grabbed a blood pressure machine and called 9-1-1.

"Asha, your blood pressure is through the roof! You are hitting stroke level! What happened?" She asked.

"T and I just changed Mr. Wiliams, that's all," I lied to her.

"Let me guess…he refused to use that lift, didn't he?" She said.

"Yes, and you know we can't make them," I told her.

"I know, but I would have made his big-self get in that machine. Asha, you pregnant now; you have to think about your baby," she fussed.

I texted Prod to meet me at Rockford Memorial Hospital. They had the best neonatal in Illinois, so I was at least grateful for that.

As soon as he got the text, he called. I knew he would; I just didn't feel like going through the whole spill over the phone.

"Babe, I know. Just meet me at the hospital they are bringing me now," I told him ending the call.

I never disrespected my man; he was my king but now was not the time for all the questions. I was just as scared as he was. All he was gone do is make me more nervous.

By the time I arrived at the emergency room, it was three o'clock in the morning. They brought me through the ambulance dock into the E.R., but I could hear the commotion from the waiting room. I could tell by the cries and screams someone had been shot. Unfortunately, this had become the norm in Rockford.

I laid in the bed as I watch the many doctors in white coats walk past me. The paramedic was giving the staff my vitals and letting them know my status.

They all moved me to the bed in my room.

"Arrrrgghh. That hurt. Oh my God!" I screamed.

I didn't care who heard me.

"Where does it hurt?" The nurse asked me.

"It's sharp pains shooting from my back around to my stomach, and it feels like my stomach tightening up," I cried.

"You are having contractions. We are going to get you changed and cleaned up. Once we're done, you will be hooked up so we can monitor the baby," she explained.

Just as she was finishing, Prod walked in and he was a wreck.

"Babe, what happened?"

His touch moved from my body down to my hand.

"I'm not sure. T and I lifted a heavy patient together and I think that's what did it," I explained.

My voice quivered from lying more so than the

pain.

To be honest, I think it was a combination of my patient and Brian attacking me.

I still didn't know what that was about.

Prodigy already beat him up before we got together and told him to stay away from me. Prod was more reserved, but he could be a savage. I was guessing that's how his family's last name was derived back in the day.

Prod and I were there all night into the next morning.

Prod had dropped the kids off at my mother's. She was calling every hour to check on us.

I was going through my Snap Chat. People loved yelling "no makeup" but be filtering the mess out of their pictures.

Prod was on the verge of cursing my doctor out. My doctor was all over the place like he hadn't slept in hours. This E.R. was jumping so I wasn't surprised they were exhausted.

I could see through the crack in the curtain of my room two police officers guarding the room of the victim that was shot. He was finally getting ready to go up to surgery. I honestly felt like they would let him bleed out right there if they could.

You could be caught in the line of fire and they would treat you like a criminal.

"Prod, who got shot?" I asked him.

He always had an ear to the street so I assumed he knew.

"I'm not sure, bae. To be honest, I've been focused on you. I'm sure I will hear about it the next time we meet at the warehouse," he said not taking his eyes off of the T.V.

He loved watching Law and Order.

My doctor finally walked in.

"Ms. Wilde, we've monitored the baby and it looks like you got a fighter. You have to understand when you stress, she stresses," he explained.

"She?" I asked in shock.

"Oh, I'm sorry, did you both not want to know?"

He apologized, placing his hand over his mouth.

"Well, if we didn't, you ruined that now," Prod said.

"Prod…please," I tried to soothe him.

He was pissed because he wanted to do one of those big gender reveal shindigs. This was his first child, so I understood.

The doctor ignored his rudeness and focused his attention on me.

"You both have a little fighter. She is just fine, but I am putting you on bed rest. I will send the orders home so you can give your employer a copy," he explained.

"Okay, thank you, doctor," I said.

The doctor nodded and headed out. Even with being nearly done with my nursing degree, I was a nervous wreck when I thought I was losing my baby. I couldn't think straight.

Prod helped me get dressed so we could leave. He said we could stop at the Walgreen's on Charles Street since it was 24 hours and get my prescription filled. He offered to drop me off at home first, but it was on the way, so it didn't make sense to have him come back out.

I was being a brat anyway. I wanted to be under him. It was weird that I didn't hurt as much when Prod rubbed my stomach. He had a way of making everything better.

"Prodigy," I called his name, tracing his hand with my fingers.

Our eyes met, "Baby, I'm so in love with you. You have made me a better, stronger woman that I never thought I could be. You have been a blessing to my children and me."

"Our children Asha. There is no yours and mine...only ours," he said.

We pulled into the parking lot of the pharmacy to park. My heart gave a nervous jolt as Prod leaned over and planted the most passionate kiss I've ever had.

He devoured my lips while blessing the inside of my mouth with his tongue. If I weren't in so much pain, I would take him down tonight kissing me like that.

I'm on bed rest for now, but as soon as I'm feeling better, it's on and popping.

PRODIGY

I hated leaving Asha at home alone, but her mom should be by soon to sit with her. Thank God she was retired. I couldn't miss the Back to School Hair Cut Event. I held it every year for the underprivileged kids in the area. Doing this always got me amped up. The local biker clubs contributed backpacks.

"Wassup everybody!" I yelled, walking into the shop. "Y'all ready to get these kids squared away?" I asked them, unable to hide my eagerness.

"Man, ain't nobody geeked about these bad kids running around the shop stealing and breaking stuff!" Darryon complained.

"Man, shut up!" I laughed.

We took the night before to set-up so there would be no rush before the event.

As soon as the doors open, the people piled in. The atmosphere was filled with the many chunk-chunk-chunks of barber chairs being raised by foot pedals.

We were all cracking jokes and having a great time despite Darryon's comment. He always had something to say so that was normal.

I looked up to see Austin David, a kid whose hair I started cutting when I stopped him from fighting in the jets one day.

He was a good kid; the hood made you hard in order to survive. If you were weak, you would be eaten alive.

I always remembered his name because he had two first names. At least it wasn't ghetto, I guess. He was twelve years old and like most young boys his age in the hood, the streets were raising him.

I started mentoring him last year and he has improved a lot. I'm trying to get him to play a sport to keep his butt out of trouble.

"Wassup, dude?" I asked shaking up with him.

"Nothing, chillin'. I'm about to pull me a new dip with my new haircut!" He said laughing.

"Boy! Don't be calling them girls out of their name. What's wrong with you?" I said popping him in the back of his head.

"Alright!" He yelled.

I took his backpack and hung it on the back of the chair.

"A.D., what is this?" I asked him through baring teeth.

"Man, mind yo' business. I came to get a haircut, not have you going through my stuff!"

I snatched him up out of the chair and dragged him to the back along with his bag.

Slamming the door, I turned to him. "Are you trying to go to Juve? From there, they're going to send yo' black butt into the prison system they designed for our black men such as yourself."

A.D. just stood there as if what I was saying was going in one ear and out the other.

"That's what's wrong with this generation! No one can tell y'all nothing. Y'all so tech-savvy you think you know it all because you can Google something," I continued to scold him.

I calmed myself down because I could feel my blood boiling despite the cool Illinois breeze.

"You gone give it back to me or not P?" He asked.

"Not! You shouldn't have brought it to my shop. I will take you school shopping instead. Deal?" I propositioned him.

A.D. was a good kid so I hope he took my offer. I didn't care if he didn't because he wasn't getting this gun back, regardless. I wanted him to at least feel like he got something out of the deal.

"Hell...I mean heck yea!" He screamed, giving me dab.

"Alright, well you can hang around here and just sweep up and direct the clients to an available chair," I explained to him.

"Aight, bet!" He said, heading out of my office.

I exhaled and placed the gun in my Gucci backpack. I had to get rid of it because I wasn't sure if it had bodies on it or not.

That was the thing about these guns off the street; either they were stolen or had a body on them. You get caught with it; that's your time.

Illinois dirty as hell; they will nail you on the strength that you're worth more to them in the system than free.

Not only for what they make off you being in there but your family as well. The fees for the phone call and them putting money on your books. It all adds up over time.

My squad and I ran through the heads that came in. By the end of the day, we were exhausted!

"Darryon, I'm heading out early. It's slowing down, and I need to take care of some business before everything starts closing," I told him.

"Okay, you know I can hold it down," he assured me.

Darryon was equipped to handle everything in the shop. He moved like Izaak in the shop.

"A.D., let's go," I said, motioning for him to follow me out.

Heading to the car with A.D. had me wishing that Asha was having a boy. I was grateful just for a healthy baby, but it would've been nice to have a mini-me.

No worries, Asha and I would have to just keep trying until we got one. I've always wanted a big family, regardless of being the only child.

"Buckle up," I told A.D. as I watched him, making sure he complied.

Yep, I think I will be a great father.

I took A.D. to every store he wanted,

running up a check close to a grand. The gun wasn't worth that much, but the smile on his face was.

He could just be a kid and enjoy school shopping with someone who cared about him, even if it was for a moment.

The sun was going down by the time I dropped him off and made my way home.

"Awweee...hell nah!" I screamed to myself.

I was halfway home when the cop pulled me over.

Man!

They always messed with me because of my dad. He gave them hell before they finally caught him.

When they did get him on the murders, he beat six cops up in that interrogation room.

They busted him on the back of his head with their steel rod knocking him unconscious.

When he came to, he was back on the same thing.

The supervisor came down himself just to see who was causing so much trouble.

Needless to say, the Le Savage name is not common, so whenever it came across their screens, they found a reason to mess with me.

"Mr. Le Savage, I need to see your license and registration please," he asked, being fake polite.

"Sure, I'm just going to grab my license out of my wallet," I warned him.

They were finding every reason and sometimes no reason to kill a black man these days.

I pulled out the information he requested and handed it to him.

"Can you step out of the car? I need to search your truck?" He said.

"You don't have probable cause to search my vehicle! You haven't bothered to explain to me why you pulled me over," I yelled.

"I pulled you over because of your broken taillight. My probable cause is the white substance laying in your passenger seat in that baggy," he replied, shining the light next to me.

"I'll be..!" I cursed under my breath.

There it was, a small bag filled with a white substance that looked like cocaine tucked into the crack of my seat.

I never carried that on me, so it had to fall out of A.D.'s backpack.

I complied with the officer's order.

He walked me to the back of my truck and had me place my hands on his hood, why he called for backup and the K-9 unit.

My body locked up in rage. My entire life flashed before me. Asha was on bed rest, and I couldn't trust Izaak at the moment due to his resentment of me not stepping down. This was horrible timing.

Within minutes the units arrived. They tore my truck apart on E. State Street.

Nosey people were hanging out of their windows recording.

I swear people felt everything needed to be shared on social media.

No regard or concern for people's situations.

They soon became a blur as fear started to claw its way through me like a bear on an unwanted camper caught slipping in the woods.

I saw them take the gun out of my bag and place it in an evidence bag. They pulled out a kit and tested the white substance.

I saw them weigh it then place a portion in a tube that contained a clear liquid. They waited for it to change colors and once I saw the color, I knew it was a wrap.

"Mr. Le Savage, we're charging you for possession of a controlled substance and the gun in your possession was reported stolen," he explained.

I lowered my head in defeat as he walked me around the back of the car and placed me in the back seat.

I had to turn my legs to the side because it was tight back here.

On top of that, it smelled like the last person they had back here didn't bathe. The smell of old body odor and hot garbage permeated my senses.

I watch them have my truck towed before we headed to the station.

Once I was booked, I was put into a holding cell. I know I wouldn't have a bond, but they still held me until I went before a judge.

When I walked in, all eyes were on me. Most of them niggas I knew from the hood. It was a couple of known enemies to my squad in attendance as well.

This was going to be a long night.

I reached through the bars to use the payphone on the wall.

I sighed as I listened to the phone ring. I prayed Asha picked up.

"Hello?" I heard Asha say.

"You have a call from the Winnebago County Correctional Facility. Press 1 to accept or 3 to block all calls from this facility," the automated system announced.

I heard Asha select her option.

"Prod? What the hell is going on?" I could hear her panting on the phone.

"Babe, calm down. I have to be quick. This call is not going to be that long. I took A.D. to get some stuff for school. Long story short, the gun I took from him at the barbershop was in my truck, along with something else. Neither was mine, but we both know that doesn't matter. Call my attorney and let him know what's up. Call Izaak and let him know what's up and that I will be in touch. Lastly, but most importantly, please don't stress yourself out. It will kill me if you lose our daughter while I'm stuck in here. I'm not sure how this will play out. Once this call ends, it will transfer you so you can set up an account. Put enough on here so I can call you as much as I need to love. Don't worry; it will all be fine."

Asha was silent and I could hear her crying on the other end.

"You have one minute," the lady came on the line to announce.

"Babe," I called out to her.

"I'm here. I...I...what am I supposed to do without you? I can't sleep without you," she cried into the phone.

Before I could respond to her, the phone disconnected, plunging me into despair.

I made my way over to the hard bench next to a drunk.

I set my face like stone; the last thing I needed was these niggas putting the word out that I was locked up.

IZAAK

I was in the trap when I looked down at my vibrating phone. Why is Asha calling me? We have each other's numbers, but she rarely calls me.

In all of the two years she has been with Prod, she has only called me twice.

Other than not encouraging Prod to get out of the business, she and I never had beef.

I hope Uneek didn't run her mouth and tell her I was the one upstairs when she popped up.

Uneek and I had been messing around for a lil' minute.

Uneek was chocolate with a nice lil' shape on her. Besides sitting in front of her house with her friends or family, she stayed in the house with her kids.

She could throw down in the kitchen too. She worked and came home. No club hopping or popping off at the mouth.

I was playing with fire because she stayed up the hill from Cam and me. If she found out about me creeping, she would be beating this girl door down, trying to bang her.

I finally got the nerve to answer, "Wassup Asha?"

"Prod is locked up!" She said, bursting into tears.

"What happened, Asha?" I asked her.

I tried to stay calm so she would calm down.

I needed to know exactly what happened and what message he sent through her.

"I don't know... he said something about he took a gun from A.D. earlier so when they pulled him over to searched his car; they found it and some work."

"Asha, you have to calm down. You know we have a business to run so I need to know exactly what came out of Prod's mouth," I reiterated.

"Okay," she took a deep breath. "He said to let you know what happened and that he will be in touch."

"Okay. I don't have a record, but I won't be able to see him. I don't know how this will play out; if he doesn't have a bond, we will send messages through you. I will teach you our different code phrases, so you will understand what he means. He says he will be in touch, which means they are not on to what we are running in the traps and warehouse. I was pissed at Prod for bringing you in; now I'm glad he did," I consoled her.

"Thanks, Izaak. Whatever y'all need me to do, I got y'all!"

"The first thing you need to do is keep that baby safe, girl. Prod ain't coming home and killing me for not looking out for you and the kids. If y'all need anything, hit my line. Asha, I'm not playing with you because I know how stubborn and prideful you can be," I fussed at her.

"Thanks, Izaak. I will keep that in mind. Is there anything I should let him know when he calls back? I put money on the phone."

"Tell him I have to work, but I will check with you to see how he is doing. That will let him know I got his message and will communicate through you," I explained to her.

"Okay," was her only response.

Her voice trembled as she spoke. You could hear the worry and fear in every word she said.

"Asha, he will be okay. I will call his attorney first thing in the morning. You try and get some rest."

"Okay, talk to you later, Izaak," she said hanging up.

Asha and Prod were the only ones who called me by my government; everyone else called me Bug.

I took a big swig of my Hennessy bottle.

"Where my money nigga?" A.D. spat.

He's been my shadow since he did what I paid him to do.

Well, I paid him half and promised the other half when I got confirmation that Prod's was locked up.

He should've stuck to his word and got out the business when he said he was. I had to take matters into my own hands.

At the end of the day, I was the one up at eight in the morning, making rounds at the traps and making sure everything was smooth. I was the reason this business was thriving, not him!

"Shut up! You got a whole wardrobe out of him anyways," I yelled at A.D. throwing the cash in his lap.

I knew how Prod loved them kids so I knew he would want to save A.D.

That further shows how out of touch with the

streets Prod was.

We all knew A.D. was the most heartless twelve-year-old in Concord Commons.

He was beating kids unconscious in pissy corners since he was in elementary.

We kept him on the squad so we didn't end up killing the youngin'. If groomed properly, he could be a righteous weapon out here on these streets.

I sat in my truck smoking a blunt while contemplating how well my plan worked. I couldn't have been executed any better.

I had already tipped the detectives off just as a backup. I sent them over to his house even though I know he didn't keep work there. I just needed him on their radar; that's all that was required to get them poking around.

One way or another, Prod was going to come off this business.

I looked down at my phone again as Cam's name flashed across the screen.

"Wassup, Cam?" I said, licking my next blunt that I was rolling up.

"What's up is this thirsty chick in my inbox on Facebook asking why I made you block her. Who is

Wanessa? Why does her profile say she's married, but she has time to ask me about you? She looks like her cat smell like sour Mac sauce from McDonald's. You love these nasty girls that be throwing that free coochie your way. Do you ever stop to think that if it's easy, it may be cheesy?" She yelled through the phone.

Wanessa was no one special. To be honest, Prod and I got drunk up one night and ran a train on her.

I'm not sure how she managed to find a nigga to marry her but kudos. I never knew she was married because I could get the cat when I wanted.

Some of these females ain't about nothing, just like some of us niggas.

"Man, Cam I don't know what you talkin' about," I lied.

Cam would have to catch me in a female before I confessed anything. Forget that.

I wasn't going down for Wanessa. She smelled like she was working in Da' Catch all day frying catfish for hungry black folks. That was the reason I stopped smashing with her.

"You know what Izaak? Come get your stuff from in front of my door. This was it for me. You can have these whores in the street. I'm good. I have a nigga trying to wife me anyway. So…yea…come get ya' trash dusty nigga!" She calmly communicated.

I pulled the phone away to look at it because, quite frankly, Cam had me messed up.

I don't know what she smoked today, but I was on my way to choke some sense in her.

Cam had hung up on me before I could cuss her out. She knew how to get under my skin.

I was speeding, trying to get to her so I could wrap my hands around her neck. They don't call me Chief Choka for nothing!

I ran lights and nearly hit an old man on one of them scooters.

I don't know what made them ride those things around the city like they are cars!

I swear if Cam threw my stuff out and them crackhead steals it! I'm poppin' off!

I don't know what's this about her having some nigga trying to wife her, but he will return her soon as she opens her mouth. Crazy woman.

I sped into the parking lot, and those bad kids knew to get out of dodge or become a speed bump. I wasn't in the mood.

My temples throbbed with rage as I pulled up and seen my clothes sitting on Cam's porch.

"Cammmmm!!" I screamed, barely giving my car time to shift into park. "Get out here, trick!" I yelled stomping up to her front porch.

BAM!

BAM!

BAM!

"You hear me knockin'!"

I turned around and noticed a cop car pulling in.

Dang. I thought to myself.

"You called the police on me?" I said, peeking through the crack in her blinds. "I see you standing there," I threatened.

A tall, dark-skinned cop got out of the car. He was bald with a strong jawline. Nigga looked like a Morris Chestnut reject. No hating involved. He was bigger, though; as a matter of fact, he was an easy two hundred ninety-five pounds of all muscle.

"Is there a problem here?" He asked, walking up to me.

"Yeah, my girl and I are just having a misunderstanding. That's all."

I made sure my agitation was evident in my voice.

"Your girl?" He repeated sarcastically with a throaty laugh.

My thoughts trailed off when I saw Cam appear from behind the closed brown metal door. It was impossible to kick them doors off the hinges; that's why I didn't try.

"Hey, baby. You good?" He asked, pulling her into him.

"Baby? What th-"

Before I could finish, Cam cut me off.

"How long you think I was going to keep looking stupid out here in these streets? Just because you felt like no one wanted me, Izaak didn't make it true. I tried to stick this out for our son, but you don't deserve me. He and I have been together for a while," she said placing a hand on his chest.

I mean mugged him but remained cool when I noticed he had his hand on his gun.

Cam knew to mess with a cop, or else I would've let her have it and him as well for the pure disrespect.

All these nosey people in Fairgrounds were outside in the middle of the night for some reason.

Well, they stayed out all times of the night for this very reason, to see what went down and who was creeping with who.

I spat at Cam's feet and started to grab my clothes. I knew it wouldn't last, and she would come running back to me. Cam was her own worst enemy and lacked the oomph to stay out of her own way.

Now I had to go and crash at my mom's house.

I didn't have my own crib, but I did buy my mom a home on the East and paid her property taxes up.

If I got killed in these streets, I didn't want her to lose her house over property taxes.

I bashed my fist on my steering wheel. After the years of cheating on Cam, I never thought she would leave, let alone get a new nigga.

Let me call this slut and tell her not to have that nigga round my son. Cop or not, I didn't want him around him.

I waited for Cam to pick up. I wasn't sure if she would.

"What," she answered with a dry tone.

"Don't have that nigga around my son!"

"Nigga, you ain't even around your son! The hell! Now you want to be a daddy? I got a real man now it's a problem? Boyyyy...get off my phone before I block your number," she said before hanging up in my face yet again.

I pulled into my mom's driveway and her 2003 Burgundy Lincoln Continental sat in the driveway. She rarely drove it now, but I kept the maintenance up on it for her.

I need to quit messing around and get my own place. I never needed one because I was either at the trap, Cam's, or at the "telly" with a random chick.

"Hey ma," I said, dragging into the house.

I didn't bother bringing my stuff in because I had clothes and everything at my mom's.

"Hey, baby. What are you doing here?" She asked, kissing me on the cheek.

"Cam kicked me out," I whined.

"Again?" She made sure I didn't miss her sarcasm. "You know I ain't never liked that lil' fast tail girl. She got a smart mouth."

My mom never liked Cam. She repeatedly told me that she was bad for me.

I sat on the couch next to her while she rambled

147

on about my relationship. Her eyes never left Wheel of Fortune but she had plenty to say.

I tuned her out as my mind wondered if Cam was really done with me this time. Maybe, it was best for both of us.

ASHA

It has been a week since Prod has been gone. I secured James "The Bulldog" Moore as his attorney. He was a beast in the courtroom for criminal cases. He favored Professor X from the X-Men movies with his bald head and stern looks.

Prod had a court date but the only thing they did was set another date a month out.

Despite Prod not having a record, they still refused his bail. It was because of his last name, no other reason.

I feared Prod would suffer the sins of his father in the worst possible way...prison.

I tried to keep hope alive, but you know the prison system is not built to favor the African American male. Any African American.

I remember I was fighting a case for Attempted Obstruction of Justice. The D.A. was trying to give me time for it.

I got the case in the first place when I first met Brian. I didn't know he owed back child support for his other kids.

Once his baby mama found out we were together, and he was trying to move in with me, she called the cops on him.

He had an outstanding warrant for missing court for Child Support.

When the cop came to my door, I was out at the grocery store.

They said they had a report of a minor being home alone so they had a right to enter.

I assured them that was far from the case. I went back and forth with the officer, trying to gain clarity more than anything.

He was irritated, so it escalated, resulting with me in handcuffs.

I was back and forth to court over a low-level misdemeanor. My public defender was this black chick with locs who never came to court.

I remember one time I was in there and they called me up.

Some young white boy who appeared to have just graduated law school stood next to me.

My chances of beating my cases were slowly dwindling.

"Is Attorney Smith absent for court yet again?" The judge asked my attorney's colleague who was standing in for her.

"Uh, yes Your Honor. She was out sick today," was his response.

"Of course she is. Let's set this for a continuance in hopes that she will show up for her client," he said slamming the gavel.

After court, the substitute attorney pulled me to the side so we could talk. He gave me hope. He educated me that I was being charged with the wrong thing.

He went over my options and a plan on beating this case to keep my record clean.

Well, I never kept that attorney because my bootleg attorney showed for the next few court dates. I ended up copping out because I couldn't miss work.

As long as I stayed out of trouble for twelve months, it would fall off of my record.

I never shared my doubt with Prod. When I was on the phone with him, I only spoke positive words. He didn't need my doubt at this time.

I'm sure it was hard enough for him to be away from his family just as I'm about to give birth to his first child.

I blamed me not eating on being on bed rest. My mom didn't buy it at all. She had practically moved in to help with the kids.

"Mommy," Amor called out creeping into my room.

My mom had braided her hair and placed it in a ponytail with a big purple bow.

My mama gelled down her edges and had swooped them down in two separate directions.

She had my baby looking like she was back in the '80s with them edges.

"Lawd, what your granny do to your edges?" I asked her.

"What mama? They pretty. I like them a lot," she said, rubbing her tiny hands across each side of her hair.

"What can I do for you, little lady?" I asked, swooping her into my lap.

"Are you okay, mama?" She asked, fiddling with her fingers.

She did that when she was nervous.

"Of course, muffin! Why you ask me that?" I inquired of her.

"You stay in bed all the time now. We never play anymore. I'm still your muffin even though you're having a new baby, right?" She whimpered.

"Oh, my baby! Of course, you are! You will always be mama baby! You are my firstborn. You are my world Amor; no one will ever change that. I will always be here for you. Always!" I assured her.

"When you get home, I will teach you how to make your own doll clothes. How does that sound?" I asked her pressing her nose with the tip of my finger like a button.

Amor was so happy she jumped up and down in my bed. I grabbed my belly and braced myself until she calmed down.

"Okay, my love. Time to get to school."

I needed to pull it together, but I missed Prod so much. He spoiled the kids and me. Amor asked for him more than her own daddy.

Brian started calling more once he found out Prod was locked up and may not be getting out anytime soon.

"Yeah, that nigga ain't here to save you," he would say.

"I don't need my man to save me. This .38 special will my nigga!" I yelled before hanging up in his face.

My mom snapped me back from reminiscing on the wack phone calls between Brian and me.

"Okay baby, I'm off to drop the babies off, then I'll be back to make you something to eat. You WILL be eating today," she stressed before walking out of my room.

"Hey, Izaak," I could hear my mom say in a dry tone.

She hated Izaak with a passion. She said he had the eyes of a snake and wasn't trustworthy. She said being addicted to drugs, she had learned by looking into a person's eyes to tell if they were dangerous. I couldn't help but wonder if there was more to her story when it came to Izzak.

She had already surprised me when she told me she dated Prod's dad.

I personally never had any bad vibes from Izaak.

He loved the streets and the women were the only things I knew.

Prod never volunteered much more outside of that.

"Asha...," his voice trailed off and his eyes were filled with pity.

This was rare for Izaak because he didn't show emotion at all.

A lump jumped in my throat. I could feel my face become flushed by the rush of heat to my cheeks and ears. I was embarrassed.

My twist out had fallen and my hair was wild. I was thankful it hid my face so Izaak couldn't see my full face.

I let myself go since Prod has been gone.

"Asha, you know Prod would lose it if he saw how little you have gotten in just a week. You pregnant girl. You already having problems, what are you thinkin' man?" He fussed.

I lowered my head as Izaak went in on me, and for the first time since Prod's been gone, I broke down.

I was a blubbering mess.

"Man...I'm sorry Ash. A nigga didn't mean to hurt your feelings. I'm about to get on your nerves because if I ain't at the trap, I'm gone be over here. You know ya' mama don't like me so you gone have to deal with us beefin' every now and again," he warned me, holding me in his arms.

It felt good to be held.

Izzak smelled of Versace cologne and pure seduction. His chest was firm, with his muscles bulging through his black t-shirt. He paired it with some distressed white pants and black Air Max.

I could see why Izaak had the women falling over themselves. He was like a brother to me so I was glad he cared enough to help me through this rough patch.

It has only been a week and I had no idea how I would deal with Prod being locked up.

If they make him do hard time I will lose my mind!

I didn't see my life working without my love being right here next to me.

He is having his first child; he had to be here for every single moment.

It was all good just last week. My life was nearly perfect.

It was crazy how fast things changed.

IZAAK

I broke my own cardinal rule…never come to this jail. My arms were folded across my chest and my face was twisted up to warn people not to try me.

I could feel my chest rising and falling with rapid breaths in anticipation of one of somebody going against the grain.

If they did, Prod and I would be sharing a jail cell because jailhouse or not, I'm giving these hands to anyone that wants them.

It was Sunday, so as I expected, it was slow.

The room was filled with chairs and monitors that looked like those computer labs back in the day.

The monitor flickered and then my boy appeared on the screen. He no longer had the fresh mohawk with the fade, but it had turned into a mini fro. He had a good grade of hair so it wasn't so bad.

"What you doing here?" His jawline tensed as the vein in his head pulsated.

"I know. You think I would be here if it weren't

important nigga! It's Asha…she not doing good man. Normally, I wouldn't even add this to yo' plate, but you need to talk to her. She trippin'. She lost a lot of weight even though she pregnant. She has always had meat on her but at the rate she is going she gone start looking like she getting high off your supply!"

That's the first thing black people said when you start losing weight fast, that you on crack or you got that package.

God forbid if you just decide to turn to a healthier lifestyle because your doctor found out you're pre-diabetic or just plain tired of your current state. In Asha's case, just plain stressed out from life.

"I know you don't owe me nothing bro, but I need you to look out for my family until I get out of here. To be honest, I'm not sure when that will be."

His neck appeared to shrink as he lowered his head and spoke.

He massaged the back of his neck as if he was trying to stop the words I just spoke from taking root in his brain.

This situation was breaking him down. Inside I was happy to see that my plan was working! Prod was one of them niggas that always spoke about a man walking with his head up and looking people in their eye and whatnot. One of those black empowerment types.

He was in the streets, but he ain't never have to survive like many us.

Yes, his dad did raise us like brothers, but he didn't do as much for me as he did for Prod.

I wasn't trippin' about it; it just made me a better hustler.

Prod, on the other hand, that nigga had it all handed to him.

His dad really didn't want him in that street life unless it was a last resort.

He was really grooming me for it because he knew I want anything but this street life.

I was born, raised, and was sure I would die in these streets.

I made my peace with that a long time ago.

It was nice to see him off of that high horse.

Yea, get down here with the rest of us. In reality.

I couldn't have planned this any better and I was enjoying every minute of it.

I didn't want to come and tell him about Asha, but the curiosity was killing me.

I wanted to know if he broke yet…and he did.

Them county and prison walls could break the strongest of niggas. I prayed that they ate him for breakfast, lunch, and dinner.

I hoped that his mind would turn on him and that he was tormented from looking over his shoulder for his enemies.

I wanted to apply as much pressure as I can.

Now that I added the stress of Asha to his plate. I knew he would give up sooner rather than later.

The counter came on the screen, letting us know we had five minutes left.

That nigga was hunched over looking like he was about to cry.

"Yo, our time almost up. I'm gone head out. You stay up bro," I put my fist up to the screen.

He didn't return the fist bump but only nodded in understanding.

"Oh, how the mighty have fallen," I thought to myself as I strutted out of the jailhouse.

A nigga felt on top of the world!

PRODIGY

Being in the county was the most life-altering experience a person could have. Being trapped behind bars with a bunch of ruthless repeat offenders had me ready to bust somebody's skull open to the white meat.

For the most part, people knew not to disturb me; those who didn't were warned by others.

Even though I was locked up, I still had a squad behind me.

No matter how much I tried to escape this life, I always end up knee-deep in the sewer. It was gutting me from the inside out.

I've done everything in my power to go the other way and still ended up behind bars.

Izaak thinks I didn't see that smirk he was trying to hold in.

I was so mad at our visit that I had to put my head down so the tears wouldn't fall.

I'm as real as they come, so a nigga like me don't fold under any circumstances.

I may have to regroup and replan, but a nigga never fold.

"You tryna' play me?" I heard one inmate yell to another.

All this testosterone pinned up in one place along with the hormones they pumped through this food had niggas banging left and right.

Most of them knew they were on their way back to the penitentiary, so they didn't care one way or another.

A nigga with nothing to lose was like quicksand to every other man around him. It was worse than crabs in a barrel. For a person to desire someone to stay locked up just as long as they were, was a warped mentality.

I saw one of the guards signaling for me.

"Your attorney is here to meet with you. Turn around," he told me.

They treated you as less than a man in here and I hated it.

It was always some going on in here because they constantly demeaned us as if we had no value.

It didn't matter if you were innocent or guilty. In correctional officer's eyes, we were all equally garbage.

I arrived in the small room with the peeling yellow paint and sat before my attorney.

"Hey, Prodigy," he greeted me.

James, my attorney, worked with so many black people he had a swag to him.

If he didn't like black people, you couldn't tell.

"Hey, James. What you got for me?" I asked, leaning back in my seat, clasping my hands together.

"The D.A. is willing to give you a deal. They are offering five years. If you take it to trial, you risk doing fifteen. The gun didn't have a body on it, but it was stolen. I was able to get the drug charge taken off with an agreement that you would go through treatment while incarcerated. I know the gun wasn't yours, but the young man you had me contact is denying everything," he explained.

"Nah man," I exhaled.

"Prodigy, we have to be in court later today with our decision. So what are you deciding? It's your future," he peered over his glasses, waiting for an answer.

"I need to call my fiancé and let her know. I need to talk this over with her. When I get to court, I will have a decision for you. It's not fair that I'm losing five years of my life trying to save someone else's," I complained.

I was brilliant and I just wasn't saying that to gas

myself up. I always figured something out when there appeared to be no way at all.

I couldn't find my way out of this though. There was no way around doing this time.

I heard the hardest time to do was the time you didn't deserve.

Once I was back to my cell, I called Asha.

I wasn't ready for this conversation, but I had to have it.

"Hello," Asha sounded so sad and hopeless on the other end of the phone.

"Hey, babe. How are you and the kids doing?"

I didn't want to just jump in with the news I had for her. I did want to know how they were doing.

Izaak said she wasn't keeping weight on her.

"We're doing, babe," I could hear her sobbing.

"I'm so sorry for getting us into this, babe. I will make this up to you. I have court today. They offered me a deal for...five years."

The line went silent.

"Asha. Did you hear me?" I asked her.

"Five…years…," was all she said. "No! No! No!" She screeched in my ear.

A rush of pain filled my body as my legs buckled. I've never felt so helpless in my life.

"If I fight it, I risk doing twenty-years. I need you to tell me what we should do?"

"We?" She said.

"Yes, you are the mother of my child; you are my family. I want you to one day be my wife once this is all over."

"I don't think you should fight it. Your dad's name rings bells down there; it's no way you would get a fair trial," she explained, pulling herself together.

"I was thinking the same thing. Babe, I have one more thing to ask of you. Once you have the baby, I need you to take over the business."

"Take over the business? Won't Izaak be mad? I don't want to be in the middle of no mess, Prodigy," she rebutted.

"You won't. Just tell him what I said. You know how to stand your ground. I taught you everything there is to know. The shop will be in good hands. You got this," I assured her.

"If you say so," was all she said.

"I know you won't be able to come to my court hearing today, but I'm going to request they let me come home to get my affairs in order. I'm hoping that with me owning the barbershop, they will let me come home. I would just have to turn myself in hopefully in a couple of weeks."

"Babe, that would be awesome! Then I could hold you one more time and make love to you," she sounded much better.

"You have to eat, babe. I need you to take care of yourself. I can't be in there worrying about you and the kids and keeping them niggas from shanking me." I laughed.

"I promise I will do better. I was thinking we name her Legacy. The baby," she said.

"I love it. Prodigy and Legacy. I'm feelin' that, babe."

I needed that encouragement right now. It was something simple but I needed that hope.

"Babe, they about to turn the phone off, so I will call you once I get back from court."

"Okay, my love."

I didn't let Asha know about Izzak just yet. I had my suspicions, but for now, that's all they were. Suspicions. If I find out Izaak crossed me, I will make him suffer.

* * *

I walked into the courtroom, shackled by my wrist and ankles.

They escorted us all to the empty jury booth to our immediate right.

I didn't bother scanning the courtroom because I knew no one was there to see me.

They called my case number on the docket, and I was escorted to the small wooden podium.

My feet shuffled across the dark brown carpet that was beyond the need of a good shampooing.

"Mr. Le Savage, from my understanding, you have agreed to take the plea deal, is that correct?" The judge asked me.

"That is correct."

"Have you been read your rights, and do you understand that you have a right to a trial of your peers?"

"Yes, your honor," I responded.

"Okay. Is there anything else?" She asked the

attorneys.

"Yes, one more thing. My client is requesting a two-week furlough to get his affairs in order. He is a respected business owner in the community with no prior offenses."

"Request denied. A respected member of the community would not be in possession of a stolen gun and heroin. The defendant is to be taken into immediate custody," she said, slamming her gavel down on the hardwood block.

I was pissed! She had no reason other than my last name for denying my request.

I looked back and saw Asha in tears. She wasn't supposed to be out of bed.

I'm guessing she thought I would be coming home and wanted to be the first to see me.

My vision blurred with tears as I watched Asha's mom help her out of the courtroom while she held her stomach. Her body was frail, just as Izaak said.

This would be the last ounce of emotion I showed for the next five years.

By the time I got out, my daughter will be five years old, and she wouldn't even know who I was.

If I'm going to survive the next five years, I had

to get my mind right.

I had to live as if no family was waiting for me outside of those cement walls.

ASHA

Three Months Later

The past few months have been a blur. Despite my mom and Izaak not getting along, they have been working together to help me. I was due any day now and as big as a house. I kept my word to Prod and picked my weight back up.

I wrote Prod every day once he got settled. He sent me these homemade cards all the time. They were really creative and pretty.

There were so many talented men locked up in the prison system—what a waste.

Legacy was growing healthy and kicking up a storm in my belly.

To my surprise, Izaak didn't fight me on taking Prod's spot on the team.

I told him he could take point and I would have his back.

I couldn't wait to drop this baby, so I can get back to working and staying busy.

I only had my clinicals left for my nursing degree and worked it out to do them after the baby.

My grades were excellent and my professors understood with my medical documentation, of course.

I had planned once I obtained my Nursing Degree to go PRN to conduct my street business.

Darryon was handling the shop, so there was no reason for me to go there.

It's not like I could anyway. I was still on bed rest, trying to let my baby girl keep baking inside.

Izaak dealt with him anyway.

"Hey, big head. What's going on?" Izaak said, jumping in the bed with me.

"Nothing, ready to have this dang on baby!" I complained.

"Let my niece bake as long as she needs to. Don't be rushing her," he said, rubbing my belly.

Izaak had been a God sent since Prod was locked up.

They shipped my baby off without allowing him to say goodbye or come home to get his affairs in order.

It was hard, but Izaak did his best to keep my mind off of it.

He was even nice enough to pick Uneek up and sometimes bring her over when he was coming this way.

I guess things have cooled off between her and her lil' boo from a while back.

I heard from her a lot more, and she was over here just as much as Izaak.

"Izaak, you sure be over here a lot," Uneek said, rolling her eyes.

"I told my boy I would take care of his family. I keep my word, ya' feel me. Mind ya' business Uneek. If I didn't come this way, how would your non-driving self get here?" He said, cutting his eyes at her.

I'm not sure what their problem was, but it was quite intense.

"Chill out Izaak. She didn't mean anything by it," I placed my hand on his back to calm him down.

"Girl, I'm not worried about him!" Uneek lit her another Newport.

"Uneek, you know you can't be smoking around me," I said, motioning for her to go on the porch.

"Girl! Ain't nothing gone happen to that damn baby because of a little smoke. My mama smoked while she was pregnant with me and I'm just fine," she spat, popping her neck and waving her hand on her way out.

"You're not just fine...you crazy as hell, Uneek!" I yelled after her.

I turned my attention to Izaak, who was strolling through his Facebook feed. His feed was full of butt naked women who I'm sure were fake police profiles.

"Cam still haven't taken you back?" I teased him, thumping his forehead. "She still with RoboCop?" I laughed.

"Yeah, she engaged, she claims. He did move her into this big house on the Eastside."

His eyes drifted away from me and I imagined he was envisioning Cam with her new life...happy.

"How you feel about that?" I pried.

"What you mean? A nigga don't care at all. I still see my son; I just don't mess with his mama anymore. To be honest Asha, I didn't want that life with Cam. The family thing. That's why I treated her the way I did. I just honestly didn't want nobody else messing with her, that's all," he shrugged, lighting his Black & Mild.

WAP!

"Girl! You gone set us on fire!" He patted the bed, trying to put out the cherry from the Black.

"I just made Uneek go outside; you ain't' special negro!" I laughed, watching him trying to put out the small flame.

"Are you happy for her? Cam?" I pulled my hair into a messy bun waiting for him to answer.

"I gotta be. She's the mother of my child. She never did anything but try and love a nigga in hopes of making him an honest man. I wouldn't give her what she wanted, so she found a cat that would. To be honest, it's better now. It's just about Jr. plain and simple."

"Izaak."

"Wassup Asha?"

"Ummm...my water just broke."

"What?! Ms. Wilde! Ms. Wilde! Asha's water just broke!" He yelled, jumping up from the bed.

I pulled the covers black, exposing a puddle of fluid. I was in too much pain to be humiliated.

Izaak threw my bag on the bed.

"Ms. Wilde, I can stay with the kids while you

174

take Asha to the hospital," he suggested, pacing the floor.

Izaak was nervous like I was having his baby. It was quite amusing.

"You can drive us and Uneek can watch the kids," she countered.

"Okay, I will take her bag to the truck and wait why she gets dressed," he grabbed the bag and darted for the door.

"Izaak…your keys," I extended my hand, catching him before he was out of sight.

"My bad."

My mom was fussing at Izaak all the way to the hospital. She was a church lady now, but I'm sure Izaak almost made her backslide.

When they got me up to my room, I was almost where I needed to be to push my daughter out.

Izaak got ready to leave once they transitioned my bed so I could deliver.

"Wait. I want you to stay." I asked him.

"Baby, don't you think that will be a little inappropriate." My mom interjected.

"Your mom right Asha, I can leave." I could tell

he was disappointed.

"Izaak, you've been here just as much as she has and I want you in here. I need you to stand in for Prodigy. He would want you to be here as well," I reached for his hand as I got ready to push.

Three hours later I was looking at the most beautiful little girl... Legacy Le Savage. She was perfect and looked just like her dad. I was one proud mama bear.

Once I was settled in my room, my mom was ready to leave to relieve Uneek.

"I'm going to take your mom home so I can drop Uneek off. I don't want her to have to bring the kids out this late," he leaned over and hugged me on his way out.

Izaak's Gucci Guilty cologne flooded my nostrils. My cheek brushed up against his. I never noticed how soft his skin was.

My eyes traveled the length of his body, getting stuck at his lips.

These drugs had me tripping. I relaxed my head on my pillow, trying to convince myself that I wasn't "that" girl.

You know...the one that sleeps with her man's best friend.

Prod hasn't even been gone that long.

Izaak has been my rock since my world came crashing down. I'm sure this was just my hormones.

Legacy was sleeping next to me. She was such a good baby. Here I was doing this all over again...alone.

"Hey, Asha," Brian said, walking into my room.

"Brian, how did you know I was here?"

Anger seared through my very being. I hated Brian with a passion.

I had my hand on the call button.

"I'm not here for trouble. I know ya' baby daddy locked up and you need a man around the house. I can be that man," he argued.

"You've never been a man all the time I've know you," my eyes darted up to him.

"You slut!" Brian mumbled under his breath with his hands firmly clasped around my throat.

I clawed at his hands, trying to get loose from him. My eyes teared up as the oxygen was deprived of my body.

"You steady tryin' to kick me while I'm down, huh? You ain't gone be happy until I kill you!"

"What the-!" I heard Izaak say as he entered the room.

Izaak charged into the room, punching Brian dead in his mouth! Fist to teeth.

Once Brian hit the floor, Izaak kicked him a couple of times in his ribs.

"Nigga get out of here before I blow your cap back. You think because my boy locked up, you gone disrespect his woman?"

"Ugh. Ugh," were the only sounds that escaped Brian's mouth.

Izaak picked him up from the floor and threw him out.

It was late, so not that many people were left on the floor. Visiting hours were over, so people had already left.

"How long has that nigga been bothering you?"

I lowered my head in shame. "Since Prodigy has been gone, it's been a lot. He calls and threatens me. When you're not there, he pops up and tries to see his kids that he doesn't take care of. I stabbed him the day I was rushed from my job to the hospital. That's what caused me to start bleeding, forcing me on bed rest. He caught me behind the building and tried to jump on me. I'm not the weak woman that he was accustomed to jumping on. I get with him now with no problem. If I weren't off these pain meds, I would've got with him again."

Izaak started laughing at me, "You wanna be a thug so bad. Asha, you ain't never been about that life. Prod already told that nigga to stay away from you!"

"Look, I'm tired. I don't want to talk about it anymore."

I turned over to try and get some rest. I knew Legacy would be up soon to breastfeed.

"Aight. Well, I'm going to stay with you tonight. When your mom comes, we can switch out. I'm not leaving you up here alone just in case Brian tries to come back up here and mess with you."

As I was drifting off to sleep, I saw Izaak pick Legacy up out of her hospital crib. He held her close and rocked her back to sleep.

Izaak was making it harder and harder for me to fight my feelings.

IZAAK

I'm gone end up killing that nigga Brian. I can't believe I came in here to find him putting his hands on Asha again. He did that to her in front of everybody in the projects.

Prod had me watch his back when he checked him about dragging her out the house.

I ain't no saint, but what Brian was tryin' to pull was foul. He was intentionally trying to humiliate her in front of everyone in them nosey projects.

They talked about that for weeks. Asha still held her head up and handled her business though, like a boss.

Asha had come a long way since then. She was confident and beautiful. She's always been gorgeous to me and I wasn't into heavier chicks.

Asha could draw any man in though. I watched her treat Prod like a King. She never disrespected him or made him feel less than a man.

Despite school, work, and the kids, she still managed to keep a hot meal on the table.

I watched them together, and secretly I wanted that. Just not with Cam.

Asha was not part of the original plan. I just wanted to take the business from him, but now I think I want his girl and family too.

I'm doing all the work anyway.

This nigga about to be gone for five years at the minimum.

I ain't gone lie when Asha gave me Prod's message about her stepping up in his absence; I thought I was gone have to off her as well. No lie.

After being around her these past few months, I can see why Prod decided to stay in the game.

Asha made a nigga feel like he could walk on the moon if he wanted to. Nothing was impossible with her by your side.

She always knew the right thing to stay and she was extremely strategic. She thought of resolutions out of the box.

Asha was a chameleon; she became whatever you needed. She had heart too.

Brian caught her coming off that high from the drugs, but I bet money she was gone get him back when she gets out.

I picked up Legacy when I got back to the hospital in hopes that she would take my mind off of Uneek.

I argued with her the whole way home! We just freakin' and she was acting as I owe her an explanation or something.

"You and Asha are getting mighty close. You do know that's yo' boy woman, right? Not that you care because you've always been foul as hell."

Uneek cut her eyes at me while she attempted to clear everything on her chest.

"First of all, it ain't even like that. Second of all, I don't owe you an explanation! You're not my woman Uneek!" I snapped.

"Well, that's craaazyyy because we do everything like we are a couple, Bug! Asha out of your league anyway. She sees right through you. What do you think she will do once she finds out that you set her man up? You think she will hold you in high regard once she finds out you did it to have the businesses all to yourself?" She spewed, reminding me that I needed to quit running my mouth after I laid pipe to her.

"You repeat that and I will kill you. Try me. What I do know is you better strip as soon as we hit this door. I got something for all the energy you have," I said, smoking on my Black & Mild.

Uneek's mouth curled up into a smirk. She stayed in the house and all that, but she was as gutta as they came.

I was shocked at her other side. She could be ruthless. She knew about the setup because she helped me put it together.

She said she watched me for years put in the work to build our empire why Prod walked around like some entitled brat.

"I'ma give you some NoDoz nigga," she laughed.

"For what? I don't need that." I had no idea where she came from with the stuff that fell out of her mouth.

"Cause you sleep on me, my nigga," she kept laughing.

Uneek was goofy. I hung around her because we laughed all the time at the most random things.

She was what you call a guy's girl. Uneek loved basketball. Not that watch it cause you watch it type, but she was ready to fight over LeBron if it came down to it.

She loved her Jordan's and jeans but kept her

hair and nails done.

Uneek was like one of the homies with a vagina, ya' feel me.

No one knew it, but we had been messing around for a while off and on.

Once Cam left me, we were together more.

"Long as you don't cross any lines with Asha, we good," she threatened again.

"We gone be good regardless because you don't run nothin'. You know what? I'm cool on you; we need to chill out. You can find your own ride to Asha's house. You got me twisted, and I'm tryin' not to put my hands on you. You try me and I will burn you down like a Swisher Sweet," I pushed her forehead with my finger while my mouth tightened with anger. "Get out of my truck!"

Uneek slammed my door after she jumped out. I wasn't worried about her saying anything; she knew better.

To be honest, I was growing tired of these hood chicks popping off at the mouth.

That used to turn me on, but since I've been helping Asha out with everything, including the kids, it has changed me.

A female popping off at the mouth all the time instead of communicating how she feels on an intellectual level ain't cute.

I sat back and watched how some of these hoodrats moved. Always looking for a come up and most would let you smash when you just showed them a little attention.

They didn't make a nigga work nothing these days. Titties and booty meat stayed on display with all the see-through clothes they wear now.

You ain't have to imagine anything because it was out front and center.

Asha and I have been coming up with some ideas to expand the business. We've just been waiting for her to have the baby and start feeling better.

We're thinking about expanding into Chicago. Asha has a cousin who is connected down there, and they need a supplier.

We have Rockford on lock, so we might as well go for it.

I know Asha is trying to do the nursing thing, but I know she would kill it if she goes all-in on these streets. It's in her blood. Her dad is downstate right now from moving that work.

That nigga Columbian, so he had the purest

cocaine on the streets in the late '90s. Think Denzel Washington in American Gangster. He would cut a nigga throat just because he didn't like the way he looked at him.

Asha never talks about him; when I asked her about him, she said he stopped allowing her to come to see him caged up like an animal.

He said seeing her made him weak, and he would be in there until the day he died, so it was best that she pretended he was dead.

I would never forget how she rubbed her forearms as she explained her past to me. It was as if it was cold and void of love, so just remembering it made her physically so.

Her brother was in the Marines so when he called, Asha lit up. He was always traveling the world, so he rarely called.

He always sent Asha postcards because she refused his money.

The one time I was around, I overheard her talking to him.

"Justin, please brother. The kids and I are fine. I tell you that over and over. Save your money to buy you a house or pay for a wedding so you can hurry up and give me a niece or nephew," she joked.

She hated taking anything from anybody.

Her family was everything to her. She would defend them until the death of her.

You couldn't buy loyalty like hers these days.

I watched her as she slept. I gently put Legacy back into her cradle so the nurse could take her back to the nursery for some more blood work.

Asha was breastfeeding, so she was with her mostly.

She had a vaginal birth, so we should be able to go home in a couple of days at the most.

Look at me talking about "we", it sounded cool though.

I could do this family man thing easily with Asha.

I'm gone start bringing Jr. over with me so all the kids can start getting acquainted. We gone be one big happy family in this joint.

Asha and I could sell dope by day and sit at the table for dinner as a family at night.

I'm not sure if my pipe dream would come through, but I had to go for it.

I mean, all of my other plans have gone through without a hitch.

A nigga was undefeated like Floyd Mayweather.

I had five years to wipe Prod from Asha's mind.

Females leave niggas every day B.

Ain't no real woman like her gone put her life on hold for a nigga that's gone for years at a time.

I reclined my chair and pulled the ottoman close next to her.

I turned on Family Guy and watched until I started drifting off to sleep.

Thoughts of my new family flooded my mind and I was full of hope.

Hope was something I haven't had in a long time.

I was finally the one winning and having it all.

ASHA

1 Year Later

I walked into the trap in my red bottoms and fitted red dress. I was thicka' than a Snicker and finer than frog's hair. All eyes were on me not because of all this booty meat Legacy left me with but because heads were about to roll.

Niggas always wanted to get greedy and steal. Stealing from me is like taking food from my baby's mouth and I wasn't playing that.

I graduated at the top of my class with my Nursing Degree but I did as I said and went PRN.

I only worked to keep my license active, but this street life had consumed me.

I was still on my African queen vibes attempting to build these black men, but some of them truly weren't worth the flesh they were wrapped in.

I don't know who was raising these niggas now. Most of their mamas were only in their mid-thirties to busy clubbing instead of raising them.

Since some of them lacked parental guidance, I

was about to give them some by putting my foot up their butts.

"Hot Rod baby…you keep coming up short love," I said, taking a seat across the table from him.

I crossed my legs, exposing those thick thighs that were saving lives in this twenty-first century.

Izaak was sitting back in the corner watching me run things.

I saw him lick his lips and goosebumps form on my legs. My clit fluttered at just the thought of him trailing all of this fine thickness with those soft lips.

I've been faithful to Prod, but it hasn't been easy. A woman has needs and being around Izaak every day was becoming a struggle.

I love Prod with everything in me. Would I be wrong to get me a little something to hold me over? I mean…five years is a long time.

We've been careful not to cross that line, and my mom warned me about playing with fire.

"Ms. Asha, I wouldn't steal from you. You know that! I count everything out twice before I hand it over," Hot Rod begged as the sweat soaked through his wife beater and dripped down his forehead. His body trembled in fear.

"Donte, come sit next to Hot Rod," I played with the blade of my meat cleaver bone ax. It had a nice wood handle with a shiny steel blade.

I stood up and circled them both, caressing their shoulders as I rounded them.

"Actually, Hot Rod, I knew that. My audits on you the past week proved it. Your stash didn't come up short until after your pick-ups. I'm guessing Donte figured that we would dismiss it as you were the new kid on the block as you being a thief. The only thing about that is...I know you hustle to care for your sick granny. You have a record, so I know it's been hard for you to get a job. I know you are doing this for her."

Without even breaking eye contact with Hot Rod, I chopped off Dontae's hand, separating it from his wrist.

"Arrrrgggghhhh!" He cried.

I was careful not to get any blood on me. I kept my blade sharp so it was a clean cut.

Izaak threw a towel over the crowd onto the table. Dontae snatched it up while still crying.

"Hot Rod, I have a cousin who is a supervisor at Gunite. I already spoke to him; the only thing you have to do is fill out your paperwork. If you mess over his name, I will mess over you," I said to him, looking over at Dontae.

"Are you sure, Ms. Asha?" He stammered.

"Hot Rod, everyone is not built for this. What type of leader would I be if I ignored that? You're a good kid. Like most black men, you will do whatever it takes to take care of your family. I won't allow you to be forced into this way of life. This fast life ain't going nowhere. If you need us, we will be here. Go wait for me in my office," I told him.

Bug had some of the other guys take Donte and drop him off at the E.R.

Once he was patched up, they would bring him back. He would be demoted and work through the pain with his one hand to get our money back.

My nickname on the streets was Joan Clever because I loved my ax.

I joined Hot Rod in the back.

"Hey Rod, I just wanted to give you something before you head home," I said, pulling open my desk drawer.

I had already put four grand in an envelope for him.

Rod was a really good kid and if I could kick him

out of the game before he got in too deep, I would.

"Ms. Asha, I can't take that. I don't know when I will be able to pay you back. I'm barely paying my granny bills and buying her medicine," his forehead creased with worry as he lowered his head in shame.

"First of all, Black King, you lift your head up when you are speaking to someone. I don't care what the situation is. You hold your head high. You don't have to pay this back. Take it and pay your granny bills up and get her medicine. This money will give you time to get your first paycheck and not live from check to check," I anchored my attention on him as I handed over the money.

Rod wrapped me in the biggest hug and his tears soaked my dress.

He was carrying a heavy burden on his shoulders. Rod wasn't out her making babies out of wedlock and gang banging; he was trying to hustle to take care of his granny.

Both of his parents were locked up and she was the one that raised him.

It was an unfortunate but common trend in the black community.

He even graduated high school, despite all he had to overcome.

He pulled away from me, wiping his face and stuffing the envelope in his pockets.

"I won't forget this, Ms. Asha. If you ever need anything, and I mean… ANYTHING, please let me know," he said before he walked out of my office.

Just as he walked out, Izaak walked in.

I called him Bug in front of the guys; not all of them knew his legal name, and he wanted to keep it that way.

"Wassup Jason Voorhees?" He joked.

"Shut up!" I laughed.

Izaak was full of jokes.

He has changed into a totally different person this past year.

He even brought over Jr. all the time. Since it was me, Cam didn't mind him being around us.

It was weird; Uneek hardly came over anymore since I had the baby.

She's a supervisor at a call center now, so she says she doesn't have time anymore to come over.

I only see her once every few months now. If that. Best friends don't have to see each other every day to be besties, so I wasn't worried, just missed her.

"We still driving down to see Prod, right?" He reminded me.

"Yep, as scheduled," I sighed.

"Why you sighing all hard. You not excited to go see him?"

"It's not that. I just feel I'm past this, you know. It ain't like he down there for doing something to take care of us. He down there trying to look out for someone that still ended up in Juve. So now my daughter has no idea who her father is because he was trying to save a child that wasn't his."

My frustration boiled over as I poured out my thoughts to Izzak. He only nodded in understanding.

He never spoke negatively about Prod, regardless of how I ranted.

I had no idea how I would feel once I arrived in the morning.

At first, I was going to see my man every week.

Once I even brought the kids, I didn't want them to get accustomed to seeing him that way, so that was the only time.

I didn't think Prod could get any sexier, but he did. He had been in there lifting weights, and his skin was glowing.

He must've found a barber because he managed to keep his hair cut in there.

My baby was looking like a whole meal.

Here we are, almost at two years and I'm becoming exhausted with the drives.

He doesn't say it, but it's as if he thought my life would stop while he's in there.

I explained to him time after time that I had to keep going for our children.

They can't see me stressed out and crying all the time.

That's not healthy, and I promised Amor that she wouldn't have to worry about me. So I made sure my baby girl didn't.

I loved Prod, but I learned after Brian that you have to put yourself first.

These men can switch up on you at any time.

That's why despite Prod's love and support, I still took my behind to school and handled my business.

He will never be able to put me out without me having a backup plan in place. No man would.

Prod would never do that, but I had to plan always as if he would.

"He only wants to see me this time," I told Izaak.

"Why? What's going on?" Izaak asked.

"I don't know. You know some days are rougher than others for him.

He most likely just wants to be a brat," I assured him.

"Well, I can chill in the room why you visit. I could use some rest. I reminded your mom that we leave out tomorrow for the weekend, and she said she got the kids as usual."

My mom and Izaak had finally got on amazing terms. Even she couldn't deny how great he has been with the kids and me.

I don't know if they talked or what, but it appeared that they had squashed the beef.

She noticed the fire kindling between us, but I assured her he was just another best friend for me. Nothing more.

"Uuh-hmmm," was all she would say.

I would just roll my eyes and ignore her. My mom always tried to tell me how to live my life.

I would never disrespect her, but she was strung out on drugs when I needed her advice. I had to make sure my brother Justin and I survived.

I had already packed my bags, and normally Izaak spent the night so we could leave at four in the morning to make good timing. It was a six-hour drive.

* * *

I followed the same routine as I arrived bright and early for my visit with Prod. I was felt up by them lesbian guards and treated like a convict for the next four hours.

The following morning we finally made it to Marion, IL.

We paid for early check-in with double beds at the Holiday Inn.

Prod always thought we had separate rooms, but we never did. We kicked it. We stayed up watching movies and eating takeout.

It was like our vacation time from the business. We never had sex or so much as kissed.

Izaak never made me feel uncomfortable. I was more worried about me crossing the line than he.

I pulled up to the Shawnee Maximum Security Prison. My dad made me stop coming to see him because he didn't want me to see him caged like an animal.

I missed my daddy. Things were better when he was home. It seems like a lifetime ago.

Prod said he sent word that if he needed anything to let him know.

Not that Prod was worried, but my dad told him niggas knew not to try him.

Prod's dad's name rang bells as well, so he was good either way.

By the time Prod was assigned to his cell, he already had his commissary, books, and anything else he could've imagined.

His dad had already sent word. Prod was welcomed by a squad of inmates assigned to watch his back and make sure his hands stayed clean from any dirt that needed to be done in there.

He never went into detail about what went on and I didn't ask.

I signed in the book and showed my I.D. I was taken into a small room where I was patted down and told I could put my things in one of the lockers for a quarter. Same process every time.

The correctional officers treated you like a

criminal because you support those you love doing time. They were extremely rude!

Once I arrived, I picked a table in the far back corner with my back facing the guard.

I watched the door waiting for my man; when he appeared, I fell in love all over again. He had the prettiest smile.

I was relieved that he didn't let this get him down. We knew he was innocent, and it had to be the hardest time to do to me.

He swooped me in his arms and kissed me.

"Alright now," the guard said, looking over his newspaper.

Prod sat on the opposite side of me.

"You want something from the vending machine?" I asked him.

Prod said they didn't have some of the stuff in these vending machines, so we pigged out for our four-hour visit.

They had these bomb hot wings that you could microwave. I made our food because he wasn't allowed to move.

I caught him up on what was going on with the

kids, and I told him Izaak is still helping out with everything.

"You sure have been talking about Izaak a lot. I told the nigga to look out for y'all not move in!"

He held my gaze for a moment before looking away without a word.

"Prod, he doesn't live with us. I would never disrespect you like that, baby. Calm down. We are just getting to this money, that's it!" I tried to explain, holding his hands.

"Babe, I want you to fall back on the streets. You are getting too deep in. They calling you Joan Clever in here too. Other niggas may think that it's sexy that they girl is holding down their empire, but I don't! I'm grateful, and I know I asked you to do this, but now I'm asking you to stop. Your name is starting to ring bells, and that's good and bad. Pretty soon, you will become a target. These niggas don't care about you being a female either," he warned.

"First of all, I absolutely will not fall back. I've tripled our business's income, and I've even turned that warehouse into a detail shop. The traffic there now is just as legit as the barbershop. We into the seven figures now, babe. I was built for this! My daddy had me in the kitchen cutting work up with him. I can hold my own!"

"You was built to be a wife, mother and nurse Asha! Not no drug lord. Oh, you gangsta now, huh?" He spewed through clenched teeth.

His temples were pulsating, and I could see the rhythm of his heartbeat.

"It's too late. Izaak and I have a business meeting in Chicago next week. We are expanding into the city as the new supplier. We will-"

Before I could finish, Prod was on me like hot grits!

"Are you crazy, Asha!" His hands tightened into fists.

"Inmate! Keep it down!" The guard yelled.

"Them Chicago King Pins will come together and put a hit out on you and Izaak. They will kill our whole family Asha about trying to come into their territory!" He had lowered his voice to a quiet yell by this time.

"That's what the meeting is for. The heavy hitters have agreed to a meeting with Izaak and me. My cousin set it up for me. They're going to either agree, or we gone make a move anyway. It's the next logical step."

"Next logical step? You getting power and money-hungry, Asha. We have more than enough money for our kids, kids at this point. You trippin', and I wouldn't be your man if I didn't tell you so. I can't do anything about it because I'm locked up. You know how I feel about it, so all I can say is be safe," he said, getting up from the table.

He signaled for the guard to let him know he was ready to go back.

We still had about three hours left.

"Don't bother coming tomorrow," he said, looking back at me.

I made my way out of the visiting room before my tears could fall.

Prod's never gotten that mad at me...ever.

Once I was done with the deal, he would see. He worried too much.

Being locked up has gotten him back on that 'let's go straight mentality'.

I grabbed my stuff from the locker and headed back to the hotel room.

When I let myself in the room, I burst into tears again.

Izaak jumped up from the bed to hold me.

"Asha, what happened?" He asked, rubbing my

head and pushing my hair from my face.

"Prod wants me to cancel the meeting in Chicago and pull back on being so involved in the business," I was hysterical.

Prod's opinion meant everything to me. I cared what he thought and how he felt. That was my man.

He was wrong on this, and he was underestimating what I could accomplish.

"What?! He tripping! You a beast in these streets. You were made for this, Ash! You've come a long way from that woman in the project getting clowned by her dirty baby daddy. You some pressure! Feel me! Any man would be lucky to have you being the Bonnie to his Clyde. You know Prod ain't never been about this street life in the first place. You and I had to survive in this. Baby girl, that is something Prod will never understand like I do," he slipped his hands around my waist.

My heart dropped to my toes as Izaak stroked my ego. I think it was time I let him stroke something else.

"I'm going to get into the shower and calm my nerves. Can you pour me some Hennessy and Coke? Matter of fact…hold the Coke. Thank you…I needed that reassuring. We have taken this to a whole other level, and Prod will understand once he is home."

"I know," was all he said before turning away to fix my drink.

I did my best to let the hot water wash away all of my insecurities and doubts about my next business move.

I stepped out of the bathroom in just my towel.

I made the decision I was no longer waiting for Prod to come home and satisfy my needs. I needed a man now to take away this stress and to hold me at night.

Izaak's eyes widened when I stepped out of the bathroom. The steam escaped that had been trapped in there with me. It was symbolic to me of the heat coming from between my legs.

It has been almost two years since I've felt the touch of a man, and I was horny as hell.

"Asha...umm...what you doin'?" Izaak asked nervously.

It was funny to see him at a loss for words. He always had some smart to say.

"Now I know you ain't never had some thick girl lovin', but it's gone change your life. You will never be the same... I promise you that," I said, sashaying over to the bed.

"Are you sure you want to do this? If Prod finds out he gone kill me and you both girl."

"You are here now; you've been the one through it all. All Prod does now is complain. I don't blame him; I just need more right now. I will always love him, and I will deal with it when he comes home. Right now, it's been you and I in the trenches," I grabbed his hands gently as I placed them on my thigh.

Izaak leaned in and kissed me with everything he had. I could tell he's been wanting to do that for a long time.

That kiss was the start of a three-hour sex session that left him and me both exhausted.

I fell asleep on Izaak's chest. Not one word was uttered between us both. What was understood didn't need to be explained.

Prod had been the only man I had been with since Brian, and he was my first.

I spent my life trying to survive, so sex was the last thing on my mind throughout the years. Not only that, I was so self-conscious about my physical appearance.

Not-any-freakin'-more! I would hit a trick with a hair flip in a minute.

I don't know what this meant for Izaak and me, but I wasn't trying to find out.

I just wanted to enjoy the moment. I hope Izaak could understand that no matter what, I would never leave Prod under any circumstances.

He was my forever man.

I held my guilt at bay until I drifted off to sleep.

IZAAK

The past few weeks back has taken some getting used to. Asha and I have been freakin' like rabbits. It has been well worth the wait.

The sex was just a bonus. Asha had become my favorite person over the last couple of years.

She made the fact that Cam moved on and was getting married easier. Who knows, maybe Asha and I would get married.

I had to laugh at myself.

Asha and I got it in anytime and anyplace that we could. The office at the warehouse, home when her mom was away with the kids, but most times at my crib.

Asha had convinced me last year to get my own place. I told her it would be a waste because I was always at her house or the warehouse.

She said it would be a…what's the word she used? *Pivotal.*

Yeah, that's what word. A pivotal point in my life.

Asha had been working with me on getting my grown man on.

I still wore my designer clothes but I was on my Jay Z. swag now.

Just because I was balling didn't mean I had anything to prove.

I stopped disrespecting Cam. I noticed that she no longer disrespected me in return.

I still didn't mess with cops, but her dude was cool. I had to get to know him because he would be around my son.

I was falling in love with Asha. I tried hard not to, but it was inevitable once you got to know her.

"Hey, big head," Asha said, walking into our office at the warehouse.

We were getting ready to pull out for the meeting in the city. We already put everything in the truck.

I had a few instructions and loose ends to tie up before he headed to the city.

"I'm ready. How about you? Are you nervous? You sure you don't want me to take point?" I checked again with her just to be sure.

"Yeah, my cousin has them expecting to speak with me. This Joan Clever mess is getting out of hand. They see me as some kind of human butcher."

"Mannnn....you are! You chopped off one dude's body parts, each piece at a time, until he passed out. That negro pissed and dropped a deuce in his pants twice before giving up the ghost."

"Why are you staring at me?" She asked.

"I don't think I ever seen you wear your hair straight."

I'm not sure if it was permed, pressed, or what they call it-blown out, but she looked amazing.

"You really trying to get us killed. If any of these niggas try to hit on you at this meeting, it's going to be trouble...trouble," I did my best Bernie Mac impression.

I loved that about her. We laughed all the time. We are so goofy together.

"Boy, ain't nobody thinking about me," she pressed a hand to her mouth to stifle her giggles. "Let's hit this highway before this traffic picks up. It's Friday; I want to check in and grab a drink before the meeting."

Two hours later, we were pulling up downtown to the Hyatt Chicago on the Magnificent Mile. I loved staying at this hotel.

There was a bar on all three floors. Even the pool room had another bar with super-sized Jenga pieces set up to play. The drinks were larger than the size of your head. They were definitely worth the forty bucks.

I made arrangements to have one of the pool rooms to ourselves. I paid the bartender and waitress to be scarce once we got ready to start the meeting.

Asha and I were no longer doing the double bed thing but opted for the king-size suite that overlooked the city.

I picked out Asha's outfit for tonight. She was just getting into designer stuff and it was my fault.

It was a compromise of me toning it down and her kicking it up a notch.

I had to remind her that she was a millionaire even though we had to be careful about how we moved.

Nothing too flashy in Rockford, but when we were out of town, it was time to live it and stunt city all the way, baby.

I was praying that these west side and south side niggas could get along long enough to make this deal happen.

Asha and I arrived early to make sure the room was set up.

We figured no one wanted to have premade drinks available, so we paid for an open bar for them.

We were making small talk at the bar over drinks when two men came walking in. The lighting was dim but enough to see their features.

One was about five foot five with deep-set chestnut eyes that seemed to sparkle against his thick eyebrows. His locs were pulled back into two barrels twist with red tips.

"What's up? I'm Amanté," he extended his hand to me.

It was a bit unexpected. I thought it would be some kind of general shake-up or a fist pound.

I shook his hand and turned to the other, who was about six foot three.

He looked more like a bodyguard than a King Pin; I guess he fits the description for both.

He was bald with birdlike eyes. This nigga looked like he wasn't wrapped too tight. I found out his name was K'eon.

I wasn't worried because Asha and I both were strapped. I'm sure they were too.

It was so many people at the hotel. Each level was packed with those passing through and those looking for a little fun while in the city.

Chicago could have several feet of snow out and people will still be on in the mix in negative degree weather like it ain't nothing.

We wasted no time taking seats at the table.

I gave our bartender and host a nod and they made themselves scarce, closing the doors behind them.

Reserved signs had already been placed on both doors.

Asha was seated at the head of the table and I was located to her immediate right.

Her hair danced on her exposed shoulders.

"We propose to come in as the sole supplier to the south and west side of town. We offer a better product at a lower price, which in turn puts more money in your pockets," Asha pitched to them.

"Y'all already have people out on our blocks selling y'all work. Now you want to come in here and offer to be the full supplier? You Rockford scammers are something else," a flash of anger covered his face as he hit me with something I ain't even know.

I cut my eyes to Asha, trying not to let them know I didn't know anything about us having work out on the streets in the City.

"My cousin released some of our product on the streets only as a feeler. I wanted to see how our product would do on the streets in the city. From what I hear …it's poppin'," Asha replied.

"Poppin' or not, the proper protocol would have been to give to distribute to OUR people so we can see for ourselves if it's lit or not," Asante´ hissed as his expression grew turbulent.

Asha had us about to get our skulls blew back. This looked foul from any perspective.

On top of that, she didn't even let me know she gave her cousin some of our work. I couldn't wait until this meeting was over so I could get on her.

I'm her partner, not her flunky. If she started to try and handle me like Prod, it was going to be a problem. For real!

"Ms. Asha, you need to be careful in this drug business. You're new to this. People do not like the way you move. You suspect as Ms. Lady. That type of behavior will get you killed. Niggas in this line of work don't care anything about you being a female; you bleed just the same," K'eon threatened.

"Don't threaten her!" I stood from the table, reaching for my gun.

"Izaak, it's fine. I can handle it. Black Kings can you put the guns away. Please finish what you were saying," Asha interjected.

"Besides, all of our blood, sweat, and tears it took to build up our blocks will not be just handed over to you because you got some cheap cocaine," Asante´ followed up behind him.

Their eyes darted over to Asha as she slipped her hands into her purse.

"Easy guys. I bought something for you. If you think this has been stepped on and is garbage, I will be out of your hair for good. My father is Sabastian Moreno. I'm not sure if you're familiar with his name, but you will find out where my roots come from if you ask around. We have connections in Columbia. I've revolutionized what my father couldn't back in the day. I've solidified transport into the U.S. of pure product. It was honestly not my intent to offend you by releasing my product on your streets without your knowledge. I just didn't want to waste your time or ours if there was not an honest demand for the product," she explained, leaning over, exposing nearly all of her breasts to them.

They were so lost in her sauce they forgot they were just mad enough to threaten her life.

Asha laid out some lines for them with her fresh

set of gel nails. Her red polish glimmered against the white powder.

The way they hit it, you could tell it was free.

We watched them clean the extra from their noses while they waited for it to kick in.

"This is good. It's pure as anything that's on the streets right now," K'eon said.

"Well, let us talk this over with our other partners. We have your numbers, so we will hit you up in about a week or so with our decision," Asante´ confirmed.

"Sounds great," Asha cooed.

I had to remind her that she was selling drugs, not cat, once they left.

We knocked back a couple more drinks then they both left.

Asha and I ordered a shrimp cocktail the size of both of our heads put together.

"Next time, don't have me blindsided like that. I need to know all the details regardless of how small you think it is. We a team; I need you always to remember that. You have helped turn this boy into a man. You call me King some much, and I'm starting to believe it. You even got me carrying myself differently. I'm trying to learn big words like you and everything," I laughed.

"I won't do that again. I am so caught up in making moves that I forget. Charge it to my head and not my heart. This move right here is it. Today we became some of the heaviest hitters in the Midwest."

As she leaned over the pool table, she exposed those chocolate mounds again, this time for me.

"Yeah, that's cool and all, but don't be seducing these niggas Asha. I saw how you were leaning over that table, showing them your tits," I invaded all of her personal space as I walked up to her. Our lips were nearly touching.

"Okay, King. I understand," she said, devouring my lips with hers.

Russ' *Losing Control* played softly through the pool speakers.

She's falling in love now, losing control now
Fighting the truth, trying to hide
But I think it's alright, girl
Yeah, I think it's alright, girl. Ooh
She's falling in love now, losing control now
Fighting the truth, trying to hide
But I think it alright, girl
Yeah, I think it's alright, girl. Ooh

I laid Asha on the fuzzy green pool table. She stared up at me with those doe eyes as I removed her panties. I spread her legs with my hands, caressing her smooth skin, making my way to her glistening middle that invited me in.

The way she handled that meeting had me wanting her something serious.

I ravaged her with my tongue. Every flick of my tongue showed her how proud I was of her.

"Oh, umm-"

We both jumped up from the table when we heard the hostess come in.

She nervously turned around so we could get ourselves together.

I slipped her three hundred dollars on our way out.

We started cracking up laughing on our way down the hallway.

We stopped to have a couple of bottles of Moet sent up to the room so we could finish what we started.

Man, I never thought I could be so happy.

PRODIGY

I hated this ugly prison-issued looking scrub. They were nothing compared to the quality threads I was accustomed to draping over my body.

These cheap loafers I wore around were so thin you could feel the cold concrete through them. I saved my Nike's for when Asha visited.

I've rarely seen her in the last six months. She claims to be busy with the same business I asked her to fall back on.

Since the day of the fight, things have been rocky with us. When I call, she keeps it brief. I rarely catch her around the kids.

I was getting the impression that her mother was raising our children, not her.

I'm sure Ms. Elisha didn't want the kids around the kind of business Asha was conducting. She has always been vocal about our lifestyle choice.

My lungs felt constricted as I thought of what Asha was really doing. I didn't trust Izaak, but I did trust Asha.

There wasn't shit to do in here but think. You think of where you went wrong and all the time you wasted.

I couldn't wait to see my baby girl. Asha stopped bringing them completely, which was no big deal because I didn't want her early memories of me being caged like an animal.

It was one excuse after another. I could feel the distance grow between us.

I only received cards on the holidays. Her letters now are no more than a paragraph. That's if she even decides to write to me at all.

The streets have been whispering about her and Izaak. I'm not liking what I'm hearing.

They said they out there making moves like a hood Bonnie and Clyde.

Everybody talks in Rockford, so people had no problem telling me they think they are screwing too.

I haven't confronted Asha with it because there was nothing I could do about it, even if she is. I was locked up in this cage with no end in sight.

Once they unleashed this beast, there would be hell to pay.

Two inmates arguing brought me back to the reality of the hell I was living in.

I stayed in my cell except for going to chow or hitting the weight room.

I refused to be like these other niggas here, jacking off or sneaky linking with these other niggas. It wasn't that serious. These niggas acted like they couldn't survive without being inside of something...anything.

I remember my first night here. The sound the doors make when entering behind these walls. The gates slamming echoed your detachment from society.

We were made to strip, bend over, and spread our butt cheeks. The most humiliating experience ever. To have grown men looking up your butt crack.

I was untouchable because of my dad. I wasn't worried about anything but doing my time.

The other fresh fish with me had a rough entry into the prison system.

As soon as lights out came, I could hear one of the young guys that came in with me yelling at the top of his lungs.

He was in for killing his baby mama and some of her people were in this facility.

I don't know how they made it happen, but they had him put into a cell with a nigga bigger than Deebo off of the movie Friday.

I later learned his name was Dekion. Inmates

called him "Big D".

"Yo! Get off me, bro!" We all heard him yell.

WAP!

WAP!

WAP!

He was hitting the young dude so hard you could hear the punches that connected with his face echo through the halls.

His screams were muffled and we all knew what was coming next.

Although his face was crammed somewhere, you could still hear the heart-piercing squeal as Big D had his way with him.

It went on for hours. The kid didn't even have a voice left by the morning.

He limped passed barely alive, with two C.O. holding him up. He couldn't walk on his own.

Word came back that he needed twenty stitches in his anus. He was beaten and raped within an inch of his life.

That didn't happen as much as people thought. The real niggas just took it out on the weights.

I shouldn't be in max, but it didn't matter where they put me at; I would be solid either way.

I wouldn't wish another man being raped by another man on my worst enemy.

I don't care how they tried to justify it in prison. It was a reflection of their true desires.

Niggas needed to just live in their truth and be done with it.

I laid down, looking at the underside of the bunk above me. I had photos of Asha and the kids tuck between the metal. I wanted them to be the first and last thing I saw every day.

I tried to figure out what I could say to Asha to help her remember why she fell in love with me.

I know it was selfish of me to want her to ride this out with me, but I needed her.

She was the only thing that gave me hope in this hell hole.

It was visiting time. I made my way out to the rec area and waited for them to call my name.

My heart was pounding out of my chest because I had no idea how Asha would react to what I had to say.

They were moving slow today so once I made it to the visiting area, Asha was already there waiting.

She looked stunning. She was wearing her hair straight these days.

She had it pulled up into a high bun, which highlighted her facial features.

Her make-up was immaculate and not one eyelash was out of place.

I'm not sure when she started wearing red bottoms. I'm sure Izaak had something to do with that.

I could tell by her demeanor that she didn't want to be here.

She looked irritated, like she would be counting down the minutes until she could leave.

It was as if she was in prison with me when she was here. I remembered when she once enjoyed these four-hour sessions.

They were nothing like our love-making session, but we had time to be with one another.

"Hey, babe!" I was happy to see her, but she didn't even bother to stand to hug me.

"Hey," was her only response.

Asha was unenthusiastic and her responses were dry.

I guess what they were saying on the streets was true; she was freakin' Izaak. I could tell by her demeanor.

I couldn't prove it yet, but I knew that nigga had something to do with me being here. Soon as I get out, I was going to return the favor.

"How have you been?" I asked, taking my seat across from her.

"Good and yourself?" She asked.

"I'm cool...look, Asha. I don't care about what's been going on out there. I need to know if you still love me. Do you still want us?"

There was pleading in my eyes. I leaned forward and held her hands.

"You know I want us. You are my heart Prod. I've just been caught up in the business."

"Do you remember the first time we met?"

"How could I forget?" She lowered her head in shame, remembering the day Brian dragged her out of the house by her hair.

"I knew from that day I wanted to protect you

and build a family with you. From then up, I've watched you grow into this amazing woman filled with love, loyalty, and strength. You a beast in these streets with a hood name and all. Remember the story I told you about your name?"

"Yeah, you said the king and queen wished for her," she repeated the story I told her years ago.

Her face softened as the memories of us falling in love flooded her mind.

Asha began to light up right in front of my face.

"Asha, after everything that we've been through, you have to know that I will always love you. You are my air baby, and I'm so empty and incomplete without you. My world revolves around you and our family. I know being without me has been hard on you. Raising our children has been unbearable at times. Looking into Legacy's eyes and it's like me staring back at you. The tears that you cried that I couldn't wipe away, baby, I'm sorry," I confessed my love to Asha.

"It's not your fault," Asha's words were getting stuck in her throat as the tears fell from her eyes.

"I'm all in. When I get out, I want us to get married. You have a month to plan."

I wanted to see if she caught on.

"A month? Prod are you serious?" She yelled.

"Shhhhh!" The guard watching us snapped.

"Yep, they gave me good time. I wanted to tell you in person. I've been helping teach the G.E.D. Class. When I told them I had my bachelor's degree, I convinced the Warden to let me teach the class. I haven't been in here fighting or none of that. I did that all for you and the kids, Asha. So like I said, woman…you have a month to get EVERYTHING in order," I stressed the everything. "End it with Izaak today, Asha," I demanded.

Her face dropped. "What you thought the streets weren't talking. Every nigga in here knows what they girl is doing. Everybody knows somebody that knows somebody. Feel me? I heard y'all like the new Bonnie and Clyde out there. End it…today!" I reiterated.

"Prod…I…," she attempted to explain.

"I don't want to know. I just want it over. I will deal with him when I get home about the rest," I told her.

We rambled on about any and everything over the next few hours. I haven't seen her in so long; she had a ton of stuff to go over with me.

She filled me in on how she was able to move the cocaine into the U.S. using her dad's old connections.

Apparently, she went to see him that day after she and I got into it.

He had already heard how she was moving in the streets and he was proud.

Justin wasn't with the drug life, so Asha was his pride and joy.

Despite him staying away from her once she got older, she still followed in his footsteps.

Sometimes things are branded in our children that we can't erase later down the line, I guess.

She went over the Chicago meeting and the new niggas she would be doing business with.

Chicago got a taste of that pure white girl and couldn't get enough.

"Asha, be careful. They will kill you as soon as they figure out your connect! Who all have you told?" I was curious to know.

"I'm the only one that knows. I told Izaak that my father wouldn't allow me to tell anyone else, or he would treat me as if I wasn't his daughter and have me killed. I wasn't lying because he did say that. My daddy can be ruthless. I'm not sure if I was supposed to tell you."

"Well, keep it like that. We will figure everything

else out when I get home if needed," I told her.

"Times up!" The guard yelled.

"Look, I put something authentic in your life. Nothing will ever replace our love," I told her.

I smiled, looking down at her cleavage. A noticed a portion of my name was showing. It was tattooed on her left breast, which made me smile.

Asha ended our visit the way it should've started.

I witnessed the hope come back into her being. Her man was coming home and she was excited.

She jumped up, hugged me, and washed the inside of my mouth with her tongue.

"Aaayyee!" The guard yelled again.

"Alright, love, I will let you know the specifics on when I'm getting out. I sign my papers tomorrow," I assured her.

"Alright, boo!" She sang.

I watched Asha make her way out the doors. Pretty soon, I would be back in her arms and hold my daughter for the first time ever.

ASHA

I cut a step to my car. My man was finally coming home.

Shoot, I pulled a Keyshia Ka'oir and tripled Prod's empire. Wait until I tell Iza...

What was I thinking? There wasn't a happy reunion for the three of us.

Izaak was crazy and we have developed some feelings over the past couple of years.

He's been there and I can't take that from him. I needed to be careful about how I handled his heart.

Man! I need Uneek.

I was making a turnaround trip so Izaak didn't come along this time.

Besides, we both haven't had time for any mini-vacations with our new business in the city. We had more people to watch and more product to distribute.

That six-hour drive felt like three. I was pushing nearly one-hundred miles per hour the whole way.

I told Uneek I had an emergency and that I was on my way. She's been shady lately, but that's still my girl.

I pulled up to the spot in front of her door. I beeped my horn before getting out.

Uneek pulled the door open and waited for me to grab my purse and lock my doors.

I almost tripped. I was moving so fast, trying to spill this tea.

"Girl, where the Remy at?" I asked her.

"Dang, is it that bad?" She asked, going to the freezer to retrieve the cold bottle of libation.

She poured us a couple of shots, but I was sure I would need to take that bottle to the head.

"Prod coming home next month!" I said it as if I was still in disbelief.

"Okayyy….?" Uneek looked puzzled. She wasn't sure what the problem was.

"The problem is I've been sleeping with Izaak," I finally confessed.

"So it's true? The streets have been talking, but I told them that there was no way you would screw your man's best friend why he's locked up. I told them you the most solid female I know," she ranted, crossing her arms in disapproval.

"It just happened. Izaak was around all the time,

and things kinda' developed between us. Feelings involved now, Uneek. I have to end it before Prod comes home. He told me to end it tonight!"

"He knows? Girl, Izaak ain't worth the skin he's printed on! He and I were messing around for the longest and I bet he didn't tell you," she blurted out.

"What…why didn't yo' ass tell me?"

"Because I didn't want to assume you were sexin' him. I wasn't going to volunteer the information because we were just kickin' it. It was nothing serious."

"I'm shocked. You two were always arguing. I never thought you two would take it there."

There's more Asha. He set Prod up. He's the one that paid A.D. to come in the shop and leave the drugs in the truck. He wanted to take over the business. The only way he felt he could do that was to either kill Prod or get him locked up."

"Ksshhhhh!"

I took that Remy bottle and busted her head open. She was leaking everywhere.

The bright red blood soaked into her dingy white linoleum.

"You sat there and watched me cry over my

man being locked up? I was all lost at how it could've happened, and you knew the whole time this nigga set my man up! I had this snake nigga around my kids Uneek!"

I towered over her, still holding a piece of the broken bottle. I strongly considered slicing her throat and calling my cleaning crew.

Uneek was still dazed from the blow across her head.

I grabbed my purse to leave, and soon as I turned my back, I felt a sharp burning sensation flashing through my body like lightning.

No lie, that taser brought me down. We both were stumbling around.

"If you would've let me finish, I could've told you that he threatened to kill me if I said anything. You know he's crazy! I got kids too!"

Once I got myself together enough to speak, I let Uneek know my plan.

"Uneek, I'm on my way to his crib now to end this and let him know I'm telling Prod he set him up. I got my gun if that nigga tries anything," I was nervous, but I was ending this tonight.

"Asha be careful! That nigga a live wire when you threaten him. He hates that!" She warned.

"I know. I'm already foul as hell for laying up with him. I gotta handle this like a woman Uneek. You know how I get down."

I was mad at Uneek but we would eventually chop this up. I knew how deadly Izaak could be. I understood her fear and it was valid.

I prayed that Prod called me tonight before they cut the phones off in there. I was telling him everything!

I was speeding over to Izaak's like I was a contestant in The Indie 500, which turned my twenty-minute drive into a fifteen-minute one.

Everywhere in Rockford took twenty minutes for the most part. I texted him on the way, letting him know I was on the way.

He thought he was about to get some of this soft and gushy, but I have a surprise for him

"Hey, bae!" He greeted me at the door.

I hugged him and walked inside.

"I have something to tell you. Prod is getting out in a month, so we have to stop the extra."

"A month?! How did he pull that off?" He coked and eyebrow in surprise.

"Were you ever going to tell me you set my man up to go to prison for something he didn't do? Or was the plan just to steal his life and not say anything? You could never be Prod! You are the epitome of a low life!" I drew my fist up like angry stones.

Smack!

"You ungrateful ass winch! I helped you with them bastard kids and tripled your so-called man's weak business. If it weren't for me, none of them nigga in the streets would've listened to you. They didn't try you because of me! Prod ain't getting this business back! It belongs to me now! Thanks for letting me know he's coming home. Now I know how to move. This is going to be a war. Now get out of my house, you fat trick!"

I was in his house, so I couldn't shoot him dead, but I had something planned for him. He must've forgotten who my daddy was.

I've never called on my dad when it came to issues with my men, but I wanted Izaak dead for what he has done to my family.

I initially planned to let him down easy until I found out why my daughter didn't know who her father was!

I was sick to my stomach at the thought that I allowed the man who snatched my man's future away to sex me down every night.

I couldn't go up against him alone. I wasn't sure whose allegiance was to me and who was with Izaak.

I had no other choice but to chill and try and develop a plan. Hopefully, I could figure out something before Prod came home.

I grabbed my purse and headed home.

ELISHA

Asha didn't go into detail about what happened between her and Izaak. I loved my daughter but I worry so much about her.

This fast life was consuming her, but I was relieved that her and Izaak's fallout forced her back into nursing.

Asha went back to picking up more hours nursing. She told me she just wanted to stay as busy as possible until Prod came home next week.

She wasn't quite herself lately. The glow she once had was now replaced with gloom. Her countenance had changed drastically. I wasn't' sure if the job was exhausting her or if she missed Izaak.

Asha can try and act like the last couple of years never happened, but we all know they did.

She was working so many doubles we thought it best if I keep the kids through the week and switch off to her on the weekends; unless she didn't have to work.

When I was cracked out, I wasn't there for my children. I try to be there for my grandchildren as much as possible. It was the least I could do.

I made Asha a promise long ago. I would do everything in my power to keep my word.

I loved the bad boys, just like Asha did when I was younger. Her dad and I were inseparable until he went to prison for life.

I didn't bother divorcing him because I felt I was past the marrying age in my mid-fifties.

I know women are doing it, but I couldn't see myself starting over.

Her father, Sebastian Moreno, and I were high school sweethearts. He was very intelligent but loved the street life. He dropped out our junior year.

He was Columbian and black. I stayed fighting over him back in the day.

I remember one instance very vividly in high school.

"Bash, are you kidding me?" I yelled, pulling the passenger door open.

"Aaaahhhh!" I dragged the skinny white girl by her long blonde hair out of my man's car.

"I told you to stay away from him, you scalawag! I told you that you would have to see me if I caught you sniffing around him again!"

A kick in the mouth reinforced every few words. I did my best to stomp a mudhole in her face. I was something else back then.

He made me finish high school even though he dropped out.

When he got mad, he started talking in Spanish. It was more like Spanglish because he would say some of it in English.

We didn't have the translating apps back then like the kids have nowadays. I was sure he was calling me everything but a child of God anyway.

Over the years, I learned enough to get the just of what he was saying.

Bash connected with his family back home and found a way to move massive amounts of cocaine through Rockford, Chicago, Freeport & South Beloit.

He threw me this graduation party. That was the night I first tried cocaine. I was hooked after that.

All the money Bash started bringing in caused us to live a fast and dangerous life. I didn't care. I was numb from the cocaine.

Somewhere in between the babies came. I still didn't slow down.

Bash would have addicts wash their clothes, feed,

and change them.

Nothing mattered to me more than my next hit.

Bash spoiled Asha the most and treated Justin like a red-headed stepchild. He said it was because he was a boy, but I didn't let him come down on my baby like that when I could help it.

When he got raided, the kids were in school. I was out running the streets. We returned home to a trashed house.

We went to a shelter for a few months and was placed in the Fairgrounds Housing Complex shortly after.

The projects were good to us. We fed each other, laughed, and cried together. It was a sense of community back then. Now, it's every man for themselves.

I pulled up to Asha's and Amor's little butt could barely wait until the car stop before she jumped out.

She loved having her house key. I rounded the car to get Romello and Legacy out of their car seat.

"Aaaaahhhhh! Mommy, wake up! Granny mama hurt!" She yelled as I was making my way up the sidewalk.

When I stepped across the threshold into my

daughter's home, her house was in shambles.

Her furniture was turned over and it looked as if someone had been fighting.

Her glass table in the living room had been shattered. There was a trail of blood leading to Asha's room.

I sat Legacy down and joined Amor and Romello in Asha's room.

"Oh my God! Nooo, baby! Asha wake up, baby! Please wake up for mama," I yelled.

I was shaking all over as the tears blurred my vision. My heart drummed in my chest like a solo act during a Sunday Morning Service.

My only daughter was lying in her bed, naked with a gunshot wound to her head.

I had no idea why I thought she would wake up or come back from a headshot.

Amor must've taken the pillow from over her face. The kids were lying on her dead body and were now also covered in her blood.

"Amor, take your brother in the living room, baby. I'm going to call help for mommy," I assured her.

Amor was smart as a whip and was old enough to understand what was going on. I know she was aware that something was not right.

She followed my instructions and led Romello to the living room.

"Hello, I need an ambulance at my daughter's house," I told the 911 operator.

I rattled off Asha's address and prayed they could save my baby.

Blood splatter was all over her room with chunks of her brain.

I was desperately trying to hold it together.

"Why God? Why my baby," I mumbled.

I curled up next to her on the bed and gently rubbed her hair.

As I leaned in close, I noticed something. The tattoo of Prodigy's name was cut from her left breast.

What in the world? I thought that to be strange.

Everyone loved Asha? Who would want to her hurt her? This didn't make any sense whatsoever.

I was rattled from my thoughts by the paramedics bursting into the room.

The police officer escorted me to the living room as the paramedics worked on Asha.

"Do you know of anyone that would want to hurt your daughter?" The police officer asked me.

"No...no...everyone loved my baby," I was hysterical. My thoughts were all over the place.

I kept staring at her blood on my hands. Panic assailed me.

"I don't have time for this. I need to follow them to the hospital. She's going to be looking for me when she wakes up. She will want to see her babies. We need to be there," I was fighting back the urge to throw up as fear twisted my guts.

"Ma'am, I'm sorry to inform you that she is gone. The paramedics have declared her dead. We're waiting on the coroner to pronounce her."

The room started spinning as the last word escaped his lips.

"You a damn lie!" I said, pushing past the host of law enforcement.

I bolted to Asha's room where they had covered her with a sheet. It has been declared a homicide. They were waiting on the forensics team.

Snatching the sheet off, I yelled to my baby girl.

"Please wake up, Asha. You can't leave these babies. They need you, Asha. I need you, baby!"

I shook her body as if she could be raised from the dead like Lazarus.

I heard the story so many times on so many Sunday mornings. I needed a right now miracle.

"Ma'am, you have to come out of here. This is a crime scene. We need you to answer our questions. It could be the key to catching the person who did this." The cop tried to explain as he dragged me from the room once again.

"Ma'am, you need to get it together. I know you just found your daughter dead, but your grandchildren are watching you! They depend on you now!"

The handsome Caucasian cop tried to talk some sense into me. His crystal clear blue eyes were calming like the ocean.

I looked over to Amor, who held her brothers in her arms with a face full of tears.

I hurried over to embrace them.

"It's okay granny baby. It's all okay. I promise," I said, kissing her forehead.

I did my best to answer all of their questions.

"Asha didn't say anything. She was exhausted from work. Once she got off, she just told me to bring them home later tonight. She didn't mention having company of anything," I explained.

I zoned out as they bombarded me with more questions.

I couldn't think of anyone who would want to hurt Asha. Anyone.

DETECTIVE HASSIM MORGAN

I walked into the home of Asha Wilde, who even in death, was so very beautiful. Pieces of her hair were stuck to her head due to the drying blood. I slipped on my latex gloves so I could examine her more closely. She had several defensive wounds, including a missing patch of skin. Based on what remained surrounding it, I could tell it was once a tattoo.

The forensics team was collecting evidence from under her nails. Blood was all over the house. My eyes went to Elisha as I canvased the crime scene.

She was still sobbing, trying to hold it together for her grandchildren. Her heartbreak was written all over her face. She was a beautiful woman with long flowing hair. I was guessing she was in her early to mid-fifties. She was exhausted. This ordeal was already wearing on her. I'm not sure why, but I was drawn to this woman.

"Is that her mother?" I confirmed with the first officer to arrive on the scene.

"Yes. Poor woman found her like this. Could you imagine finding your child like this with your grandchildren?"

His heart went out to her and it was evident by the compassion in his voice as he explained to me the details.

I made my way over to her. "Hi, I'm Detective Hassim Morgan," I extended my hand to her as I introduced myself.

"E-Elisha Wilde," she stammered. "I would shake your hand but I have blood on them."

She looked at her hands as tears flowed more heavily from her eyes. They were trembling like the rest of her frail body.

"Ms. Wilde, can you please take the children home? We need to gather evidence to get started on finding out who did this to your daughter. Here is my card. Can you call me tomorrow so I can update you if we find anything here that may lead us to your daughter's killer? I will also come by to take an official statement from you. I know this is difficult but time is of the essence. The first forty-eight hours are the most critical when it comes to catching a murderer," I explained to her.

"Okay. I will call you tomorrow. Asha and I were all we had. I was her babysitter. We don't trust anyone else with the children. That's the only reason I'm leaving this house tonight while my baby's body is still in that bed."

"I understand. We can talk privately once I stop by."

"Come on babies, let's get you all home."

"Is mama going to the hospital?" The oldest girl asked her grandmother.

"No, baby. We will talk about it more once we get home over some warm milk. How does that sound?" She told her.

I helped her gather their things as they headed out.

I could see the weight of the world on her shoulders.

My heart went out to her. She had raised her kids and was now starting all over with her daughter's children.

It took us several hours to process the crime scene. We were hoping that the perpetrator left behind some form of DNA that would make this a slam dunk.

We could only hope.

I fumbled through a crate of letters she had. The name Prodigy Le Savage was written as the sender on the envelope. He was at the Shawnee Correctional Facility. That was a maximum security facility.

I took a notepad out and wrote down the information. I also made a note to see what he was convicted of. Maybe someone came after her in retaliation for something he did.

After I was done with the crime scene, I made my way home. Some years back a murderer retaliated against me and killed my wife and daughter.

I could never prove that Sabastian Moreno killed my family, but I always knew it.

I understood more than anyone what Elisha was going through and what she was in for.

I hated going home some nights because my wife and daughter's love no longer resonated through the house. I remember it like it was yesterday.

"Baby, I have the pizzas!" I yelled as I fumbled through the door.

It was Pizza Friday at our house. It was the one night I dedicated to my family since I worked so much. The night was only interrupted by anything my partner, Ryan Grey, couldn't handle.

Ryan was my partner for more than fifteen years. He was a Caucasian man that you could tell grew up on the black side of town. Ryan was more than my partner; he was my best friend and brother. He is always there to pull me back in when I'm about to go overboard.

He helped me through my drug addiction after I lost my family. He walked through it with me every step of the way. He never gave up hope that I would find my way back.

I can also get a bit aggressive when I deal with criminals. I've been hit with so many excessive force complaints that my Captain doesn't bother to address them anymore.

On this particular family night, I made the biggest bust of my career earlier in the day. I still managed to be on time for family night.

I will never forget the smell of the pizza as it hit the floor. It was a mixture of Italian sauce and wood polish.

"Felicity! Journey!" I cried as I ran over to their bodies.

They both were still restrained and shot execution-style. At that moment, I wasn't a detective; I was a devastated husband and father. Sobs flooded my throat as I cradled them both in my arms.

They were lifeless, but the dead weight felt light as a feather as I held them.

I cried like a baby for hours before I called 9-1-1.

I secretly hoped they could overpower death and come back to me.

I needed them. My wife was the reason I was the man I am today. I was a hot-headed boy full of ambition. She harnessed it and helped me become a man.

My fellow officers questioned me for hours. I

didn't have anything else to tell them, though. I was just as lost as they were.

I had them bring in Sabastian Moreno for questioning. We didn't find any prints or other DNA in my home. I had a gut feeling it was him. I had taken down several of his operations and was currently working an informant that assured me we could take him down.

Sabastian waltzed suavely into the interrogation room. I watched him from the other side of the two-way mirror.

"Hassim, we're only allowing you to go in there in hopes that you will trigger him to say something that we can use to put him behind bars if he did this," Ryan explained.

My throat muscles tightened as I attempted to let him know that I wasn't going to mess this up. "I'm cool. I got this," I boiled with fury as I stood to my feet. I ground my teeth and clenched my jaw so tight, it hurt.

"Sabastian Moreno here in the flesh. I'm glad that you could take time out of your busy schedule for little ole' me," I said sarcastically, entering the room.

Our posters encouraging perpetrators to snitch was peeling off the walls along with the eggshell paint.

The worn table had dents from past assailants and officers who mixed it up, trying to get to the truth or avoid it.

I could feel my pulse speeding and my heart pounding underneath my button-up. I did my damnedest to hide my true disdain for this man.

"I was deeply sorrowful when I heard about your family," I didn't miss his snide tone and the smirk that accompanied it.

"Deeply sorrowful, huh?" I scoffed. "We both know you killed my family, man!" I growled, slamming my fist down on the table, nearly causing one of the legs to collapse.

"I don't know what you're talking about, detective. Honestly, truly," his thick accent reminded me of Giancarlo Esposito, the dude that played Esteban in that movie Fresh. He even favored him a bit.

"I know you killed them!" I yelled, dashing across the table, securing a firm grip on his throat.

"Hey! Hey! Hey!" Ryan yelled, hurrying from the corner. "I told you this is a conflict of interest, and you ain't supposed to be in here!" He pushed me out of the room as he scolded me for my behavior.

"I know he killed them. I feel it in my gut. He did this!" I thrust my fist in the air.

"I know you are hurting man, but we have to do this by the book. His lawyer on his way as we speak! We don't have, jack! You hear me! Nada!" He grabbed his hair in frustration.

I looked back over my shoulder through the small window into the room. Sabastian had an arrogant sneer on his face as if he had won.

"I will have the last laugh, Moreno. Mark my words," I

said as if he could hear the whisper of words.

He was now downstate serving consecutive life sentences, but I still felt no justice served my family.

I now only had the company of my Rottweiler, Ceaser. He was trained to go and very obedient.

He greeted me at the door as he did so many nights when I dragged in.

As I sat in my Lazy Boy, I couldn't get Elisha Wilde out of my mind. Even in heartbreak, she was so beautiful. I was, unfortunately, familiar with her pain. She would need a support system to survive her daughter's death and be there for her grandchildren.

It had been years since I even thought of another woman. My wife and daughter have been dead for over ten years, but it feels like yesterday since I've lost them.

I decided to just throw myself into my work since then.

I went over my notes from the crime scene, trying to get a head start on who the killer could be.

On paper, Asha Wilde appeared to be a loving mother who worked as a nurse.

I would have to find out from her mother if she was romantically involved with anyone since her fiancé was locked up.

I pulled up Prodigy Le Savage in my system. I'm guessing this is the son of Francois. We never got him on the drugs, but we got him on three murders.

Let's see if he was anything like his father. I read over his case and filtered through his file.

It didn't make sense that a college graduate would have a stolen gun and cocaine on him during a routine traffic stop.

His attorney had submitted documentation that he was a pillar of the community, but his father's sins were at play in his trial.

The court only saw a man headed on the same path as his father. They were ready to cut their losses.

I made a mental note to contact the warden first thing in the morning. I wanted to notify Prodigy myself of the death of Asha. I wanted to see his reaction and hoped he would blurt out something in his anguish that would help in this case.

I poured myself another shot of Jack Daniel's as visions of Asha flooded my eyes. I've seen a lot as a detective, but a woman brutally murdered only to be found by her children and mother was never something you got used to.

*   *   *

I awoke the next morning to Ceaser licking my

face. I had drunk so much until I passed out, which was nothing new for me.

I popped two Advil as I got ready to start my morning so that I could head to the correctional facility and get back in time to stop to visit Elisha Wilde, hopefully.

The drive felt longer due to my hangover. I tossed back several bottles of water on the way, trying to sober up.

I called ahead to make prior arrangements. The warden welcomed me to speak with Prodigy with no problems. We had worked together on other cases, so we were pretty much acquainted.

He insisted on having the correctional officers and the counselor in attendance as well.

I pulled up to the prison and made my way inside. Some juveniles sentenced to boot camp were mopping the front entranceway as I made my way inside.

I was escorted to a room in which Prodigy shortly walked in after.

"Mr. Le Savage, my name is Detective Hassim Morgan. It is with my deepest regret to inform you that your girlfriend Asha Wilde has been killed."

"What type of game is this? Y'all trying to set me up so I throw my release date in three days?" He laughed.

"Prodigy...this is not a game. Asha was brutally murdered and found by her mother and children on last night."

"Are you kidding me?" He yelled, flipping over his chair. "Asha baby noooo!! Baby nooo...," he sobbed.

He started banging his head on the table. Blood began to run from his forehead.

The correctional officers quickly grabbed him to calm him down.

"P, we need you to calm down, man. We don't want to have to put you in the hole," They sympathized with him.

"Get the fuck off me! Get the fuck off me! They gone pay for this! I promise you that! I put that on my daughter! They're going to pay for hurting my baby!!"

He finally broke down as if his knees buckled under the news of his girlfriend's untimely death.

"That was my baby man! She was my everything! How am I supposed to breathe without my air?" He cried uncontrollably and without shame of his love for his woman.

He was curled into a ball, gasping for air like it had been snatched from him.

My heart jumped into my throat as I watched his heart evaporate as mine did when I lost my wife.

From what I was seeing, Prodigy Le Savage was nothing like his father. His father was more sinister and cold—void of all emotion.

The C.O.'s helped him into the chair across from me as the counselor handed him some Kleenex.

"Prodigy, who do you think wanted to hurt Asha?" I asked him.

"Man, I've been in here. I don't know. All she told me was that she was picking up more hours at her job since I was coming home. She wanted to take some time off. Asha was the sweetest person you could ever meet. She wouldn't hurt anyone. The kids and I were her life. Feel me?" He explained.

"Did she mention any run-ins with anyone that you remember?"

"No." He shook his head dumbly as a frown creased his forehead.

"If you think of anything before you get out, please let the warden know. You may want to contact Asha's mother. She is taking this really hard. Asha's oldest daughter was the one who found the body," I informed him.

"Amor," he said barely above a whisper.

"Are all the children yours?" I asked.

"Yes. Biologically only Legacy is mine, but those are all my kids. I love them all the same. Amor is very smart; I know this is killing her inside. Can I call and check on them?" He asked, turning to the counselor.

"That won't be a problem," she nodded.

"Prodigy, I will let you be on your way so you can check on your children. Please stay in touch once you are released. The warden mentioned you have been doing amazing with the G.E.D. program, so he is working on trying to get you out of here early."

"Thank you, Detective Morgan. I need to get home to them. I know my mother in law is going crazy," tears poured from his eyes as he spoke.

"Have you and Asha had any problems with the children's father?" I asked.

"Once Asha and I got engaged, he stopped coming around. I'm not sure if he has been in contact with her since I've been locked up."

"Okay. What is his name?"

"Brian. I'm not sure of his last name."

"Can you think of anyone else? Anyone at all?" I coaxed.

"Not that I'm aware of."

All of the life appeared to have been drained from the young man. My heart went out to him.

Buzz….Buzz….Buzz…

I pulled my phone from its holster to see who was calling me.

Elisha. I thought to myself.

"Prodigy, I have to take this, but I will keep you informed of any developments," I assured him.

"Hello. This is Detective Morgan," I said, stepping into the hallway.

I had stored Elisha's information from our database the night prior.

"Yes, this is Elisha Wilde. I wanted to see if you had time to stop by today," she asked with a shaky voice.

"Absolutely. I'm on my way. I'm coming from Marion, so it will be several hours if that's okay?"

"Yes, that is quite alright. I have some information that will help the case," she said.

Elisha's voice was drenched in sorrow.

"I'll see you shortly. We can talk about it then," I said, ending the call.

ELISHA

I did my best to straighten up before Detective Morgan arrived. I haven't quite been myself lately. I was so full of regret. I should've been a better mother to Asha instead of chasing that pipe. Now I wondered if I had it in me to be what my grandchildren needed.

I was too busy searching for the next high that I neglected to be a mother to Asha and Justin. Justin…with everything that's going on, I forgot to tell him. I was debating on whether I should notify the Marines or wait for his weekly call.

I didn't want that on his mind in the field, but he needs to know.

One thing at a time, Elisha. One thing at a time. I reminded myself.

I'm trying to cope, but I need to make time for a meeting because I feel the urge to use itching inside me. I normally don't fight these urges until the anniversary of my sobriety.

Knock!

Knock!

Knock!

Detective Morgan is early. I thought to myself as I made my way to the door.

The children were in the playroom watching a movie. Amor is so depressed. I'm thinking about putting her in therapy. She needs to work through these emotions and just praying ain't gone cut it.

I pulled my door open only to find Brian's standing in my doorway.

"Brian, what are you doing here?" I asked him, making sure he didn't miss the attitude in my voice.

He was not welcomed at my home. He never was even before Asha was killed.

"I'm here to get my kids. I heard about what happened to Asha. I'm their father, and I should have them," he said.

He was high. I know that look. He was sweating and dirty. I could smell the liquor coming out of his pores.

"Brian, you don't give a damn about them kids! You just want a check. You haven't been around them in years," I refuted his attempted request.

"Asha wouldn't allow me to be around the kids. I always tried to reach out to see them."

"Yes, when you wanted to try and have sex with Asha. When she moved on and got with Prodigy, she told me all about it," I shot back.

"I'm not about to argue with you about my kids. I

will come in there and take them if I want you cracked out, witch!"

I was so focused on Brian that I didn't see Detective Morgan walk up behind him.

"Is there a problem here?" He asked, flashing his badge.

Brian's got in line quickly.

"Yes, officer, I'm here to get my children. She won't allow me to take them," he tried to explain.

"I was at the scene when the children were released into her custody. If you want your parental rights, you will have to file a motion in the courts. You are their father, but that isn't an automatic that they will go into your custody," Detective Morgan explained.

"Aight. I'm going to get on that," Brian said, walking off my doorstep but not before cutting his eyes at me.

Something tells me Brian is going to be a problem. He doesn't want these kids. He's just spiteful.

"Please come in, Detective Morgan. Thank you for intervening. Brian makes me uncomfortable."

"Is he always like that?" Detective Morgan asked, taking a seat on the sofa.

"I've never seen that side of him, but he and Asha have had issues in the past," I told him.

"Ms. Wilde, I've been doing my best to piece together your daughter's life, but I'm going to need your help."

"Anything I can do to help. I'm more than willing."

"Did Asha have any enemies that you knew of?" He asked.

I didn't want to say that my daughter was selling drugs at one point because I didn't want to open up a can of worms that would hurt her case more than help. I wasn't about to have them sweeping my daughter's murder under the rug because they felt that she was just another drug dealer who succumbed to the life she was living.

"Not that I was aware of. As I said, everyone loved Asha. She was good people. You can ask her best friend, Uneek. She lives in Fairgrounds. She would know more about that. She and Asha were thick as thieves."

"Do you have her address?" He said, writing her name on his notepad.

"Yes, 1011 Hess Court."

"Great. What about relationships? I visited her boyfriend-,"

"Fiancé," I interrupted.

"My apologies. Was there anyone else while Prodigy was away?"

I thought long and hard about Izaak. *Could he have done this to Asha? Is that why I haven't seen him lately. Did she break it off with him?*

"I'm not sure what was going on with her fiancé's best friend and her. They grew close over the last couple of years while Prodigy was away. They had a really good relationship. I can't see Izaak hurting her."

"Had?" Detective Morgan asked with wrinkled brows.

"Yes, I haven't seen him in about a week or so. I'm not sure if Asha wanted space since Prodigy was coming home this week or if he's just been busy. He's been running the barbershop while Prodigy has been away, so he may just be busy."

"Where is the shop located?"

"It's on North Main," I told him.

"Okay, great."

"I feel like I'm not helping at all," I confessed as tears formed in my eyes.

"You are helping more than you know. I also want

to let you know that you should get a lawyer. That Brian character does have rights if he is the father. The laws have changed in Illinois, so it's not automatic that the parents get the child. You have rights as the grandparent as well."

Detective Morgan reminded me so much of Blair Underwood. He had cold black hair with waves deep enough to make you seasick. His cinnamon eyes had a fire behind them, but sadness echoed in his iris. His strong cheekbones and smooth chocolate skin called out to me to taste a sample.

Elisha...girl, get it together.

"Are you okay?"

Lord, this man was so fine; just the appearance of him drew me into him.

"Yes, I'm fine. Thank you for asking," I did my best to gain my composure.

It has been years since I've been this attracted to a man. Once I got clean, I was too scared to get into a relationship in fear that I would relapse on drugs if it didn't work out.

I found it easier to commit my life to God and hide in him.

I definitely would need some prayer after lusting over this fine specimen that sat before me.

My eyes traveled the span of the rest of his body as he continued to take notes.

His body was athletic, but he had a bit of a stomach. I'm guessing it was from eating out because there wasn't a woman cooking for him.

His nails were manicured. I noticed because that's one of the things that attracts me to a man. If he has clean nails or not was on my checklist.

"Ms. Wilde-"

"Elisha. You can call me Elisha. I meant to correct you earlier."

"Thank you. I will keep you informed on every step of this case. Please call me if there is anything else that you need. I mean anything," he said, standing to leave.

I watched him walk to his car. Once he was inside, I closed my door.

I haven't started making arrangements for Asha yet. Prod will be home in a couple of days. I want to include him.

I'm praying that once Brian knows he is back in the picture, he will back off. I don't have money for an attorney right now.

I went back over to check my phone. I heard it vibrating when the detective was here.

I had a missed call from my Pastor's wife.

To be honest, I had given up on God. He took my baby from me. I know they say we are not supposed to question God, but why did he have my baby die in such an inhumane way.

As I was checking my voicemail, a call from Justin was coming through.

"Hello, baby."

"Hey, mama. I'm just calling to check on you. Asha butt didn't answer her phone."

"Baby…I have to tell you something. It's your sister…someone killed her," I burst into tears.

The line went silent. "Hello, Justin? Are you still there?"

"I'm here, mama. I'm on my way." He said disconnecting the call.

Since Justin had been in the Marines, he's more like a robot. Still sweet, but I could never tell how he was really doing. My son now possessed this look in his eye. A look that revealed he had taken life.

I know the look all too well. Their father had it, so I was accustomed to it.

I could imagine he was surrounded by death more than I cared to imagine.

Justin was in special forces, so we rarely knew where he was stationed. I just had to wait until he got here.

"Gram Gram," Amor said, standing in the hallway.

"Yes, baby."

"I miss mommy. I'm trying to be brave for my brother, but I miss her so much. She was supposed to be my best friend forever. She promised she wouldn't ever leave me. She promised!"

Tears were streaming down Amor's golden bronze skin. She stood there, fiddling with her fingers as she spoke.

"Come here, baby. It's okay to cry and miss your mama. She will always be watching over you to protect you. Just because you cry doesn't mean you aren't brave. You have been my big helper since your mom has gone to heaven. We just have to take it one day at a time."

Amor nodded in understanding.

*   *   *

The children were sound asleep as I stood in the doorway.

They had their room already at my house from when I kept them through the week. It wasn't too much of an adjustment since Asha's been gone in that aspect.

My baby is gone.

I closed the door as my tears began to consume me as it had the previous night.

I made my way back to my room, where I stared at the sea-green walls.

I could really use a hit right now. I remembered why I didn't like Izaak when he initially started hanging around.

It played on the walls like a movie with no sound.

"Lisha, I ain't giving you no more credit until you pay me! I don't care that you mess with Francois," Izaak yelled at me as I sat in his car.

Francois had started cutting me off because I was doing too much. I started getting hits from Izzak.

I heard of Prodigy, but I never saw him because he never hung out at the dope house. I was so high back then I wouldn't know the boy if he stood in front of my face.

"Man, I can do something for you. You ever have head from a cougar?"

"You mean an old woman?" He laughed.

"You gone let me do it or not?"

"Hell yeah!" He sang.

I watched Izaak release himself from his jeans. I pulled my dry wig off so it wouldn't get in my way and did what I promised.

He needed to put the Hennessy down and pick up some fruit.

He pulled my hair ferociously as I worked for my drugs.

The warm thick liquid slid down like a loogie on a car window.

I thought it was over but he didn't stop. Unbeknownst to me, round two started without warning.

"You got some fire head for an old lady. That experience is everything I see," he said, handing me my work.

I didn't say anything to Izaak. I grabbed my wig and hopped out of the car. I just wanted my drugs so I could get high.

When he started hanging over Asha's during her pregnancy, I was constantly reminded of my past.

I was blessed that I didn't contract HIV. I caught other STD's out there but nothing that penicillin couldn't cure.

Izaak finally pulled me to the side one day at Asha's. "Elisha, I don't want any problems. I know you a different person now from back in the day when I was young. I respect you now. I'm proud of you. A lot of people don't make it off that shi...stuff."

"Thank you, Izaak. I must admit my animosity was due to the constant reminder you represented from my past."

"I know, that's why I wanted to clear the air and let you know we good."

Izaak hugged me, and we never spoke about it again. Our relationship was smooth sailing after that.

He was a good guy once I gave him a chance. He was so amazing with Asha. He was attentive and nurturing. He was a rock for her while Prod was away serving his time.

Asha insisted on living that fast life. I felt a little better that Izaak was watching out for her.

I'm not sure how he managed to do what Prod couldn't by making her quit hustling, but I was ecstatic.

I need to call him to see if Asha made any enemies that he knew of. To be honest, I was willing to take justice any way I could get it, through the system or on the streets.

As long as someone paid for my daughter having to be put six feet under...I didn't care how it got done.

I curled up in my bed waiting for the news to come on. I would normally pray and read before I went to bed, but I haven't felt much like praying lately.

"Breaking news. Last night a mother of three was shot dead. Sources say her mother and children found her in her home on the Eastside of town. If you have any information on this horrible murder, please contact Crime Stoppers."

I laid there looking at Asha's picture on my dresser as her story leaked to the rest of Rockford.

I was hovering between sleep and despair. My eyes were burning due to the crying and exhaustion.

"Asha? Is that you?"

If I was dreaming, I didn't want to wake up. Asha was sitting at the foot of my bed like she had done so often when she would stop by to visit me at night.

She placed a hand on my foot as she always did.

"Mom, they need you. I see you struggling, but you got this. Don't fail them, mama! You are all they have left in this world! Don't let Brian get my babies no matter what! I don't care what you have to do! Please!" Asha pleaded as she burst into tears.

As I blinked away the tears, Asha was gone by the time my vision had cleared.

"I won't fail you or them, baby. I promise," I

continued to cry.

I pulled my Bible from the dresser and put on my glasses so I could read Psalm 23.

I needed forgiveness for what I was about to do.

PRODIGY

The nurse gave me something to calm me down. I was then placed in solitary confinement, where I was put under a suicide watch.

"Man!" I yelled, punching the brick walls.

I was so zoned out that I didn't realize that my hands were bloody.

I collapsed on the thin worn mattress as thoughts of Asha and I flooded my entire being. That's all I had now…memories.

"Asha…why you leave me, baby? Why?"

I cried so much my eyes were now swollen and nearly shut.

The only time I would see Asha now was in my dreams. I could feel whatever the nurse injected me with was kicking in. My eyes felt as if bricks weighted them.

"Asha, is that you?" Now it had me hallucinating. What did she give me?

My mind and eyes were playing tricks on me because Asha stood right in front of me. She glowed around her. She looked so sad even though she didn't speak a word.

"Help me," she mouthed.

I'm not sure how I was able to understand her, but I did. Maybe it was our bond. She was reaching out to me.

I don't know if this is real, but I'm going to find out who killed my baby!

"I got you, Asha. I promise they gone pay with their lives and the lives of their children."

My heart leaped from my chest as she disappeared just as mysteriously as she appeared.

I laid back on my bed, anticipating my release in a couple of days.

The old Prodigy died with Asha. Rockford was about to feel the wrath of Prodigy Le Savage, whom he was originally groomed to be.

My first stop is to check on my kids. Once I'm done with that, I'm going to track Izaak down.

I know Asha broke it off with him. That nigga don't take rejection well. If he hurt my baby, I will end him and his child. I'm killing him regardless for screwin' her in the first place.

*   *   *

"P! Get up—you out of here. I'm going to escort you to your cell to get your stuff. We will process you out. I heard about what happened to your girl man, sorry to hear that," he expressed his condolences with sincere remorse in his eyes.

"Thanks, man. They let me out early?" I clarified.

"Yes, the Warden gave you what would equate to a compassionate release. You only had a few more days left anyway, so he just let you out. Your work with the G.E.D. program helped as well. Like I said, you were out of here soon either way."

The hallways smelt of sweat and mildew as I made my way down them. I know it was all in my head, but to me, the muttering of other inmates among themselves was about Prodigy Le Savage.

Anyone familiar with our family understood the savagery that was about to be unleashed once my feet hit the ground outside that gate.

Once I made it there, the guard stood on the outside and waited as I packed. I didn't want any of this crap, just my letters and pictures from Asha.

My celly and I had already agreed that he would just take my commissary. I pulled some strings to make sure he could get my T.V.

"You have five minutes Moreno," I heard to guard say. I turned to see Asha's father, Sabastian Moreno, coming into my cell.

His Columbian decent was evident with his long

salt and pepper colored hair. You could tell back in the day his hair was cold black.

He was a slender man knocking at the door of his 60s, but his body structure would confuse you.

His old butt looked like he hasn't missed a day in the weight room since he got here.

My roommate excused himself without being asked.

The guards stood in the hallway, making small talk about one of the other female guards.

Since I've been here other than the message noting I would be safe even with the guards, I haven't seen or heard from Sabastian.

"I heard about my baby. Did you know Asha was my only daughter?" He asked me, his hands clenching into a fist.

As far as I know, Bash didn't have a beef with me, but his body language is saying otherwise.

I stepped back and answered, "Yes. She told me."

My face was hard, but my heart skipped a beat on the inside.

"Someone sent me the pictures of her from the crime scene. It's messed up what they did to my baby. They carved her tattoo from her chest before they shot her in the head. I still hold weight in the streets, so I got some info for you."

"They did what? My name was tattooed across her chest."

Bash stepped into me to the point our noses were nearly touching.

"I heard yo' brother or friend whatever he is...I heard he the one did it. Something about her breaking it off with him: he ain't take that too well. I'm hearing he was already moving funny on the business side before she even broke it off with him. Izaak Coleman...yeah, that's the name they told me."

He stood back so he could take note of my reaction.

He did a once over of me from head to toe and continued, "Now, I understand that you may have a conflict of interest, so I wanted to offer my services. I still have favors owed to me in the streets. I can call upon any one of them to settle this. You can keep your hands clean so that you can raise my grandbabies."

"With all due respect, Mr. Moreno-"

"Bash. Call me Bash," he interrupted.

"Bash, there ain't no such thing as a conflict of interest when it comes to Asha! That nigga was dead when he tried to take what's mine!" I explained through clenched teeth. "He will suffer…I promise," I assured the man who was almost my father-in-law.

"Understand this…if you don't handle it…I will," he said, turning on his heels to walk away just as quietly as he came.

I followed behind with a small brown box that held what little I wanted to bring with me into the free world.

My heart was full of so many emotions that I felt as if it would explode.

I was excited to be free—no one telling me when and what to do.

I would meet my firstborn, my daughter, Legacy.

Asha always said, "Every Prodigy should have a Legacy."

The worst part about getting out of this hellhole was that I had to put my baby Asha six feet under.

I was on the same page as her father. Izaak better give his soul to God because his body belonged to me!

Bash confirmed something I had already got wind of. I knew Izaak was moving funny even before I told Asha she better end it.

I didn't bring it to her because I ain't want her

trying to solve it herself. She thought she was some type of female drug lord.

Once I started calling and realized she was back nursing, I was at ease.

I had planned to settle the shit when I got home.

I'm done with this drug shit once and for all after I get revenge for Asha.

I'm all my children have left in this world. I ain't letting them down.

I took the bus home. I didn't trust anyone to pick me up and I didn't want to bother Ms. Elisha.

Once I got to Rockford, I could move how I want.

The bus ride was cool. It was a couple of other people released with me.

They only talked about all the cat they were about to hit up once they got to Chicago.

I had imagined the same thing so many nights thinking about my arrival home to Asha.

I could still envision her waiting for me in the lobby of the prison.

She would be in something sexy, rocking a natural fro. She knows that turns me on when she wears her hair natural.

We would stop by a nearby hotel and get a few rounds in because the drive home would be too long of a wait to be in each other's arms.

"Screw you!" I heard one of the guys yell, snatching me from my daydream of what could've been but will never be.

All the passengers turned to look in his direction.

"What y'all looking at?!" He yelled back at them.

"Yo, man chill out," the guy sitting with him whispered. "What happened nigga?"

"Man, Cynthia talking about don't come to her house. Talking about, I better go to Nikki's house," he said, handing the stranger he had finessed back their phone.

"Who is Nikki, bro?" His homeboy asked him.

"My other baby mama. I had both of them putting money on my books. On top of that, I was freakin' both of 'em before I got locked up. They have been fighting while I've been locked up. Nikki gone let me come to her house though anyway. She doesn't give a fuck long as she feels like she got one up on my other baby mama," he laughed.

They were around my age of twenty-seven, but my mentally was totally different.

I've always yearned to love just one woman. I

wanted one woman to give my all to and trust with my heart.

At the end of the day, a variety of women is just that…a variety. There's nothing else to it. I'm beyond pointless sex. I wanted to touch the soul of one woman.

I did that with Asha, and I doubt if I ever will find that again. I don't know if I will be able to open myself up again.

It was something about Asha that drew me to her from the jump. Our bond wasn't something you came across every day. You were blessed if you found it in your lifetime.

We loved each other like husband and wife. We fought and played around like a brother and sister. Last but most importantly, we were each other's best friend. I didn't hide anything from Asha. I kept it a hundred in the door and she followed suit.

The ride home was grueling. Detective Morgan left word with the Warden that I could go home, but he suggested I go somewhere else and have someone come clean the place up before I go in.

To be honest, I wanted to see it all: the struggle, her blood, and where her body was found. I wanted to take in all of it. It would ultimately be what I wanted to flash in my mind when I got ready to pull the trigger.

After hours upon hours, I finally arrived back in Rockford, Illinois, wearing the same thing I did the night I took A.D. home.

I needed to find him so I could get some answers to my questions.

I suspected Izaak was behind me getting locked up, but I had to be sure.

There's no way this nigga was this much of a snake right under my nose.

Asha and Izaak were all I had in this world until Legacy was born.

I never knew my mother. She bounced when I was a shorty.

I thought about going to look for her, but my dad always said she had her reasons for leaving.

Izaak had made one thing perfectly clear. We weren't blood. As much as my love and loyalty resided with him…his wasn't with me.

I have a code I live by and Izaak is aware of it. I adopted it after my father was locked up.

Death before dishonor. Dissociation before disloyalty.

I called a cab once I made it to the bus station. I'm sure this is the only place in the city that still had a payphone.

I prayed the money I stashed at the house was still there.

I didn't tell Asha about it because I wanted it to be there in case of a true emergency.

My baby was a boss, though. She took what I left and flipped it all. Last I heard she was bringing in seven figures easily.

Once I got to the house, I had the cab driver wait until I went around back. I had some petty cash in my tool shed.

I opened it and went to my tool drawers. I pulled out the third drawer and pulled the envelope taped to the top out.

I pulled out enough cash for the driver and stuffed the rest in my pocket.

My hands shook violently as I tried a few times to get the key into the lock.

Once I stepped inside, I couldn't breathe. The room started to spin, and tears burned my eyelids. A tiny tremor ran all over my skin.

The keys fell from my hands almost in slow motion as I took in the crime scene.

Asha's blood was everywhere. It was no longer

bright red but almost black; it was so dark.

The house smelled of death and it was cold. Not the usual cold I was used to living up north, but this was something else.

"ASSSHHAAAAA!!!" I screamed at the top of my lungs. I hoped she would appear to me again.

I didn't care if the entire neighborhood heard my cry of pain and sorrow. I was coming undone at the seams by what I was seeing.

My baby suffered. Someone wanted her to be in complete agony in her last moments on earth. I couldn't imagine anyone having such hate in their hearts other than some niggas from the streets trying to get her out of the way.

But niggas in the city had to know I was on my way, so if they wanted to pop her off, they would've done it from the jump.

Izaak was worse than a nigga from the streets. He was jealous. That is colder than the grave.

I laid on the floor until the sun started to set. I didn't have the strength to go into our bedroom.

I was told that's where they found her. She was naked with my name carved from her skin.

They're not saying it, but I think Asha was raped too.

I'm going to the police station to talk to Detective Morgan first thing in the morning. I wanted to see the pictures from the crime scene and the reports.

I forced myself up from the floor and headed down the hall to our bedroom.

Nothing had been touched. I know Ms. Elisha didn't have the stomach to come back here after Asha was killed, so there was no one else to do what I was going to have to do.

One hand firmly gripped one side of the door frame. It was doing its damnedest to support the weight of my paralyzed body.

I was stuck and twisted up by what I saw. Asha's blood was drenched and dried into our white bedsheets. We always did white everything with our bed linens.

It made us both feel like we were sleeping in the clouds.

There was a bullet hole in the bed and the lamps were turned over and broken.

The room looked like a burglary gone wrong.

Out of the corner of my eye, I see a wicker basket lined with white linen that contained every letter and card I sent to my baby. She kept every one of them.

As if I had no control over my body, out of

nowhere, the senior citizen dietary food I had at the prison shot up my throat when I saw chunks of Asha's brains on the wall.

I thought about grabbing my keys and heading to a hotel room, but I couldn't. I just wanted to be close to Asha.

This is where she spent her last moments. I wanted her; however I could get her.

I went to the garage and our cars were parked in there. I turned the lights on because it looked like some changes had been made to my truck.

Asha had my Range detailed and customized. She had the white leather seats with black trim put in, and she got new rims put on.

My heart crumpled in my chest when I thought about how considerate she was. Asha always did stuff like this. She still surprised a man who, to the world, seemed to have everything at one point in time.

I walked closer to the car and there was a note on the dash.

I pulled the door open to see what it was.

It was a note from Asha.

Surprise baby!!

I know how much you love your Range, so I took the chance of giving her a make-

*over before her daddy got home. I hope
you love it! She hasn't been moved since
you left her. I took her to get a tune-up
and oil change as well. She's the only
one you're allowed to cheat on me with!
LOL!!*

"Why they take you from me, Ash..."

I cried like a baby in my truck. I was so tired of
crying. I have cried so much my side was hurting.

I didn't have an appetite, but I at least tried to
drink water when I thought about it.

"Boss up, Prod! Get this done! You have kids that
need you!" I scolded myself.

I pulled myself out of the car and made my way
back inside the dead house that once felt like home.

I went into the utility room and pulled out the
cleaning supplies.

No one was expecting me home tonight, so I
would take this time alone to grieve. It was my time
to go down memory lane once more with my Ash.

Being in my line of business, you learned the most
effective ways to remove blood stains.

I went room by room. Once I was done cleaning
one room, I closed the door and went to the next.

I saved our bedroom for last. I doubt if I could

sleep in here tonight, but I still needed to clean it up.

The mattress was impossible to move. Asha's blood had soaked all the way through, so it weighed a ton.

I finally gave up and concluded that I would just hire some people.

The more I cleaned, the colder my heart grew.

I poured myself a couple of shots of Hennessy once I was done to calm my nerves.

I couldn't determine if I was shaking with rage or hurt.

No one knows I was released today. Now is the time to pop up on Izaak.

I jumped up from the couch and went to our closet. My clothes were still there like I left them.

I put on a black hoodie with black pants and shoes.

I didn't want to drive my Range because people would possibly recognize it on the West.

Asha mentioned he got his own crib, but she didn't say where.

I bet Uneek knows. If I went to the Grounds, word would hit the streets that I was out.

I grabbed my keys and headed to my storage garage. I prayed my other cars were there.

Izaak knew about it but I doubt if he came by.

Once I arrived, I entered my access code and drove around the back to my spots. I pulled up the doors, and all my cars were there.

I bought this beater that no one knew about. It's what I drove when I was incognegro.

I pulled the keys from the visor and it started right up.

I arrived at the projects in about twenty minutes or so.

I knocked on Uneek's door at about eleven at night. It was a Wednesday, so no one was out.

Her country butt usually hollered from the top window, but this time she just opened her door.

"Prod?! I thought you were somebody else. Come in. Did you hear about Ash? It's messing me up for real for real," she whimpered.

"Messed up, don't begin to put in words how I feel right now. Yo' you know where that nigga Izaak stay?"

My eyes were staring into her soul, daring her to lie

to me. I didn't hit women at all, but I was not about to play if I felt someone was standing between me and justice for Asha.

"Prod...I don't want to get in that! You know Izaak is crazy as hell!"

I stepped to Uneek and pulled the nine from my back. I placed it against her temple.

"You call yourself her friend? Even in death, you ain't loyal. You think I didn't catch the way you tried to flaunt around in front of me when Asha wasn't looking. I just knew you were all she had. I would bury you if you broke her heart by trying to come for me. Now...I'm...going...to ....ask...you....one more time! Where that nigga at?!" I pressed the gun deeper into her temple.

Uneek's tears didn't move me at all. I didn't have feelings anymore. I was dead inside. They wanted a savage they got "The Savage"!

"Okay, Prod! I need you to calm down. Take the gun from my head! I will tell you everything that went down while you were gone."

Uneek grabbed her damn Remy and commenced to telling me all the shit that went down in my absence.

She confirmed my suspicions of Izaak setting me up, how the streets were saying Izaak and Asha were like the ghetto Bonnie and Clyde. My spine stiffened just hearing that.

It killed me knowing that nigga had my baby in a way I refused to give her.

I didn't want Asha in this life. I was starting to go with it, but when I got locked up, it reminded me of my original desire…a wife, kids, and a quiet life.

Asha, on the other hand, got a taste of that life, and it consumed her.

I didn't recognize the Asha that Uneek was describing to me.

Asha was out here, dropping bodies and torturing niggas. Both friends and foes…apparently she didn't care once you crossed her.

"Prod…she was in love with Iza-"

BOOM!

Before she could finish, I had Uneek pinned against the wall by her throat.

"Don't you ever in your life repeat that in my presence Uneek. Ever!"

I could see my spit on her face as I spoke.

I wasn't normally this disrespectful towards women, but Uneek knew better than to say that to me.

She nodded her head because the grip on her neck was too tight to speak.

She burst into tears once I released her. I felt bad for putting my hands on her.

"Uneek…I'm sorry. This situation is really messing me up. Asha was all I had," I cried again.

I couldn't stop these tears from falling.

"Prod…she told me if anything happened to her, Izaak did it. She went to confront him when I told her he set you up. She was hot! You know her mouth. Ain't no telling how that went down. When I talked to her on her way home, she said she had something for him, but she would lay low because you were coming home in a few days. I know you think I wasn't loyal, but I told the cops what she said about him. I had my girl back. I wasn't sure about telling you because y'all are like blood brothers."

We both were standing there, missing the hell out of Asha embracing one another.

I almost forgot how it felt to have a woman in my arms.

Uneek's body was soft and smelled of pears.

She looked up at me with tears in her eyes. She genuinely missed Asha.

I gently wiped the tears from her eyes as she licked

her full lips.

I've never noticed how light her Cognac colored eyes were. She wrapped her hands around mine and kissed them.

I felt my manhood rising as if I was no longer in control.

BOOM!

BOOM!

BOOM!

I jerked my hands from Uneek, snapping myself back in control.

"I'm going to head out of the other door. Don't let nobody know I'm out yet...okay?" I asked Uneek.

"I got you, Prod," she said, going to open her front door.

I'm not sure what was happening with Uneek and me, but I wasn't ready to let another woman close to me. It would be dirty to even mess with her on that level knowing she was Asha's friend.

I brushed it off as being locked up, and she was the first woman I've seen in a couple of years.

I doubt if that nigga Izaak was home. Knowing him, he already somewhere laying low.

He already knows how I'm coming. Izaak has only seen this side of me once, and it's the reason he will never come at me head up.

I rode to the address that Uneek gave me. A lowkey up and coming black neighborhood on the West.

I sat there for hours, but there was no movement at all.

I finally gave up and went back home. I wasn't worried about anyone popping up on me because the word is already out on the street—its blood for blood with hate coursing through my veins.

I walked into my home and the bleach stung my nostrils. It no longer felt like a home but just four walls that sheltered me from the elements.

I didn't bother to go into the bedroom; I just collapsed on the couch, nursing my glass of Hennessy until I drifted off to sleep. The only place I was able to see Asha.

IZAAK

I sat at the bar in Central Tap, throwing back shots of Patron. I've been drinking myself into oblivion since I found out Asha was dead. I felt guilty that her last encounter was me calling her out of her name and disrespecting her.

Prod would be home soon. I would have to deal with him one way or another. I should've killed him a long time ago. This wouldn't be an issue right now if I had.

People were staring and whispering all around me. I wasn't trippin' about it because none of them dared to say anything to my face. I had my banger just in case one of them did after they got some liquid courage.

I tried to go back and mess with Camille after Asha and I called it quits. She wasn't tryin' to deal with a nigga, though. That cop she with done proposed and put her in this big house in Poplar Grove.

I don't know how he can afford that because cops don't make that much money.

I've been picking up random chicks here and there, but none filled Asha or Camille's shoes, so I didn't sleep with them. They were more company than anything.

I missed Asha and contrary to popular belief…I didn't kill my baby.

I loved that girl. I've been asking around and putting the word out, but everyone thought I did it, so no one took me seriously.

I had to figure this out on my own.

"What's up, man?" Lino said, taking a seat on the stool next to me.

I knew him from around the way but I ain't never kicked it with him or nothing.

"Wassup bro, how you been?" I attempted to make conversation with him.

"Man, they saying you killed ole' gi-"

Before he could finish, my pistol was going upside his head.

WAP!

WAP!

WAP!

I pounded his head repeatedly as his blood baptized my face.

"Nigga don't you ever come at me sideways!" I said, standing taking one last kick to his head.

I grabbed my keys and got out of there before the cops came.

I honestly didn't care if he was dead or alive.

I made my way home in record time but noticed a familiar car.

That couldn't be Prod's beater because he ain't out yet. Or was he?

That nigga slick like that.

Instead of taking the chance, I bent off my street.

I pulled out my cell and called the one person who would never refuse me.

"Hello," Uneek answered.

She sounded asleep but I didn't care; she had to wake up.

"Yeah, I'm on my way; leave the door cracked," I told her.

"You ain't coming here, nigga!"

"What you mean? I will come kick your door in! Stop playing with me!"

"Do what you gotta do, but the cops going to be waiting for you, my nigga! Believe that! You aren't my man. We haven't even been freakin' for that matter.

You left me for my girl, remember? My girl, that niggas in the street saying you killed!"

Uneek better be glad I'm hot in these streets, or I would try my luck and kick her door in.

I don't care if we haven't been messing around. Her box garbage anyway.

I circled back around to my house and the car was gone. Maybe I was just paranoid.

"What are you doing in here?" I asked Camille. "I gave you that key for emergencies only."

"Did you do it? Did you kill Asha?" She asked.

When she asked, it didn't anger me as it had earlier.

I took a seat next to her on the couch.

"No. I didn't hurt Asha. It's not like anyone believes me, though."

"I had to look you in your eyes and ask you. I know what you do in these streets, but Asha was family. We weren't close, but we didn't have words either. She was great with our child and I needed to know for myself. A detective came to my home asking questions. I didn't know anything, but he asked me about you and Asha's relationship. As far as I knew, y'all were good. I heard Prod was coming home and wasn't sure how that was going to work between you and her."

"Yeah, she broke it off with me. She found out I set him up and she lost it! She felt like I betrayed her."

"You what? I know you wanted that top spot all to yourself, but I didn't know you would go through with it."

Camille always knew my plan to take over. She was all for it because she wanted to be the first lady.

She has always wanted the money and everything that came with it back then. She has changed so much now since she got with that dude.

It was amazing that we were everything to someone that we could never be for each other.

Her skin glowed and she was genuinely happy.

"Yeah, I'm the one that sacrificed and built it. He never gave me my proper respect, so I had to take what was mine," I said, lighting my blunt.

I hit it a few times and passed it to Camille. She hesitated.

"Forget it," she said, taking it.

"Why you got that little skirt on coming up in here. You trying to give me some of that coochie or something?"

Whether Camille knew it or not, she wasn't leaving until I was swimming in her guts.

I placed my hands on her thighs and ran them up until I reached that sweet spot that I missed so much.

I missed her something serious. She was as naked as the day she came into this world under her skirt.

I pushed her back on the couch while she smoked.

She gasped as I explored her body with my lips. I missed this woman so much. Now that I couldn't have her, I wanted her more than anything.

"Izaak...I gotta get home," she said, pushing me away.

"What you mean you gotta go? Do you think you about to get some head and bounce? Who do you think I am, Cam?"

I snatched the blunt from her and put it out because it was about to get real... fast!

"Just what I said. You're lucky I let you taste it! I ain't about to mess up what I got going on with my good man over you!"

I snatched Cam by the back of her head. I had a hand full of her weave in my hand when I bent her over the end of the couch.

She tried her hardest to fight me off.

WAP!

I smacked her to let her know I wasn't playing.

"Look, this about to happen whether you want it to or not! You got me messed up if you thought I was gone warm you up only for you to bust it open for that nigga when you get home!"

I rammed myself inside Cam with no mercy. I wasn't getting what I needed out in these streets. Quality cat is hard to come by these days.

Cam cried as I took what she use to give me so freely.

When I was done, she wiped her snot and tears with the back of her hands. She bolted out of my house. She didn't do so without throwing my key on the floor.

"Cam!" I yelled after her.

I honestly thought she would get into it after I started. She use to like it rough, but I guess she wasn't feeling me anymore.

If she tells that nigga he gone bury me under the jail just to make sure I'm out of the picture!

I called Cam's phone over and over, but she just sent me to voicemail.

I texted her that I was sorry but she didn't respond.

This was the last thing I needed. What was I thinking?

* * *

BAM!

BAM!

BAM!

"Man...who is beating on my door like the poli..."

My words were cut short by a detective and two police officers standing on my doorsteps.

I still had cold in my eyes from sleeping so hard.

Man! Cam really called the cops on me.

"Izaak Coleman, you're wanted for questioning in the murder of Asha Wilde."

I zoned out as they read me my Miranda rights.

Despite what people thought about Asha and me, I really did love her.

It was killing me that the last time I saw her, I said

some messed up stuff.

It pissed me off how she came at me. I was foul as but the truth hurt. Everything she was saying cut like a knife!

They stuffed me in the back of that small cop car as they searched my house. I didn't have anything in there but some weed, and I doubt they can find it.

The ride downtown was long, and my legs were starting to cramp.

He had the cuffs so tight they were digging into my wrist.

I was just ready to get this over with. I know they ain't have anything on me because I didn't do it!

I waited in the interrogation room for about thirty minutes until a man that looked like a fake Blair Underwood walked in.

You can tell his cool self use to have all the females back in the day.

"Mr. Coleman, I brought you here to ask you some questions in regards to you and Asha Wilde's relationship. Where you two romantically involved?"

"You have been asking around about me, so you tell me," I snapped back.

"People can say a lot of things, but only you can

tell me facts."

"Yes, we were involved. We got close after her daughter's father was sent to prison. She broke it off recently," I told him.

"How recently?"

"About a week or so before she died."

"How did that make you feel?"

"How you think? I was mad but not mad enough to kill her. I always knew when her dude got home; she was going to end it."

He just wrote on his notepad as I explained my side of things.

"Her dude, huh?" He looked up from his notepad and started flipping through pages. He looked back up at me with raised eyebrows. "I was told you two were raised like brothers."

"Yea, we were close before he left, but when I got with Asha, I didn't mess with him anymore like that."

"So just like that, you cut your brother off over a girl?"

"Asha wasn't just any girl. She had a way of making a nigga feel like he can fly. She brought out the king in you. Made you believe in yourself despite people telling you that you were nothing. That girl was the truth," I explained, trying to speak over the lump that formed in my throat.

I ain't never put in words how I felt about her until just now. It made me relive when I got the call that she was dead.

I will never forget the way Elisha cried into the phone.

"They killed her!" She sobbed. "They took my Asha from me!" She was hysterical.

"Wait? What?"

"They shot her in the head. Amor found her in the bed naked. They humiliated my baby and took her life. They left her there like she was nothing."

I was at the warehouse. I collapsed in the chair behind my desk.

"I'm on my way," I told her, ending the call before she could refuse.

I ran every red light getting to Elisha's house.

Once I got there, I saw the kids with Asha's blood on them from where they must've touched her or something.

Amor's eyes were puffy and red. She looked exhausted and sad.

"Bestfran," I tried to joke with Amor.

That's what we called each other. Asha watched Kendall Kyndall on Instagram for her Love & Hip Hop highlights, so that's where we got it from.

Man, it hurt my heart when Amor looked up at me with those sad eyes. Crocodile tears were rolling down her fat cheeks.

When I kneeled in front of her and opened my arms, she jumped right in them.

I tried to hold it in, but I broke down with her.

"I'm going to miss yo' mama to baby girl. We gone get through this."

Amor nodded in understanding.

I helped Asha's mom get them in the tub and in bed. She gave them something to help them sleep because there was no way they would be able to go on their own after seeing their mom with a bullet in her head.

I couldn't imagine finding my mama dead.

"Mr. Coleman. Mr. Coleman," I tuned Detective Morgan out.

I had no idea what he'd been saying the last few minutes. My mind was somewhere else.

"Yeah. What did you ask me again?"

"Do you know of anyone else that would want to

kill Asha?"

I honestly thought it was those niggas from Chicago. They probably got another plug and put a hit out on Asha's to dead the competition.

I got into it with them during our last business meeting.

"What do you mean Asha is out?" Amante´ asked.

"She out, like I said. Something came up, so she had to pull back," I reiterated.

I wasn't one for explaining myself, but this was business.

"Our original agreement was made with Asha! If this organization is not stable, then we need to find another connect and dead all this right here right now!" Amante´ threatened.

"We both know that I got the purest product for the lowest price. Now...you are more than welcome to take your business elsewhere if you like," I said, leaning back in my chair.

Amante´ just stood up and walked out without saying a word. He'd already paid for his product. My crew loaded him up while we were in my office.

His partner was out with them, verifying the weight.

Ain't no way I was telling this detective that!

"Man, her baby daddy Brian is crazy. I caught him trying to jump on her after she had the baby. He ain't been around though, so I don't know if he would do something like that. I don't think he's that crazy, but I know he was harassing her," I told him.

"Thank you. You're free to go. We didn't find anything in your house, but please don't leave town just in case I have more questions for you," he said, removing my cuffs.

I got out of there so fast I left rubber marks on the linoleum floors.

For some reason, I didn't think about them niggas from Chicago until the detective asked me who I think would want to hurt her.

It's time to take a trip to Chicago. That's for sure!

PRODIGY

Even though I was out of prison, I still felt confined. My couch felt better than the thin worn mattress I've slept on for the past two years, but the smell of Asha still consumed me. No amount of bleach could drown it out. I didn't want to, but it was also a painful reminder that she was no longer here.

Without trying, Asha left just as my mother did. One of the things that drew me to her was that she took such good care of her kids. I knew after seeing that side of her that I wanted her to be the mother of my children.

"Asha, you left me here to do this alone. How will I ever do what you did for our children?" I spoke as if Asha was sitting next to me.

It was strange because at times, I swore that I could feel her near me.

Today is the day I see my children. I had to put my revenge on the back burner for now and take care of them.

I know Ms. Elisha would always help, but I had to do this on my own.

I won't abandon my kids as my mom did me. Ever!

So I had to pull it together and be what they

needed me to be.

I know Brian will put up a fight knowing damn well he doesn't want Romello or Amor.

Last I heard that nigga going from house to house. He still doesn't have his it together.

I was dreading charging my phone back up. Asha and I were on a family plan, so she paid the bill even though I was locked up.

I put most of our bills on autopay, so she didn't have to worry.

I didn't get caught with any major work, so my assets weren't frozen.

My feet felt like I had ankle weights on as I walked over to my phone. I turned it on and waited for all of the alerts to come through.

I didn't do the social media thing, so all of my notifications were mostly emails and messages from Asha the night I got locked up.

I strolled through them. *"Don't cry this time Prod,"* I attempted to coach myself.

"Babe... I'm worried about you! Call me! You should've been home by now!"

The rest were just random messages; she texted me while I was locked up. It was almost like a diary.

They all were timestamped with the current date.

"I miss you so much. Today they sent you off but just know I got us!"

"Having some issues with the baby, so they put me on bed rest. Wishing you were here."

"Izaak has been a big help. He's doing what you asked of him. I never knew he was so cool."

I cringed as I read her message about Izaak. She was falling for him and didn't realize it.

"Legacy walked today!"

The next message gave my heart pause as I read it.

"Know that I never meant to hurt you. I never expected what happened between Izaak and me to evolve into anything serious. My heart was and is always with you. I broke it off with Izaak as I promised. I can't wait for you to come home, baby. I'm done with the extra. I just want you and our family. I'm so sorry for everything!"

That was the last message I had from my baby.

It's all my fault. I should've found the courage, stood my ground, and got us out of this life as planned.

I'm not too fond of Izaak's right now, but to be

honest, ain't no telling who killed Asha.

Now that I've talked to Uneek, I understood how Asha made herself a target.

Izaak probably said she was falling back because I was coming home, but I need to find him ASAP because I'm tired of playing Blue's Clue's trying to put this together.

I strolled through my contact list until I found Uneek's number. I wasn't sure if she had the same one, but I had to try.

I felt so bad about how I treated her and the things I said.

Uneek never moved funny around me. She was always on the up and up.

She lived in the projects but she stayed to herself. Based on what Asha said, she worked and stayed in the house mostly.

She wasn't out thotting around in these streets but she had a degree as well. She was a Medical Assistant and worked in a doctor's office.

I only knew because Asha felt some type of way once she started working.

"Everybody ain't able to have their man move them out the projects to the Eastside Asha. Some of us have to work hell," I would hear her laugh through the phone when Asha

313

would call to check on her.

I took a deep breath and pressed the green button.

"Hello," Uneek said.

"Hey, it's me, Prod. How are you doing?"

I attempted to make small talk. I was never good at apologies because I rarely made mistakes.

"I'm okay. I cursed Izaak's out last night. He called me after you left. Can you believe he thought he was going to come to my house and layup? We don't kick it like that no more."

Uneek grew quiet on the phone once she realized she let it slip to me that she was messing around with Izaak.

"You was sleeping with him too?"

"I was sleeping with him on the low when you and Asha were together. He use to pick me up and bring me to your house when Asha was put on bed rest. We were already smashing before that though. Once he…"

She was afraid to make the same mistake she made last night so she chose her words wisely.

Smart girl.

"Uneek, you can speak freely. I was calling to apologize for how I acted last night. I make no excuses for my actions because that was foul of me to put my hands on you."

"Well...when he started falling for Asha, he stopped talking to me altogether. I watched how he treated Asha. He never treated me like that. The way he looked at her. It was like she could do no wrong. She even made that business deal in Chicago on her own. Izaak didn't even know she already had work out on the streets in the city. He didn't care, though. Like I said...she could do no wrong in his eyes."

My flesh crawled, hearing Uneek describe more to me how close Asha and Izaak were.

"Well, I wanted to let you know that I apologize. I need to get myself together to go and see my kids."

"You haven't seen them yet?" She asked, clearly shocked.

"No, I came home and cleaned and tried to catch up with Izaak. I wanted to get my mind right as much as possible before I see them."

"Well...Amor found her. She's taking this really hard. Ms. Elisha can't get her to eat. I've been over there on my off days and after work to help out. It's all bad, Prod. It's so sad over there I can barely hold myself together and be strong. I'll be praying for you. If you need to talk, you know I got you."

"Thanks, Uneek. Good lookin'. I'm going to catch up with you later. If you see that nigga Izaak hit my phone."

"Bet."

I was relieved that Uneek didn't bring up that little interaction between us last night.

Every time I entered our bedroom, I could feel my heart on the tip of my tongue.

It was a constant reminder to never fall in love again and that's exactly what I needed.

I put on a button-up and jeans. I grabbed my pistols from the coffee table and headed out.
Once I walked out of this door, and people saw my Range, I was sure word would spread like wildfire in California during the summer.

I was ready for anything.

*　　*　　*

Within twenty minutes, I had arrived at Ms. Elisha's house. I didn't call her because I didn't know what to say.

I also didn't want to hear her cry over the phone and again when I got there.

My heart couldn't take much more at this point. I

was barely hanging on. What I have left I had to give my kids.

Ms. Elisha had been the mother I never had, along with Izaak's mom. They were the world to me. They would always be family.

I sat in the truck, trying to get the balls to get out.

I knew once I did that it would all be on me. Everyone in that house would be looking to me for answers and protection.

Protection was no problem but I didn't have answers for any of them.

Just as I placed my hands on the doorknob, the door flew open.

Amor jumped into my arms and cried. Not just an ordinary cry but one of those deep cries from your soul.

The loss of her mother would forever change her.

I could imagine the thoughts of her lying in a pool of blood would haunt her for a lifetime.

I held Amor tightly as Romello hugged my leg. I did my best to get inside with them hanging on me.

"You okay baby girl?" I asked Amor.

"I'm okay," her voice was weak and void of the joy she once possessed.

Ms. Elisha stood there, holding Legacy. She was the spitting image of me.

I put Amor down and reached for Legacy while hugging Ms. Elisha.

Legacy was smiling, revealing a full row of teeth. Drool ran down her chin as she tried to kiss me.

It was like she knew I was her daddy.

Legacy is too young to know what's going on, and for that, I'm thankful.

"How are you holding up?" I asked Elisha.

"I'm just doing my best to hang on."

"Me too. How have the kids been since everything happened?"

"I can't get Amor to eat. Romello has been acting out. He tries to fight the girls and he throws things."

"You not eating Mo?" I asked Amor.

"I just don't be that hungry."

"Well, I'm taking you to your favorite spot, and we gone see what's up!" I said, tickling her so she laughed.

"Amor, can you help Mello get dressed? I will dress Legacy," Elisha said.

"Sure, Gram Gram," she hopped off of the couch and bolted toward the bedroom.

Amor loved JMK Nippon's. It was a Japanese Hibachi restaurant. I had no idea if she liked the food or if it was the fact that they cooked the food in front of her.

Either way, I was willing to do anything to see a smile on their faces.

I picked up Romello, "You causing trouble lil' man?"

He just laughed and tried to swing on me with his bad butt.

I was excited to spend some time with them. I know Elisha probably needed a break to process all of what has happened as well.

Just as I was pulling out, Brian pulled up in a beat-up Toyota.

"I know my kids better not be in that truck!" He yelled, jumping out of his car.

I threw the truck in park and jumped out to get dead on him.

"My nigga, who do you think you're talking to? These just as much my kids as they are yours. You ain't been nothing but a damn sperm donor. You must want me to beat you down again nigga!"

"P, I don't want no smoke but them my kids. I got rights!"

"Man, if you don't get out of here. These kids have been through enough. You selfish!"

"Asha would still be alive if it wasn't for you, P. Let's just keep it a thousand around here!"

WAP!

WAP!

WAP!

"Prodigy! Stop!" I faintly heard Elisha yell.

For a moment, I forgot that the kids were in the truck. I only saw red as I beat some sense into Brian in the front yard.

I administered several kicks to his ribs. I could've sworn I heard something crack but I didn't care.

At that moment, I lost track that I was all my family had. I couldn't afford to go back to jail.

"Please stop!" Amor cried.

I didn't realize she had gotten out of the truck. The last thing I wanted was for her to see me like that.

I climbed off of Brian and turned to Amor. She was no longer smiling. Tears were flooding her face.

"Get out of here, Brian," I said, walking towards Amor.

"Y'all can't just keep me from my kids. I'm filing charges, my nigga!" He screamed before jumping back into his raggedy car.

I tried to make my way to Amor, but she just jumped back in the truck.

The look of disappointment on her face tore an even larger hole in my heart.

"I'm sorry you had to see that," I told Amor.

"Can we just go?"

"Amor...do you want to live with Brian?" I asked her.

"No. He's not nice to us. I want to stay with you or Gram Gram."

Despite me acting a fool, she still wanted to be with me.

I was so thankful for her love. I needed her right

now.

*   *   *

JMK Nippon was jam-packed. We sat at a table with other people for all of the seats to be filled.

Halfway through dinner, I see Izaak walk in with some girl.

I couldn't believe this nigga had the nerve to be out in public like he wasn't the last one to see Asha alive.

I gritted my teeth, causing my jaw bone to twitch. I had my kids with me, so I couldn't act up.

I've been waiting to get at this nigga.

"Amor, I will be right back. I'm going to speak to your Uncle Izzak," I told her.

Legacy was in her own world with the chopsticks and fruit I ordered for her.

I strutted over to Izaak. I watched all the color seep out of his face.

"What's good with you?" I said, inviting myself to take a seat.

The girl with him had no idea what was going on

322

as she smiled at me.

"How long you been out?" He asked.

"That's neither here nor there. We got business to take care of. I need to meet up with you tonight. I prefer not to have to look for you," I told him.

"Nigga you ain't ever gotta look for me. I stay in plain sight! Don't come in here with flexin'! I've been waiting to get at you anyway! I did you a solid having you locked up instead of having you carried by six."

"You a coward nigga! Always have been, always gone be!"

It was taking everything in me not to slam Izzak's face flat on the burning grill and make him the special of the night.

"We gone see who laughing last Izaak! She knows you kill women who reject you, or are you saving that for the second date?"

His date looked at him as if she wanted him to refute what I was saying.

"Oh, you waiting for him to say something? Nah, lil' mama. Nigga will body you, no doubt," I laughed as I walked off.

I wasn't sure why I laughed because I was mad.

I couldn't let Amor down again. I could see her

watching me from the other side of the room.

I made my way back over to them and did my best to push Izaak out of my mind.

The only thing I wanted more than vengeance is to see my kids smile again.

"You said hi to Uncle Izaak?" Amor asked when I got back to the table.

"Yeah, something like that." I lied. "Amor, I'm sorry about what happened with your dad earlier. I was out of line for that," I choked out.

"It's okay. Daddy is a bad person. He makes me sad. He hurt mommy."

It hurt my heart that Amor witnessed her dad putting his hands on her mom. That was just another thing on the list I couldn't undo.

"He's still your dad. Sometimes even though we are adults, we still have issues that we deal with that can make us act ugly on the outside because we are sad on the inside," I attempted to explain to her.

"I understand."

"How about we just focus on having fun. How about that?" I offered.

"I'm with that," she smiled.

"Oh, you're with that, huh?" I laughed. " When did you get so hip?" I asked her.

"I don't know."

I loved Amor as if she was my own. That little girl had a way of making things okay.

It was amazing that she was so mature for her age.

We spent the rest of the evening surprisingly laughing and catching up.

Kids have no filter. It was interesting to get her point of view of things while I was gone.

"Uncle Izaak was cool. He kept us safe, so my dad didn't come around. He and mommy worked a lot, but they took us a lot of places. We started living with Gram Gram so she could get me off to school and everything."

"Did you like living with your granny?"

"Yeah, we have our own room. It's not like how mama has ours fixed up, but it's nice still. I hear Gram Gram cry at night. She thinks we sleep...but I hear her. She misses mommy. I try to be strong for her and help her with Legacy and Mel. Sometimes..."

"What? Say it," I coached her.

"Sometimes, I think I see mommy...at night. She sits at the foot of my bed and tells me she's so proud of me for being strong and helping Grandma. She said to look out for you too. She said you would take care of us and keep us safe from daddy too. I think it's just a dream, though."

She dropped that bomb and went back to eating like she said something simple as the sky is blue.

I didn't bother to tell her about my experience.

The rest of the evening was filled with laughs and time well spent with my babies.

I kept watch of Izaak out of the corner of my eye. He talked a lot of smack, but he got up out of there quickly.

What the kids didn't finish, I had packed up to go. The ride home was quiet.

Everyone was sleeping except for Amor. That girl didn't miss anything.

Amor jumped out of the truck as she always does.

Elisha met us at the door. I had Romello in one arm and Legacy in the other.

Mel was getting big. My biceps were burning carrying him. He was asleep and I wasn't trying to wake his mean self up.

"Hey P. How was dinner?"

"It was good," I mumbled.

Except for seeing Izaak's, I enjoyed my kids.

Something was off about Elisha. She had this look in her eyes. A look I was all too familiar with.

I know she not back on drugs at a time like this. I couldn't afford for her to fall apart right now.

I'm barely hanging on myself. The last thing I needed was to have to babysit my mother-in-law.

I got the kids down in bed and sat with Elisha.

I didn't feel like confronting her right now about her possibly being high.

"Elisha, I think Izaak killed Asha. She told me she broke it off with him, and he didn't take it well."

I looked at her waiting for her facial expression.

"Izaak wouldn't hurt Asha. He has a bad temper, but he wouldn't hurt Asha. He's been that way since he was a boy," she rattled off nonchalantly.

"You knew Izaak from back in the day?" I shockingly asked her.

I never had much time to chop it up with Elisha. I was always with Asha and seen her in passing for the most part.

"I'm not sure why your father never told you, but...Izaak is your half-brother."

Elisha had to be high saying something like this to me!

"Are you high? Ain't no way my dad would keep something like that from me!"

Elisha leaned back on her couch and lit a Newport cigarette. I guess she didn't have the energy to argue or try and convince me otherwise.

"When did you start back smoking?" I questioned her.

"I've started doing a few things since my baby died. No, drugs ain't one of them! Do you think you can go to the funeral home with me in a day or so? I need to make the final decision for Asha's arrangements," her eyes filled with tears as she spoke.

"I sure can. That's not a problem at all." I assured her. "Elisha, I just want to tell you that I'm sorry. I should've kept Asha from this drug stuff. I make no excuses, but I never wanted this life. I was glad I made it into college. I felt it was my chance to escape what I was groomed for. I didn't feel worthy of complaining because my dad stayed when my mother left. He never left me. Ever. So I owed him to drop out and come home. I-"

"Prodigy.."

"Please let me finish. I worked my butt off to excel in college to prove my mother wrong about me. That she left behind a good kid, all the stuff I do in the community and the barbershop was me clawing my way out of the life. Trying to give kids what I never had...hope. I compromised and lost Asha."

Elisha had this blank stare on her face.

"What is it?" I asked.

"Prodigy...your mother didn't leave you. Izaak's mom killed her. It was long ago. You don't remember. Your father didn't allow you to go to the funeral, so in your mind, it was as if she left and never came back. Nothing was further from the truth."

"What do you mean? I would remember my mother being killed! Why was she never put in prison if she killed someone?" I challenged.

"Because it was self-defense. Your mother went to her house after finding out that Izaak's was, in fact, your dad's child. She was furious. Your mama kicked Linda's door in and beat the lady within an inch of her life. She somehow managed to grab a letter opener she had on a nearby table and stabbed your mama over and over. Your mother bled out on the floor. Your dad said she had several wounds in her heart and her lungs. She was dead before she made it to Rockford Memorial Hospital. Izaak witnessed it all. He was only about three at the time if I remember correctly."

I was sitting there in utter disbelief. I can't believe this was my first time hearing of this.

It makes sense why my dad never made a fuss when I told him I wanted Izaak to take over the day-to-day.

It explains why my dad raised us so close.

How could an entire city keep this under wraps for so long?

I can't believe no one said anything. My dad watched me cry about my mother and never once told me what happened! Even when I became old enough to understand. What was he thinking?!

I was so mad; I couldn't think straight. I was out here about to kill my only brother I had, and no one said anything!

I need to get in touch with Bash ASAP. This changes things.

SABASTIAN

He killed my baby.

The only thought that ran through my head since the day I discovered Asha was taken from me. I was a big-time dope dealer back in the day. I wasn't out here making kids I knew I wasn't going to be around to take care of.

"You good boss?" My right-hand man asked.

"Yes. Can you get the guard for me?"

"Absolutely."

Terrance walked in shortly after I made my request to Nathan.

Terrance worked closely with me when I was on the outside years ago.

Once I went down, Terrance became a Correctional Officer where I was sent.

He handled things for me and quickly got other CO's onboard once they found out how lucrative it was.

I didn't have much money left once I came in. I quickly turned that around.

I started running so many drugs through the prison that within four years in, I had a hold on the Warden.

I would've sent Elisha money, but I know she wouldn't take it.

Once I heard about her getting clean and getting her degrees, I pulled some strings to get her a good job.

It was the least I could do. I got wind of all the horrible stuff that happened to her and my kids.

I was glad that Justin didn't end up in here with me and that was all due to his sister.

Elisha was so hoed and drugged out that I was shocked our kids even survived.

When I heard about what went down with that nigga Cobra, I immediately put some niggas on him.

I made that nigga cut all ties with Elisha when she was put in the hospital by one of them tricks.

That nigga act hard but he not really about that life.

A lot of these niggas out today are some Little Debbie soft frauds.

"T, it's time for Izaak to stop breathing. Make the call," I instructed him.

"Okay, boss," he said, turning and walking away.

"T, get word to Prodigy Le Savage that his time is up. I will take it from here on out. Let him know if he interferes, then he can get this work as well."

"I understand," T confirmed.

My baby girl had defied all odds despite her mother and me. She didn't deserve to die the way she did.

I stopped Asha from coming to see me because I saw her starting to give up hope and crawl up in here with me mentally and emotionally.

She had always been that way, even as a child.

"You got this, Asha. You can ride without the training wheels. Daddy got you. I'm right here."

"No, daddy. I'm going to fall and hurt myself."

"No, you won't. I'm right here. I have the back of the seat to support you."

She took me at my word and pedaled down the cracked sidewalk.

She was doing amazing until she hit a hole in the sidewalk and flipped over.

"Shoot!" I scolded myself.

That girl hollered more out of knowing the injury would happen rather than the pain from the actual fall.

She curled up in my arms. "I'm never riding a bike again, daddy! I told you I would fall!"

"Asha, whatever you believe will manifest itself. I don't care if it's bad or good. Be conscious of the things you speak and believe because they will manifest themselves in your life."

"Yes, daddy."

She didn't want to, but I made her get back on the bike. If I didn't, she would be afraid to ride forever.

Memories such as this flooded my mind on a daily.

The only thing I felt was...failure.

I've been incarcerated so long I'm skilled in not showing emotion.

The fact of the matter is I'm dying on the inside.

Izaak will understand loss as well. I have something special planned for his son.

This will not be an instant kill. No, I will drive him into utter sanity. When I'm done, he won't know who to trust.

I will pick off, one by one, all of those he loves.

There's more than one way to skin a cat and I'm skilled at them all.

ELISHA

Once Prodigy left, I just sat there looking at the white powder inside the small Ziploc bag that I stuffed inside of my bible when he arrived with the kids.

There was a sinking feeling in my stomach as I contemplated the idea of how orgasmic a high would be right now.

I've had it for a couple of days. I just couldn't bring myself to flush it down the toilet.

I traced it with my fingers to afraid to brush the opening.

I knew if I did that, I would take those same fingers and brush them against the tip of my frigid nose.

My mouth salivated at the thought of the temporary high that awaited me. I just needed an escape, just for a minute.

Each time I prepare myself to spread open my tiny version of Pandora's box, I can hear Asha telling me that my grandbabies need me.

I war within myself that I'm older now. I should have a handle on this addiction.

I was no longer the hot, boy crazy girl from a long

time ago looking for her next high.

I lied when I told Asha about how I got into rehab. I was too ashamed to admit to her what she already remembered growing up.

I would never forget the day I was beaten within an inch of my life. Once Francois got locked up, I and some people I thought were my friends at the time had a smoke party.

We were up for three days straight, getting high.

We ran through Francois' work in about a week tops.

Once it ran out, I had to find a way to support my habit. I turned to tricking.

I started hanging out on 7th Street and Broadway. The other ladies of the night, that's what we use to call them back then, didn't take to kindly to me moving in on their territory.

"Who yo' pimp?" A skinny chocolate girl with a matted red wig asked me.

"Pimp? I ain't got no pimp! Why would I pay someone else when I'm the one laying on my back," I snapped.

WAP!

WAP!

WAP!

The onslaught of punches blinded me immediately. I wasn't sure if it was the chicks questioning me or someone else.

Soon I heard him speak. "You paying for protection!"

The three-piece given to me was handed over by a man I soon found out quickly to be King Cobra. He was as dark as midnight with soulless eyes. When he spoke, it was as if the world shook from the baritone in his voice.

"Here, give me your hand."

The blood poured from the gash in my head opened by the diamond ring he wore on his pinky.

I could barely see because the tears and blood mixed burned my eyes.

I reached out my hand in fear that rejection would cause him to take my life right there in the alley.

"I'm about to take you somewhere to get cleaned up. I had to make an example of you, so these other sluts don't get any ideas. Now come on 'cause I ain't got all night," he complained, snatching me from the ground.

Cobra had an apartment right above where the girls worked so he could watch them from the window in the Winter.

He had another girl clean me up, and even with my fresh wounds, he didn't hesitate to pull his junk out for me. I was so scared, so I did whatever he wanted me to.

Every time my mouth would touch a part of his body, I could feel the burning from the tear in my lips.

Pain shot upward through my body from what I later found out to be fractured ribs.

Once I was fully healed, I was put on the strip until I was nearly killed one night.

One of my tricks was high. Normally, I never missed an opportunity for free drugs, but Cobra had warned me already.

His threats were a drug regulator. I dared not get high on his watch.

Cobra instilled in us that if we thought our trick was high enough, then go in their pockets and take a "tip".

I was a lot of things back then, but I was no thief.

My hands quivered and my face started to tic as I slid the brown leather wallet from the back pocket of his slacks.

I was horrible at this. Every time I did it, I had to beat down the empty feeling in the pit of my stomach.

I filtered through the contents of his wallet. My heart gave a pause when I opened up to the picture of his children.

For a brief moment, my heart went to my kids. I quickly pushed those feelings to the back of my mind and focused on the task at hand.

We didn't deal with the credit cards, but I fingered through five one-hundred-dollar bills, a few fifties, and some twenties.

I quickly pulled the cash from his wallet. I was so busy trying to slip his wallet back into his pocket that I didn't notice my trick walk up on me.

"Aaarrrgghhh!" I screamed as he pulled me by the back of my head with such force I could feel my tracks separating from my scalp, taking my hair along with it.

I barely had any hair as it was from being so stressed out about making sure I stay on Cobra's good side.

Ksssshhh!

He violently hurled me into the enormous painting of a red and orange flower of some sort trapped behind glass designed to keep it safe.

"You think you can steal from me after I already paid you?"

His eyes were cold and flinty as he brought down blow after blow to my face.

Brittle fragments of the shattered mirror tore through my skin, causing it to burn as if red fire ants were consuming me.

"Get off of me!" I screamed, praying others in the rundown Pump Handle Inn would come to my rescue.

BAM!

I snatched the phone from the wall and swung it with all my might!

I clobbered him so hard he staggered back, affording me just enough time to dash to the door.

I slid the security lock back and just as I reached for the other lock.

WAP!

At first, I wasn't sure what he hit me with. I just felt this excruciating pain.

To be honest, I thought he stabbed me in the head and hit a part of my brain that forced me not to comprehend the intensity of damage done to me.

I stumbled around to face him more out of distress and confusion than anything else.

My vision was blurred and these sheets of blackness were being fought back by my sheer stubbornness and a desperate desire to live.

"Got you! You gone die tonight!"

I managed to concentrate on the object in his hand. It was an iron!

He must've grabbed it when my back was turned.

At that moment, I believed what he said. I was about to die!

"Please! Please don't! I have kids! I will give you all the money b-"

BAM!

Before I could plead further for my life, he brought the iron down again across my head.

It was the last thing I remembered.

I woke up in the hospital weeks later. I was in a coma. When I came to, every machine in the hospital was hooked up to me.

That experience is what made me go into rehab.

Cobra didn't give me a hard time leaving, which

was nobody but God that touched his heart because otherwise, he would've finished the job the trick started.

A toe tag was the only retirement plan that this job came with.

"Remember your why Elisha," I whispered to myself.

I forced myself to remember that night on the bad days.

I did amazing with my addiction until the anniversary of the day I quit. Every year I would have these dreams that were what a wet dream was to a novice lover.

Ding Dong.

My forehead wrinkled as I looked over to my right at the clock.

It wasn't late, but who could be showing up at this time of night?

I stuffed the baggie full of my narcotics back into my bible.

"Lord, forgive me," I uttered under my breath as I made my way to the door.

"Oh my God! Justin, baby, you're home! You made it!" I disintegrated into my baby boy's arms.

A current of heat devoured me as I clutched my stomach.

"She's gone J. They took…they took…our Asha from us," I contended to get out.

Justin was not disgusted by the tears of anguish that poured from my eyes like a busted water line.

He tenderly held me in his arms as if I were the child and he the parent.

The despair I had been holding in spewed from me like swirling vortices in a kettle.

I had reached my max. I could no longer entomb my shredded heart that leaked with regret and remorse.

"It's okay, mama. I'm here. I got you!"

Wetness saturated my forehead. I lifted my head and gazed into his eyes. Justin's grief was setting in.

I could look into his eyes and tell that sadness was tearing at his chest.

It was my time to be a mother. He needed to lean on me. In reality, I could imagine he felt as if he lost his mama.

Asha raised Justin. She sacrificed for him. She made sure he ate and was clothed. She ensured he solidified amazing grades. Grades that afforded him an opportunity in the United States Military Academy or what most people called West Point. I was his mother, but Asha was his mama.

"I'm fine, mama," Justin jumped up from the floor, and just like that, he pushed it all back in.

Justin hated showing weakness way before the Marines. He kept so much in I often worried myself about his mental stability.

On top of that, there is no telling what he sees overseas day to day.

"Ahem...Ahem," Justin cleared his throat, reaching for my bible.

"Justin wa-"

Before I could get my words out, Justin reached for my bible on the table.

I dashed over to him and grabbed it, but it was too late.

"Are you kidding me?!" Asha ain't even cold in her grave yet. You already back using mama! These kids need you! I can't just up and quit the Marine Corps ma'! I can't be over there worrying about getting my head blown off and if you back using putting my nieces and nephew in danger! Really mama?"

Justin's chest was heaving up and down rapidly as if he was struggling to breathe.

His forehead was wrinkled in anger and hurt was flashing in his eyes like a caution light.

Calmly I attempted to answer my son's questions.

"Yes...I've been struggling, but I haven't used it at all. It's been difficult to get to a meeting with all that has been going on, but I promise you I've been fighting this thing with all I have left in me. You didn't see what the kids and I saw. Not that it's an excuse. She was lying there naked with a bullet between her eyes. They carved Prodigy's name that was tatted on her from her chest. Amor and Mel were bloody from lying on her, thinking she would come back to them. They thought she was just hurt bad. You've smelled death, son. I'm sure of it. It sticks to you like rotten fish juice. I...I...it's like the world stopped. I've been fighting to hold it together for these babies but I'm tired J. Mama tired."

I broke down once again as I stood before my son, trying to explain my transgression. Praying he would forgive me.

I couldn't afford to disappoint the only living child I had left.

J was my everything. He was my baby boy. I spoiled him because his dad was always so hard on him.

Well, until the drugs took me over. Asha then picked up where I left off.

"I grabbed the Bible because it triggered a memory from when I was little mama. I remember after you got clean, I would peek in your room at night and hear you praying. You would walk the floor with this bible, praying for Asha and me. I knew once I was in the service, I would be fine because I had a praying mother. You know Asha and I forgave you a long time ago, mom, right? That's one of the reasons I got so mad. I don't want her kids to have to live through what we did, ma'. You are better than that. You stronger than any addiction!"

"I always figured as much. You both have always been so respectful, even when I was out there in the streets. How have you been, baby? How long are you here for?"

"I'll be here for thirteen days, mama. That's the max amount of sick leave I receive each leave year. I want to do as much as I can while I'm here to make sure you and the kids are okay. Get to a meeting. As a matter of fact, go to as many as you need to until I have to leave. I got you!"

"I'm just glad to have you. We have to make the arrangements tomorrow. The service will be in a few days. I want to give our family time to come in from out of town. Your father's side will be flying in the country as well."

"Whatever you need."

"I know you're tired. Your old room is just as you left it. The kids are sleeping. I know they will be happy to see their Uncle J. Get you some rest, baby. I'm going to stay up and read a little."

"Okay, mama. I'm going to take a shower and pass out. I'm exhausted."

He planted a kiss on the side of my face and grabbed the oversized green duffle bag and threw it over his shoulder.

I was just glad to have him home. I just wish it was under more favorable circumstances.

Once I was sure he was upstairs, I went into the bathroom and closed the door.

It was no longer a struggle.

I pulled the temptation from my bible that was ironically lodged in Psalm 23. I read the passage aloud.

The Lord is my shepherd, I lack nothing.

He makes me lie down in green pastures,
he leads me beside quiet waters,

he refreshes my soul.
He guides me along the right paths
for his name's sake.

Even though I walk
through the darkest valley,[a]

I will fear no evil,
for you are with me;
your rod and your staff,
they comfort me.

You prepare a table before me
in the presence of my enemies.
You anoint my head with oil;
my cup overflows.

Surely your goodness and love will follow me
all the days of my life,
and I will dwell in the house of the Lord
forever.

God provided me a way of escape and I was taking it.

DETECTIVE HASSIM MORGAN

As I sat in my leather chair, clearing my browser history, I ran the case of Asha Wilde through my mind over and over. I was so sure that Izaak would be her killer once I did some digging.

Based on his criminal history and his reputation in Rockford, I was sure I would have a slam dunk for Elisha.

The more I researched her; the more something awoke in me that has been dead since I lost my wife.

The growing admiration I was developing for her engulfed me with a need to protect her.

What was I missing? What am I missing?

I shuffled through the papers over and over. The Expert opinions, forensic files, and witness testimony weren't telling me anything.

None of it was pointing to who could've possibly taken Asha's life.

I picked up my phone to place a call to one of my informants. He was pretty good at keeping his ear to the streets.

"Black, have you heard anything about a girl named Asha Wilde on the streets?"

"Man, I told you I was done snitchin'. Niggas are starting to get suspicious. Y'all already be letting me out early when I get taken in. Niggas be knowing wassup."

"Look, answer my question before I come to pick you up now," I threatened.

"She Prodigy's girl, right?"

"Yea, that's her," I confirmed.

"Man...they call her Joan Clever out here."

"What do you mean?" I was utterly confused.

"Man, she was known for dismembering niggas that crossed her. She was out here running the streets so anyone could've killed her. I wouldn't be surprised if one of them niggas from Chicago put a hit out on her. I mean, she crossed so many people it could be anybody. I ain't heard anything else about it. People die every day B," he laughed.

"This ain't funny. Her kids found her dead body! Have some respect!" I yelled before ending the call.

Asha was not the picture-perfect nurse I initially perceived her to be.

She was actually Izaak's partner.

The drug task force has been watching Izaak for some time, but they haven't built a case.

They don't have enough evidence to have his lines tapped. For the past few years, it has been a waiting game.

I was running out of options.

I pulled out Asha's autopsy report.

I combed through the pictures one by one. Who would carve a tattoo from her flesh?

It was late now, but I needed to speak with Elisha to find out what was on Asha's chest.

Something like that is personal. It wasn't Izaak and Prodigy was locked up. Unless Asha had another lover, I need to find the father of her children, Brian.

All of the witness reports said that he hadn't been around since she got involved with Prodigy.

I need to speak to her best friend too.

I shuffled through my small notepad to find the name I was given by one of the people I spoke with.

Uneek. That was her name. I made a note to stop by her house as well while I was out.

Ding. Dong.

The doorbell rang and I glanced at my watch.

She's on time, like always.

Fionna was six feet tall with long cold black hair she wore down to her butt. She had a small waist, which was merely an introduction to the fat backside the Lord blessed her with. Her skin was dark, smooth chocolate. She reminded me of a young Naomi Campbell. Perfect long eyelashes accented her narrow almond-shaped eyes. The top of her lips was shaped like Cupid's bow and glistened as she licked her lips.

Fionna was an escort I met a couple of years ago. I had closed myself off so that I would never fall in love, but I still had needs.

She fingered through her payment of five hundred dollars. "So only sex tonight? You don't require the extra?" Disappointment weighed her voice.

"Not tonight. A case I recently acquired is keeping me busy."

I would pay her sometimes an additional five-hundred dollars to spend the night so that I can hold her.

There were times that I missed the true intimacy that a woman provided. Her soft touch, the way her chest gently rises as she sleeps, the way they always seemed to find their way up under you no matter how large the bed was.

Fionna was the only woman I dealt with after my wife that I allowed to sleep in my bed. I've had several one-night stands but nothing serious.

I quickly grew tired of the random women in my space, so once I met Fionna, it was for me.

She was discreet and sometimes she didn't charge me. There were times she just wanted to be held. She desired something authentic as well.

Recently, Fionna has been hinting at wanting more but I always changed the subject.

I didn't care about what she did for a living because I knew it would stop once we decided to make this official. I just wasn't sure if I was ready.

Well, that was until Elisha. That woman had me feeling some type of way.

She had sustenance. You can tell that she had been to hell and back but was like a concrete flower. She was still so beautiful and unsullied by life.

I quickly pushed Elisha from my mind so I could handle my business.

Fifi dropped her black mink coat to the floor and

stood there in a red crotchless teddy.

I didn't have time to take my little blue pill before she came. I pulled one out of the Altoids container I kept them in and washed it down with the glass of water sitting on my desk.

I had no secrets from Fifi. A wicked smirked crossed her face because she knew once that pill was in my system, I was going to wear her out.

We made love most times unless I was stressed.

She unbuttoned my white shirt and traced my chest with her fingertips.

"Your body is astonishing for a man of your age."

"Oh?" I replied, swooping her up into my arms.

I had my way with her for a couple of hours before I collapsed in exhaustion next to her.

"Would you like another round?"

"No, sweetheart. I have a long day tomorrow. Thank you though."

"No worries. You have my number."

Fionna hopped off of me and put her clothes back on. I made my way to the bathroom to dispose of the condom and clean up.

By the time I made my way out of the bathroom, Fionna had let herself out.

It was not uncommon for her to do this. Other times I was so exhausted I would immediately fall asleep.

She would just lock the bottom lock and leave me be.

Ceaser was here. I didn't have any worries if she didn't.

He was familiar with Fiona so he didn't bother her. She loved him. Sometimes she would bring him treats. I told her to stop spoiling my dog. I don't need him too friendly with her.

*   *   *

I woke up the next morning with my flaccid junk hanging out my boxers.

I picked up my phone as I did every morning to see if I had any missed calls and to check my messages.

Ryan: I have some information on Asha Wilde's case. I think I have a lead. Call me ASAP!

I sat up on the edge of my bed, attempting to wipe last night's escapade from my eyes as I waited for Ryan to pick up on the other end.

"About time you wake up!"

"Man, it's seven o'clock in the morning. Go to hell. So what's the info you have?"

"Everyone you spoke with said that the father of the older children, Brian, hasn't been around since she got with the new guy. I pulled his social media and found that the day after she was killed, he was on Facebook making some very suspect rants. He deleted them, but we were able to get the retrievals from Facebook. I had a few people comb through his messenger, videos, and other social media content, but there wasn't much more."

"What did you find in the post?"

"Oh yeah! He was saying stuff like, "Anything that he touched he can touch again." "People get some clout and think they can't get touched." "I always get what I want one way or another.""

"Yeah, but it's still not enough. Do we have a location on him?"

"No one has seen him since the murder," Ryan advised me.

"I saw him at Elisha Wilde's house trying to take custody of the kids. His behavior was erratic. He appeared to be high on something. I caught the tail end so I'm not sure exactly what was said. I'm trying to get in contact with Elisha Wilde today. I will keep you posted. I will be in shortly to discuss strategy."

"Sounds good. See you then."

I hung up the phone with him and immediately called Elisha.

If I were to be perfectly honest, I was looking for a reason to speak with her.

I wanted to get to know her but not on these terms. On the other hand, these terms were the only open door that I had at the moment.

"This is Elisha."

Her voice was as smooth as satin and as calming as a crystal clear lake. Just hearing her made me smile like a little kid.

"Hellloo," she stressed again when I failed to let her know I was on the other end.

"Yes, it's Detective Morgan, Ms. Wilde. How are you holding up?"

"I'm leaning and depending on God. What can I do for you?"

"I wanted to come by and speak with you about a couple of things for your daughter's case. I know you and your family are going through a difficult time, but it's key to solving your daughter's murder."

"I understand. I have to finalize the arrangements today and an NA...I mean a meeting today," she stumbled over her words.

"Can I go with you?" I proposed.

I was a recovering addict, but my addiction vanished once I got my grief under control. I'm not sure if I'm a creep or not. I had to get in where I fit in.

"To a meeting...meeting," she was shocked.

"Yes. A meeting...meeting. Is that okay?"

"Sure. When I'm done, I will let you know where to meet me."

"Sounds good. See you then."

IZAAK

Zoya knew she was fine! I watched her as she walked past my truck with her booty meat bouncing around. I asked around and found out she just moved here from Nigeria. Man, with a booty like that, I can help her get a green card. I have been at her hard, but she won't give me any play. She knows she wants me.

"Hey Z! What's good with you ma' when you gone let me take you out, love?"

Z was about her paper. She had females coming from all around Rockford to get their hair braided and she was cold with it.

"When you learn how to approach me with respect."

Her accent drove me crazy.

"My apologies Queen," I said, stepping out of my truck to go over to her.

TAK!

TAK!

TAK!

I dived on top of Z and dragged her between my

truck and another car.

I couldn't believe someone was bustin' at me in broad daylight!! Z was screaming at the top of her lungs.

"Z, calm down. I need you to listen. When I say so, we're going to make a run behind the brick wall over there. Okay?"

"Okay."

"Shh…Shh…Shh," I exhaled viciously.

Beads of sweat formed on my brow and started to slither down into my eyes.

I quickly wiped it away before it could blur my vision.

"Now!!"

She was fast as a cheetah in the African safari. She didn't stop at the brick wall. She kept going and dodged the bullets coming at us. It turned me on! I loved a chick that could handle herself in a shootout!

TAK!

TAK!

TAK!

They were hot on me as I dipped and dodged

through the apartments.

POP!

POP!

POP!

"Arrrgghh!" I heard one of the masked men scream out as I let my burner rip.

I just had to make it to the back of the projects. I know my squad was already on go mode once they knew it was me.

They know not to make our spot hot for any other reason. That's law.

TAK!

TAK!

The flying bullets sounded like bees flying by my ears.

"Oooh!" I yelled out as the bullet tore through my flesh.

I didn't have time to assess the damage because these niggas were trying to kill me.

Whoever was after me knew where my spot was at here in Concord because they all fell back.

"Man, we ain't know that was you getting aired out! We thought you been left Bug," one of my Generals huffed. "Man!"

They knew not to use my government at all!! Some of the new niggas still didn't know my name was Izaak. Bear has been with me for years and he still didn't know my last name.

Bear stood six feet and was a solid three hundred pounds. He wore a low fro. His eyes were dark and sunken into his head. His hands were huge and had broken more jaws than I could remember. He could and has killed with his bare hands.

"They caught me off guard. Let's get inside until this dies down," I told them.

We all mobbed inside our tip before the cops rolled in. They wouldn't get here until they were sure they wouldn't get shot in the crossfire.

This particular project was nothing more than a cage for human beings the city didn't care to deal with unless they had to. It was a shame.

"Lashonte, come look at Bug's arm and make sure he gone be okay."

"I'm a medical assistant, not a doctor. Y'all pay me to tip out of here, not play nurse," she clapped back.

"We pay you to do we want you to, now over here!"

She marched over to me huffin' and puffin'.

"Look, don't touch me with that janky attitude girl," I growled.

"I'm not Bug. I got you baby, let me take a look. I was just giving them a hard time. It just grazed you. It got you good. It probably feels as if someone rammed a hot poker in your arm, but you good. Let me disinfect it and wrap it up."

"Those niggas pulled a Houdini. Did you get a look at their faces?" Bear asked.

"Man, they had masks on so I didn't see any of them. I hit one of them when I was blastin' back, but they ain't drop. Call Somaya and tell her to look out for anyone that comes in with a gunshot wound," I instructed Bear.

"Aight. Bet

"Ayyee...I need y'all to prepare for war. I think Prod is behind this. I'm not takin' no more L's!" I yelled, clenching my fist.

Bear appeared from behind the white brick wall. "Bug, let me talk to you in the backroom for a second."

I followed him as he closed the door behind us.

"Wassup, bruh?"

"Bug, we respect you running everything while P been gone, but you know we can't open war on him without dealing with Francois. We both know he touchin' niggas from inside of the prison. He built this and left it to his son. We know you've been doing the work and making sure things run smoothly but don't you think we need to play this another way? Either way, y'all are going to have to handle this among y'all. We can't get mixed up in it. Understand?" Bear confirmed.

"Yeah, you right. I ain't thinkin' straight. I'm about to get out of here and go home and wind down. I will hit you later bruh," I shook up with Bear and headed out.

"You want us to follow you home?" Bear offered

"Nah, I'm good. Y'all be easy, though."

They went and got my truck and pulled it around. It wasn't too bad. The bullet lodge in the back windshield shocked me because it didn't shatter altogether.

I was paranoid about driving home. I had a full clip so I was ready if necessary.

I needed to get to Prod and see what was up. I needed him to know I didn't kill Asha.

At one point, I ain't want anything as bad as I wanted him to be six feet under.

Asha dying put a lot into perspective for me. It meant more to me to find out who murdered her than to clear my name.

I can be selfish and arrogant but I love the people I love.

I just have this rage inside of me that I've never been able to understand where it came from.

Yeah, I was raised by a single mother, but what black man these days hasn't been.

I was the only child. I had an okay life from what I can remember growing up.

I use to get these nightmares as a kid and would wake up in cold sweats. My mom would rock me back to sleep and remind me it wasn't real.

The nightmare would play every night. It was always the same. Some monster would attack my mom and I was too small to help her. I cowered in a corner crying with pissy pants. It would all go black and I would wake up.

I just figured my anger was due to my messed up attitude. I felt like niggas were always trying to get over or think they were better than me or something.

I don't think that now.

I circled my house just to be sure the coast was clear.

I couldn't risk them following me to my mama house or some shit. On top of that, I didn't want to deal with her fussin' about my arm.

"Shhittt!!" I yelled.

If it wasn't one thing it was another. Shit been crazy since Asha died.

That girl was like a perfectly rolled purple Kush blunt on a pillow top mattress accompanied by a bad bitch that gave insane brain.

Other than taking that pussy from Camille I decided against fuckin' random bitches.

When Asha and I broke up I wasn't out here fuckin' these chicks. I mean a week or so may not seem like a long time to other people but to me, the shit was an eternity.

My ass was sick when she broke it off. Inside I knew she would do it but I also hoped she would pick me. I prayed she would see something in me worth taking a risk on.

The way I grew with Asha in the last couple of years made me question if I ever really loved Camille.

I never desired to change that way for her. I never wanted to be a better man for her.

It wasn't her as a woman. She did everything. Hell, the woman gave me a child.

Asha spoke to the man in me and held me accountable to it. She didn't take my excuses or lies. Her take no shit attitude is what forced me not to fuck over her or play with her feelings.

I didn't want to lose her. I didn't want to waste what time I had with her.

I always knew it was Prodigy. It's always him. He's always been the chosen one. Everything was always handed to him with his weak ass.

His dad, Francois, treated me just like his son but I felt it was always sloppy seconds. I was thankful because he put a real nigga on but I always felt like I was waiting in the shadows.

I couldn't complain because that wasn't my dad. Shit, he was doing what my deadbeat ass daddy failed to do…be a father!

My mom told me that he was killed back in the day but I asked around and people just look at me crazy.

There are no pictures of him, my mom or us.

It's as if he doesn't exist.

I finally parked in my garage and made my inside.

"What the fu-"

How in the fuck did this nigga get in my damn

house! Cam gave my house key back so this breaking and entering fool had me fucked up.

WAP!

WAP!

WAP!

"Pussy ass nigga!" He yelled.

Aston, Cam's fiancé, met me with a combo that rocked my shit!

At that moment I didn't give a fuck about him being a damn cop so I returned the favor landing a punch dead in his mouth.

"Aaarrgghhh!" I yelled when he did some kind of defensive move that landed me with him gripping one hand behind my back and my face pressed into the hardwood floors.

"How could you violate the mother of your kids? You already put her through hell! How do you repay her for being concerned about your sorry ass? You rape her! She made me promise not to kill your ass but I wanted nothing more than to dump your ass in the Rock River! Stay the fuck away from my family!"

"Your family?! Nigga fuck you! I don't give a damn about what you and Cam got going on but that's MY damn son!"

"Nigga your son calls me daddy because you're never around. Like I said that my damn family now so stay the fuck away or I will make your life a living hell Izaak!"

"Arrgghh!" He dug his nails into my fresh wound. I could feel the warm blood soaking through my bandage.

"Next time it will be a bullet to the back of your head. Try me," he said standing up finishing me off with a couple of kicks to my stomach forcing my Wong Wong's up onto the floor.

I didn't argue with him further because I would take this assault over prison any day.

I didn't have any guarantees that this muthafucka wouldn't still have it out for me down the road.

I knew all of the crooked cops and he wasn't one of them which is why he probably opted for beating my ass instead of planting evidence to take away my freedom.

I laid on the floor huffing and puffing trying to catch my wind from the fight and throwing up all over the floor.

"Fuck my life!"

I watched Aston show himself out. I was just ready for this damn day to be over.

I needed to come up with a plan and fast. I yearned for my life to return to business as usual.

I managed to get up on all fours and from there stand to my feet. I wiped the extra vomit from my mouth with the back of my hand.

I grabbed an ice pack from the freezer for my face. I didn't beat Aston's ass because deep down I knew I deserved that ass whooping for what I did to Cam.

I couldn't afford more bad karma with all the shit I have going on.

I need to get to Prod ass before he made another play on my life.
He must've met some new niggas when he was downstate because the ones who ran up on me weren't from around here. I could tell by their accents.

This shit was becoming exhausting!

UNEEK

I watched Prodigy stroll out of the bathroom wearing his black Ermenegildo Zegna boxers. My eyes traveled from his barrel-chest to his mouth watering abs.

As he walked closer to me I traced them with my fingers. "*1…2…3….4...5…6.*"

Each number was sealed with a kiss. I traced the dip in the center of his abdomen with my wet tongue all the way down to his hard rod.

It was so long the tip peeked out from the top of his boxers taunting me for a kiss and to be freed.

I obliged as I slid his boxers down his smooth gingerbread skin.

I never imagined in my wildest dreams that I would be taking Prodigy Le Savage into my mouth and swallowing his kids.

I laid on my back in the bed and allowed my head to hang over the bed.

The bed height was perfect. It allowed Prodigy to drop all nine inches of dick into the back of my throat.

I grabbed the base to guide him in and out of my hungry mouth.
It was my mission to suck the soul out of this man

tonight.

He caressed my body delicately exploring my full breast.

In spite of having kids they still sat up just as perky since the day puberty blessed my life.

He leaned over planting kisses down my stomach paying close attention to my belly button.

He swirled his tongue in and out. His lips were so soft almost like velvet.

He continued and I could feel the wetness on my leg from the anticipation that was building up of him devouring me with his mouth.

He finally placed his lips over my clit and a moan escaped my mouth in spite of it being filled with dick.

I raised one of my legs allowing him full access to my kitty.

He wasn't scared to eat the pussy either. It was sloppy and vigorous.

I could tell I was the first woman he had been with since he was released and I was honored that he chose me.

I didn't let his superb mouth game deter me from my goal of feeling the warm thick white liquid slide down my throat.

The fact that he was an all-around good dude and excellent father only turned me on more.

There was nothing as sexy as a black man handling his business in the home, community and bedroom.

Shit made my pussy percolate just thinking about it.

I skillfully stroked Prod's length while sucking with enough pressure to bring what I wanted to the forefront.

Within minutes we were both climaxing at the same time.

He didn't let not one drop fall on the all-white bedding the Radisson provided.

Simultaneously we both rotated so that he was able to climb on top of me and give me what I've been wanting since he showed up at my house looking for answers about Asha and Izaak.

As he slipped in and out he pulled my ankles in front of him so he could suck on my toes.

A bitch ain't never ever had that shit done before and I damn near lost my mind.

"Uuumm..." I moaned as I bit down on my bottom lip. "Why you in here trying to turn me out?" I laughed.

My goofy ass couldn't be serious for shit. I couldn't help it.

"I haven't turned you out yet baby. Just wait on it though."

Just as I was about to cum he pulled out and tapped his dick on my pussy.

"Not yet. I'm not ready."

"You not ready! The fuck! I am. I need it, babe." I whined.

"You gone get all of it…I promise." He smiled.

"Put it back in…please," I begged.

He looked at me with such an intensity it made me uncomfortable.

It was as if he was looking into my soul trying to determine if he could trust me with all of him.

"I got you," I said reading his mind.

He leaned in and kissed me as if we had been involved for years.

R. Kelly's Honey Love played in the background on my phone.

Prod sucked on my neck making his way to my

ear. He slid his tongue inside and my toes curled.

I pushed him away because I could feel myself losing control of my body.

I couldn't let all the freak out on our first go round. Could I?

Fuck it. I thought to myself. Go big or go home Uneek.

With that, I rolled over on top of Prod. I rode him to the beat winding my whips.

I leaned back using his legs as a balance so that I could use his dick to reach my G spot with every stroke.

I could feel his grip tighten on my ass signaling he was close to an orgasm.

I switch that shit up and started riding him like a porn star.

"What are you doing to me?" He moaned.

A seductive smile adorned my face. I took it as a compliment.

We were fucking like crazy. We switch from one position to the next as smooth a Cadillac on the highway.

P switched it back up on me so he was on top.

With every stroke, he went deeper and deeper.

Our chemistry was undeniable.

I wrapped both arms around his neck and pulled him in closer.

He didn't deny me access. He slowed down so that we were no longer fucking but making love.

"Put your name on this pussy P," I begged.

If I had to put it in words…imagine DMX putting it down on Keisha in the movie Belly.

"Oh..Ohhh..ssshiittt!!!" I yelled loud enough for everyone on our floor in the hotel room to hear us.

Beep. Beep. Beep. Beep.

I jumped up at the sound of my alarm.

"Shaattt."

My hours had been so crazy working two jobs I slept when I could.

"Really Uneek?" I scolded myself as I looked between my legs.

It was yet another day I had awaken to a small wet puddle of cum.

I was too old to be having wet dreams but the

shits won't stop! The night we nearly kissed was crazy. I couldn't stop thinking about what could've happened.

I'm not sure if it's right or wrong but my girl is gone.

Regardless, I can't cross that line.

I'm not sure if the knock on the door was a blessing or curse because something sparked between P and I that night.

I had so many mixed emotions and no one to talk them through with.

I was so glad I was getting ready to move out of these damn projects before I had to kill one of these hoes.

They so damn nosey!

Hoes I don't even talk to catch me going to my car talking about, "Girl, they found out who killed yo' girl?"

"Nah." I said walking fast as shit to avoid going off of the bitches.

"We heard she was fuckin' with her nigga homeboy and he killed her when she tried to break it off."

"Mind ya' fuckin' business hoes!" I snapped

getting in my car.

I stayed to myself but these hoes always wanted to try you.

They be jealous as fuck if you had any type of ambition and actually wanted to get up off the system and do something positive.

I had two kids who I wanted to be able to go outside and play without worrying if they going to get shot.

What did it for me was my lil' homie Keenan dying in my arms over the summer.

I'm rarely outside but it was my birthday so I decided to grill.

Keenan helped me bring my shit in the house and promised to come back after he made a run.

I went ahead and got everything started.

We were all having a good time. Drinks were flowing, the kids were playing and the spades game was crackin'.

The next thing we knew a car full of random dudes sped into the driveway.
TAKKA!
TAKKA!

TAKKA!

TAKKA!

TAKKA!
TAKKA!

The pit of my stomach fell as I dashed for my kids. I grabbed them both and ran inside along with everyone else who was outside.

We all cowered on the floor until the fire ceased.

We frantically checked our children and each other for injuries and by the grace of God we were all okay.

"Where's Keenan y'all?" I asked. "Where is he?!"

I quickly lost my shit when I realized he wasn't inside with all of us.

We all ran outside to find Keenan stumbling from his car.

He had been sitting inside rolling up so the Metro's would walk up on him outside.

He walked a few stepped and collapsed.

I ran over to him and rested his head in my lap. Once I positioned him I noticed my hands were full of blood.

He had been shot in the back of his head.

"I'm gone be okay Neek."

His voice was weak and his breathing faint.

"Somebody call 911 dammit!" I yelled. "Tell them to hurry the fuck up!" I cried.

I tried to remain as still as possible. I wasn't sure where the bullet had traveled or if he had been hit anywhere else.

There was so much blood I couldn't tell where it was coming from.

"Stay with me Keenan! Don't you fuckin' die on me bruh! Not like this Keenan! Not like this!" I was hysterical.

By the time the paramedics arrived he was gone.

I sat there rocking him like he was one of my kids.

"Ma'am, we need you to step back."

"Don't fuckin' touch me! Don't touch me! Fuck this shit! Fuck all of this shitttt!!" I yelled as they dragged me from his dead body.

That was the straw that broke the camel's back for me.

I sat there for hours with his blood on my hands.

This was happening all too often in the hood.

The Cease Fire initiative worked for a while but nothing last forever when there was a constant struggle in the hood to be on top.

That's when I got the second job. I had to get the fuck out the hood.

I was geeked as shit that I got approved for my house. It was a rent to own house going towards South Beloit in a quiet area.

I was actually getting ready to move in about a week or so.

My deposit has been paid and all my utilities were scheduled to transfer over.

I just needed to survive long enough to the hell up out of here.

I'm not about to get caught in the middle of Prod and Izaak's shit. I wanted justice for my girl but I have my own damn kids to think about.

I don't know who gone help me move all of this shit. I didn't feel like standing over some crackheads while they moved my shit.

I had to focus on one thing at a time though. I needed to get through my girl funeral first.

Shit Asha! Who killed you baby?

I pulled up to the doctor's office I worked at

during the day.

I prayed this bitch Nancy didn't start with me today because I was not in the damn mood.

"Good morning," I spoke as I made my way into the office.

I put my purse in my desk and locked it up. I went the list of scheduled appointments for the day so I could pull the charts.

What do we have here? The same bitch that was starting shit with me about Asha's death has an appointment today.

Let's see what she coming in for.

Bwwhaahhaha! I was dying laughing on the inside.

This bitch was burning! I wasn't surprised she stayed having one nigga leave out the front door and another sneaking through the back door.

Bitch only ended up with a wet ass because none of these niggas helped her. She was still running around the projects having her kids beg the neighbors for sugar and shit.

"Please make sure you double check the names and the dates of birth. Last time you pulled the wrong file and we almost disclosed another patient's protected health information." Nancy was starting her shit.

"That happened once over four months ago. You can let that go. I rarely make mistakes. By the way, how is the patient that you gave the injection that she was allergic to doing?" I smirked.

"She's fine!" She snapped.

Yes bitch, get the fuck on and quit playing with me you fake ass Jennifer Aniston.

Regardless of how educated or hard working a minority can be in Corporate America, they always view us as inadequate.
We always have to work twice as hard and there was no room for error.

I was for the shits though. I loved when they tried me so that a ghetto, educated woman named Uneek could put them in their place. Fuck these people.

Nancy was the office manager but she was racist as hell.

I had to leave here and go to my second job after this. I was a CNA also so I worked at River Bluff Nursing Home. Asha once worked there so she gave me a referral.

Tarshae and I hit it off once I found out she knew Asha. Her crazy ass made the time fly by on third shift.

I had to work with her tonight. I was glad because

we cleared our halls and chilled.

We alternated taking turns sleeping when we had the cool DON (Director of Nursing).

Jennifer didn't give a fuck what we did as long as we took care of the patients and answered them damn call lights.

The nights we didn't have her I was a zombie the next day at my other job.

Adderall was the only thing keeping me going. The side effect was my ass was losing weight because my appetite was obsolete when I took it.

I needed to come up with a plan before I crashed. There is no way I can continue like this. What can I say…I have to do what I had to in order to take care of my kids.

* * *

I just sat in my car as I stared at the nursing home. I was soooo fuckin' tired bro! My body was giving out on me.

I reached into my purse and pulled out the pill bottle. This girl in the project sold her kids ADHD medicine for the low. She had all they asses on that shit in order to secure a check.

She still didn't make they bad asses take it. She let them bad ass kids terrorize their teacher and other students.

They stayed roaming around the project tearing up shit because they were always suspended.

I washed the pills down with a bottle of water and dragged my disgruntled employed ass in the building.

Tarshae met me in the breakroom so we could get our first cup of many of coffee in.

"Bitch you look like a wet dishrag." She laughed.

"How the fuck can someone look like a dishrag girl?"

"You look worn out."

"I am. These two jobs kicking my ass. I barely see my kids and that shit is fuckin' with me for real girl."

"You got this girl." She encouraged me.

"I hope so 'cause a bitch is tired on my mama!" I laughed giving her a high five.

"Bitch we on Mr. Thompson hall tonight again." She cut her eyes at me.

"Fuck man! Why they keep giving us his ass?"

"You know why. We the only black chicks on this shift at night." She rolled her eyes. "When is Asha funeral? I haven't heard anything."

"I'm going to call her mom tomorrow. I think if a few days. They made the arrangements today if I'm not mistaken. I helped pick out her dress. I will keep you posted."

"You know who I think did that shit?"

"Who bitch?" I was eager to hear her take.

"Brian ass. He came up here one time. The day she got rushed to the hospital from here was because she was fighting him off in the back. She stabbed his ass and everything. This white detective reached out to me and I told him that shit too. I don't give a fuck call me a snitch or whatever but it's justice for Asha around this bitch."

"Trill shit!" I said giving her dab.

I didn't think that it could be Brian ass. I need to tell Prod about this shit because I know he doesn't know about him coming up to her damn job.

PRODIGY

I escorted Elisha and Justin to the funeral home. Chill bumps filled my arms. This would literally be my first time seeing Asha since I left for prison. I didn't know seeing her in court would be my last time seeing her alive.

My stomach was doing somersaults as my dress shoes clicked against the linoleum floors.

I could feel the beads of sweat forming under my armpits and trickle down my side.

My hands were shaking so I bald them in a fist in hopes that it wouldn't be noticeable.

"She's right behind these doors. Please take as much time as much time as you need. If you would like anything else changed about her please let us know.

I could literally feel myself stop breathing as I walked through the glass doors. It's as if all the oxygen got sucked out of the room.

There was a nameplate on the door that read "Asha Wilde services at 4747 W. Riverside Blvd.

She was in a white casket that was trimmed in gold. Each corner had a kneeling angel plated in gold as well.

"Asha…" I whispered to myself.

The tears started to flow out of my eyes and my legs were too weak to hold me up. I doubled over with my hands on my knees to catch my breath.

Elisha walked up behind me and rubbed my back.

I pulled myself together and stood up. Even in death she was the most beautiful woman I had the privilege of resting my eyes upon.

"Her stylist agreed to do her hair. Uneek helped me pick out her outfit. Traci the woman that owns Royal Glam did her make-up. I was told she was the best in Rockford so I had to have her. It was not something she does but she made an exception due to the circumstances. She did an amazing job covering up the gunshot wound don't you think?"

"She did amazing." I agreed with her.

I'm not sure what was going on with her and Justin but it was a lot of tension between them.

Justin just stood in the corner. He was extremely quiet in a creepy way. It was like his mind was somewhere else but his eyes had murder in them.

I've seen the look to many times on the streets. I was surrounded by killers all my life.

Asha's hair was flawless. She wore it natural but her hair stylist had straightened it with some big curls that rested on her shoulders.

She cut her bang to help cover up her wound so to look at her you couldn't tell she was shot in the head.

She was my sleeping beauty. I leaned over into the casket and lightly kissed her lips. I hoped it would be like the fairytales and she would wake up and make this nightmare come to a screeching halt. She didn't though. She just continued to lay there in peace. Her nightmare had finally come to an end.

"I will find out who put you here baby girl. I promise."

"We will," Justin interjected.

"How long are you here for?" I asked him.

"Long enough."

"You got a problem with me?" I snapped back.

"My mama may not be able to see it but my sister laying here because of your ass! If she never would've met you she would be still alive. My sister didn't know anything about selling drugs or none of that shit before you!"

"She was also living in the projects with a nigga beating her ass barely making it. She gave up everything for you and you didn't bother to send a single dollar home to her to help out! I loved the shit out of your sister and I told her I was giving up the drug shit for her but she wanted it! I didn't want the shit anymore I was content with the barbershop. Asha got intoxicated by the power!"

Justin walked up on me like he wanted some rounds and I posted up with the shit.

I didn't give a fuck about us being in a funeral home ain't no nigga gone disrespect me.

"Now is not the time. Y'all please let's not do this

right now!" Elisha appealed to our sensibility.

Justin stormed out of the room and we both just watched him leave.

I was wishing we had opted for separate vehicles because I didn't want his crazy Marine ass sitting behind me on the drive home.

"He's just dealing with a lot. Asha was like a mom to him and he's angry. I'm sorry he blew up at you. You know what he said wasn't true, right?"

"The things he said are the same words I have been beating myself up with since I've found out Asha was killed. I'm full of regrets." I said lowering my head.

Elisha walked over to me and gently lifted my head. "This was not your fault. Asha was a strong-willed woman and no one makes her do anything. You hear me? You hold your head up. I watched you with my daughter and I know you loved her and them kids. I was there!"

"Okay. You ready to go, mom?" I asked her.

I've never called her that but she has been more of a mom than I was ever given the honor of having.

Buzz. Buzz. Buzz.

"Excuse me, I have to take this," I told Elisha.

I stared strangely at my phone because I hadn't heard from Bear since I've been home. What could he want?

"Hello."

"Hey P, wassup with you?"

"Shit. What's good? Why you hittin' my phone?" I asked him.

I hadn't reached out to anyone because I wasn't sure which direction I wanted to take my life.

I had three kids depending on me so that changes everything.

"Somebody was bustin' at Bug yesterday and he thinks it was you. He tried to get us to come after you but I pulled him to the side and let him know that we couldn't get involved. It's between y'all."

"Man I've been busy trying to get my girl buried and being here for my kids. I haven't had time to worry about his ass. I will hit his ass up and see wassup. Thanks for the heads up."

"Bet." He said ending the call.

I just shook my head. Izaak's ass was so paranoid he actually thought it was me after him.

I knew exactly who was after him and it wasn't me. It was Sabastian.

He said if I refused to handle Izaak he would step in and I know he was a man of his word.

I had to get word to him so he could call me.

I drove Elisha and Justin back home so I could run some more errands.

Justin wanted to spend more time with the kids so I opted to see what I could find out about Asha's murder.

Buzz. Buzz. Buzz.

I looked down at my phone and it was Uneek.

Since nearly kissing her I made it my business to avoid her.

I felt like I was betraying Asha if I crossed that line.

"Yeah," I said answering the call.

"Hey Prod, I wanted to tell you something about Asha. I don't know if you know it but Tarshae said the time when Asha had to be rushed to the hospital it was because of Brian. He came up here and they were fighting. She said Asha had to stab him to get him off of her. Apparently, he was fucking with her when you weren't around and she didn't want to tell you because she didn't want to upset you. I just thought you should know."

"Good looking. Thanks, Uneek."

"No problem. Keep me posted if you catch up with that nigga. I will keep a lookout in the projects for him…well until I move."

"Oh, you moving? When?"

"Yeah, in a few days. Trying to find somebody to help me because I don't want these crackheads to double-back and rob me at my new crib." She laughed.

"I can help you."

The line went silent for a moment. "Are you sure?"

"Yes, I'm sure. I know Asha would want me to look out for you."

"Is it going to clash with the funeral?" She asked.

"The funeral is tomorrow."

"Okay good. I'm off this weekend at both of my jobs so that works. I will let Tarshae know.

"Okay. Well, I have to take care of some business I will hit you later."

"Okay, bye."

I had to find Izaak and squash this shit so we could find Brian dirty ass.

Fifteen minutes later I pulled into his driveway.

It was true what Bear had said. Izaak's truck looked like swiss cheese.

I stuffed my nine in back my holster and took a deep breath.

I prayed that this shit didn't go left.

I knocked on the door and waited and knocked again.

Izaak answered with a gun pointed in my face.

"What the fuck you doing here? Came to finally face me like a man instead of handling this shit like a coward?" I said through clenched teeth.

It looked like someone had already got to Izaak before I did. Bear didn't say he got his ass beat today when I was on the phone with him a few minutes ago.

"Man, I just want to talk. I know you didn't kill Asha. Your dirty ass set me up but we can deal with that shit later."

"Or...we can deal with the shit now he said cocking his gun."

"Look, I need you to help me track down Brian ass. I think he the one killed Asha."

"Real shit? You think that nigga had the balls to do this shit?" Izaak asked lowering his gun finally.

He stepped to the side allowing me entrance.

"Before we get to that I need to ask you something else. What do you remember growing up?"

"What the fuck you mean? You gotta be more specific my nigga."

"Elisha said your mom killed my mom a long time ago when she came to her house to confront her about you."

"About me? What the fuck you talkin' about? My damn mama couldn't kill a fly! Why the fuck is she lying on my mama bruh?"

"Just think back...you don't remember anything?"

He sat there with a stern look on his face. "I use to have this reoccurring nightmare. It was about this monster coming to our house attacking my mama. I cowered in the corner crying as my mom killed the monster. She always told me that shit was just a dream."

"It was real...the monster to you was my mama. This whole time nobody said shit."

"What you mean she came over there to confront her about me?"

"Francois is your dad too my nigga. They never told us. I'm not sure why but they didn't. They let me grow up thinking my mama left me and you grew up thinking your dad died a long time ago."

"So this whole time he just treated me like some step-child while you were sent to college and all that shit? That's some fucked up shit! I'm trying to figure out why I'm so damn fucked up in the head and it's because I saw my fuckin' mama kill somebody! Fuck!"

"That's why dad-"

"That's not my fuckin' daddy!"

"Nigga you damn near sent me away from life trying to take control of the shit he left behind. You act more like that nigga than I do and I understand why now. That's why he never said shit when I told him I wanted out and you to take over. He knew the shit was staying in the family regardless! I still don't want no parts of the shit! If you would've given me time the shit was yours. You took away my freedom on some jealous shit my nigga."

My temper was flaring and I couldn't help it. If I wasn't locked up Asha would still be alive.

"Man, you wouldn't have given that shit up with Asha by your side. You didn't see her P. Asha was worse than we ever were. She was making deals and shit on the side that I didn't know about. She expanded and contacted her dad's peeps overseas to reconnect so we could get better pricing on a more pure product. She wasn't the same Asha you left."

"I wouldn't have left if you didn't set me up!"

"You right. I violated but I just wanted my time on top that's all. I went about that shit wrong and I understand if you at my neck. I ain't on that shit no more. Asha changed me. I know you don't want to hear that shit but it is what it is. I'm glad I didn't kill yo' ass being that you my brother and shit." He laughed.

"After Asha's funeral, I want to talk to your mom about what happened. I want to ask her about my mom."

"Yeah, we can go over there together because I got some questions of my own. When the funeral?"

"Tomorrow. I'm not ready for that shit at all my nigga. Amor not eating. Mel acting out fighting and shit. Legacy to young to know what the fuck going on."

"She looks just like you but way better." He laughed.

"Fuck you nigga." I laughed. "It's one more thing. Sabastian met with me when I got ready to get out and told me that he was putting a hit out on you. I told him I would do that shit at the time because of how you did me dirty but I ain't know you were my damn brother. I guess I was taking to long so he took matter into his own hands. I sent a message to him so hopefully, he calls me. Until then nigga watch yo' back. You know his reach is long."

"I already know. So we good?"

"Yeah, we good. You can have that drug shit I gotta be here for my kids. Ms. Elisha looks like she barely holding on so I want to bring them home. When we kill Brian ass I'm hoping I can get custody of all of them. I know Ms. Elisha won't mind."

"You think so?"

"I hope so. She doesn't look like she can handle them. We can share custody if she wants but I want my kids with me. All of them."

"Yeah, I saw Amor…that shit broke my heart when she cried in my arms."

"Nigga, you not going to take them back to the same house they mama got killed in are you?" He questioned me.

"I ain't think about that part. I've just been thinking that I want to be the last place she was."

"They will never heal in that house. It's a constant reminder to all of y'all if you be honest with yourself. You they daddy man, you can't be selfish. You can still keep the house but you have to find something else if you want them to be able to move forward."

"You right." I agreed.

"The night we saw each other at JMK she said that her daddy hurt her mommy. At the time I thought she was talking about how he use to beat her ass and shit but now I think Amor may have seen something. They said she found her mom but what if she saw Brian ass leaving? I need to talk to her. You want to come with me?"

"Bet. Let me get my shoes on."

Izaak and I caught up on everything as we made our way to Elisha's house.

I hope Justin didn't give me shit because I was not in the mood.

We pulled up and Elisha was still gone.

Justin let us in and it appeared that he was cool.

"What's up? What y'all doing here? Prodigy I thought you wanted us to keep them until I leave."

"We think Amor may have seen Brian the night she found your sister dead. She told me when we were out to eat that he hurt her but at the time I thought she was talking about how he use to beat up on her."

"Wait…what? That nigga was putting his hands on

my sister and nobody said shit?"

"That's how we ended up together. I got him off of her one day in Fairgrounds. He was trying to beat her ass in front of everybody out there but me and Izaak didn't let any of that shit go down in our presence. I beat his ass right after at Larry's talking shit. He stopped coming around when she and I moved in together and I threatened his ass before to stay the fuck away from her or I would kill his ass."

"Good looking," Justin said giving me dab. "Let me call Amor down so we can talk to her."

He walked over to the bottom of the stairs. "Amor."

"Yes Uncle J?"

"Can you come down here for a minute. Izaak and Prodigy are here for you."

"Yes! We heard her yell.

She came running down the stairs so fast I thought she was going to fall.

She jumped up into my arms and gave me the biggest hug and kiss.

This little girl made my day without knowing it.

I walked over to the couch and sat her between Izaak and me.

Justin took a seat on his mama coffee table so we had her surrounded.

At first, I thought we would freak her out but she was loving the attention of her favorite guys.

"Amor...we have to ask you something that may make you sad but we need you to tell us the truth. You don't have to be afraid because we will all protect you. Do you understand?"

"Yes." She softly replied.

"When you found mommy was anyone else there?"

Tears filled her eyes and her body quivered.

Izaak and I both grabbed her hands.

"It's okay niece. Speak your truth. We got your back. We not going to let anything happen to you."

"We got to the house and I ran to the door to put the key in. Gram Gram was getting Mel and Lele so I tried to hurry to the door. When I got in I ran to mama room and she was bloody. I looked at her window and I seen daddy. He said if I told he would kill me too. Then he raised down the window."

We all sat there stunned. None of us thought that nigga had the nerve to do some shit like this.

"Is that why you said he hurt mommy at the restaurant?"

"Yes...I was trying to tell you but you didn't get it."

"We all are going to make sure we keep you safe. We promise." I said sweeping her up in my arms.

"You okay to go back upstairs to check on Mel and Legacy?" Justin asked her.

"Yes, sir." She wiped her face and went upstairs.

Justin sat in her spot. "How did we miss this? How did we not suspect his ass? Then he showed up here trying to take the kids I heard."

"Yeah, I was here when he did that shit. I got dead on his ass. I ain't seen him since. His ass probably knows we would figure it out."

"Izaak has anyone seen his ass?" Justin asked.

"Not that I heard. Shit everybody thought it was me so don't nobody know to look out for that nigga."

"Let's keep it like that. The fewer people know, the better." Justin suggested.

"Look I gotta get up out of here so I can get the kids something to wear before everything closes. Let your mom know I will be by early to help get the kids ready. If that nigga comes by again... hit us up." I told

Justin.

"Man, if he shows up here nobody will know about it. I know too many ways to dismember a man." His face was cold and he was dead ass serious.

"Aight...either way we want a piece of that nigga."

We all shook up and headed out.

"Maaaannn we own this muthafuckin' city! How we can't find one damn man?" Izaak spat in frustration.

"Bro, we haven't been looking for that nigga. We were too busy beefing with each other. His scary ass could be anywhere by now."

"Nah, that nigga shot her in the head and tried to snatch his kids back. He ain't going nowhere with his arrogant ass. We have to make sure to keep an eye on the kids so he don't try to snatch them. We need to end this shit fast." Izaak was clearly anxious.

"Agreed. You want me to drop you off or you riding with me?"

"Shit, I can ride. I can't take them four walls no more."

"You think he going to show up at the funeral?" I asked Izaak.

"Shiiittt....he might."

ELISHA

I sat there in the meeting listening to all of the brave people coming forth bearing their truths. Hassim was sitting next to me and surprisingly I felt at ease. This wasn't a side I showed people. I battled my addiction with likeminded people in this room and my sponsor.

I stood to tell my truth. "I want to say that I'm still clean but with the death of my daughter I've been struggling recently with my addiction. I've gone as far as actually buying a small amount of cocaine to take the edge off and get rid of the pain temporarily but something in me fought when I didn't want to. It was no one but God who kept me because I've been having moments that I didn't want to be kept. I know my grandchildren need me at this time so I'm trying with everything in me to stay clean. I know I can do this. I have to do this. I worked too hard to get this far and I'm fearful every single day I got through this that I may fall off the wagon." My heart was beating in my throat as I choked out the words of my internal conflict. "Please keep me in your prayers."

They all clapped and some of the others in attendance came and hugged me.

I broke down in tears. I was astonished that I had any left. Every private moment I had I broke down at the thought of my baby being gone.

I wasn't able to call her on the phone or go to her house.

I would give anything to hold her one more time. She fought tooth and nail to overcome so much.

Against all odds, she clawed her way to a better life.

I felt like my chest was cracked open with a bone saw and my heart ripped out.

How? How was I supposed to live without my baby? How was I going to raise these kids?

"Are you okay?" Hassim asked pulling me from my thoughts that I was drowning in.

"I'm okay." I lied. "I'm ready to leave I have to get back to the kids."

"Okay."

I rode with Hassim. My nerves were so bad lately I was basically sleepwalking I was so deprived of rest.

We got into his car and he looked over at me. "I know what you are going through. My wife and daughter were murdered. The man I suspected I could never prove it. It was a long time ago but I miss them every single day. The hurt is always there but it gets better."

"I'm sorry to hear that. Who do you think killed them?"

"A man by the name of Sabastian Moreno. I had an informant on the inside and was able to hear him execute three people while I was on the phone. What? What is it? Is something wrong?"

I never could hide my facial expression and I was sure my light skin was beet red at this very moment.

"Sabastian is Asha's father..." I mumbled.

"What..."

"Yes, he's Asha's father. We're still legally married but I never changed my name. He always worried that someone may try to get to him by killing us one day so I wasn't allowed to take his name. Me or our children."

Hassim sat there and I wasn't able to read him. I could clearly see that he was in shock but I didn't have words for him.

He was assigned to catch the person that killed his nemesis' daughter.

Ironic could not even begin to describe this moment.

"Hassim, does this mean you're not going to work Asha's case now?" I needed to know.

"Absolutely not! You and Asha have nothing to do with what he did long ago. Elisha, I know this is not the right time but I want to let you know that I want to get to know you. I know you are going through it right now but I want to be the person you lean on. I want to be your person. We can take it as slow as you need but I haven't been able to stop thinking about you since the first time I laid eyes on you. You awakened something in me I thought died with my wife and daughter. I feel hope again. I know you don't need this right now b--"

"Hassim, if I haven't learned anything from losing my daughter I've learned that life is short. You have to live in as many moments as you are blessed with. I would like for us to start off as friends and let it evolve organically. Does that work for you?" I proposed.

"Absolutely. We can do this on your terms. Your way."

"Thank you."

"No thank you! I did have a question for you. It's the reason for me showing up to see you today. My partner came across some messages from Brian, the father of your daughter's children. We're making him a suspect. Do you think we can speak with your granddaughter? I understand if you say no. I can't imagine what that child is going through but we need her to nail this down into something solid."

"We can try. She's been really shaken up since everything happened. She may be sleep by the time we get home but we can set something up after the funeral. Or do you think we should do it before? It may be too much for her to relive after. Let me call my son and check if she's awake."

Justin's phone rang a few times and then he picked up.

"Hey, mama."

"Hey, baby. Amor sleep yet?"

"No, why you need me to do something?"

"The detective wanted to ask her about the night Asha died and if she saw Brian."

"That's crazy! Prod, Izaak and I just asked her about the same thing. She said he was there and he threatened her. But we are going to handle it ma' don't worry."

"Okay baby….I understand." I said ending the call.

"He said that she's sleeping. She hasn't mentioned anything about her father to him." I lied.

Lord forgive me but I wanted street justice for my daughter. The penitentiary wasn't good enough for him.

"Okay. We will have to try and interview her sometime after. We need to catch her while the details are fresh in her mind."

"Okay. I will stay on top it."

The detective dropped me off and I noticed the car Brian came by in last time parked down the street.

I frantically texted Justin to let him know.

Baby Boy: I see Brian's car parked down the street. Can't tell if he's in it. I'm pulling up now. Call Prodigy and Izaak NOW!!

I prayed that Brian didn't know Justin was back and thought I was home alone.

"Thank you Hassim. I will confirm everything with Amor in a couple of days."

"I can walk you to the door."

"No, it's fine." I tried to remain unbothered.

"Okay talk to you soon."

I jumped out of the car and high-paced it to the door.

I went inside and Justin was on the phone.

I waited until he was done. "So was the Prodigy?"

"Yes. They are on their way. They left not to long ago so they not that far. I don't need them to handle Brian mom."

"I know but do you know how to dispose of the body so that it doesn't trace back to you?"

"Of course. Prodigy doesn't want me to get my hands dirty. He said that the last thing I need is the Military Police on my ass and I agree."

We waited to see if Brian would knock on the door but nothing.

"Justin go check on the kids."

I had to weird feeling that something was off.

Thump! Thump! Ksssshh!

"Gram Gram!" I heard Amor yell at the top of her lungs.

I bolted up the stairs to find Brian and Justin tussling on the floor.

Justin was trying to wrestle a gun out of Brian's hands.

I immediately grabbed my grandbabies and headed to my room.

"Amor lock this door and don't come out no matter what!! Do you understand?"

"Bu-"

"No buts Amor! Do you understand?"

"Yes, Gram Gram." She cried.

My poor baby had been through so much.

I looked down at her pajamas and she had wet herself.

She did this when she was scared.

"I will be back to help you clean up I'm going to check on your Uncle J and your dad!"

Without waiting for her response I bolted back up the stairs.

POP!

As I planted my feet on the bottom step to head back toward them I heard the gun go off.

My heart dropped and I wasn't sure what I would find when I reached the top.

I grabbed a knife and ran upstairs to help my baby.

When I reached the top Justin managed to disarm Brian and put him in a submission hold.

I ran over to the gun that was near the dresser and put the gun between Brian's eyes.

"Why did you kill my baby you bastard? You made her suffer enough already you miserable ass son of a bitch!"

"She thought I was just going to let her leave me and have a baby with another nigga and live happily ever after! Fuck her! That bitch didn't deserve happiness! I kept telling her I was going to kill her fat ass and she thought I was a joke. She had that nigga jump on me and shit. I wasn't gone let that shit ride!"

Just as I was about to pull that damn trigger Prodigy grabbed the gun!

"What the hell you think you doing?" He snapped.

"I'm avenging my daughter! Why did you stop me?!" I cried.

"Look Justin take his ass out back. I will pick y'all up on the back street. Wait for me in the alley. The cops probably already on their way if the neighbors reported the gunshot."

WAP!

Prodigy took the butt of the gun and knocked Brian unconscious.

I watched Izaak and Justin drag him downstairs out the back door.

"Mom, these kids need you. Asha would be pissed if I allowed you to go to prison! We got this! I promise!"

413

I broke down in tears in his arms. I had so many mixed emotions.

I never thought I could take another life up until this moment.

"Y'all better get out of here. That detective just dropped me off and if he gets the call he may turn around and come back."

"Okay. I'm going to pick them up. That's all you need to know. I won't tell you any details about what we're getting ready to do. Just know Brian won't bother this family anymore." I said kissing her forehead. "This is why you have sons mom. We will always protect you and these kids with our lives. Lock the door behind me."

I nodded in understanding and did as he instructed.

I sat on the couch and grabbed my bible and held it to my chest.

"Lord forgive me."

PRODIGY

When I went outside I didn't notice anything. It was normal to hear gunshots in Rockford so many people didn't bother themselves unless the bullets were flying through their home.

"Took yo' ass long enough!" Izaak complained.

"I had to make sure Ms. Elisha was okay."

"Let's handle this at the warehouse," Izaak said.

"I already know."

The drive over was quiet.

Brian was still knocked out but Justin didn't take his eyes or the gun off of him.

"Y'all think this the gun he used to kill my sister?" His voice was cold and void of emotion.

"It don't matter. This nigga about to suffer. A gun is the last thing we using on this nigga." Izaak said.

The streets of Rockford was pretty much empty. It wasn't that late but it was a Friday and people were up in the club.

It took everything in me to do the speed limit but we couldn't afford to get pulled over right now.

We arrived at the garage.

"Justin stay inside. We about this clear everybody out of here." Izaak said. "Yo' Bear let me holla at you for a sec." He yelled out of the truck window.

"Wassup Bossman? Wassup P? Good to see you!"

"Clear this muthafucka out! You stay. Tell everybody else to get the fuck on. Now!"

"Aight!" He walked away from the car and yelled, "Y'all ain't got to go home but y'all got to get the hell out of here! Moooveeeeeee muthafuckas! Now! Before I get to popping you muthafuckas off on my mama!"

Within minutes we had the place to ourselves.

Justin dragged Brian from the truck causing his head to bump against the concrete.

A trail of blood followed behind as he dragged him.

Izaak threw some water on his face as we all surrounded him.

The fear in his eye was priceless.

"Nigga I know you ain't scared! You was talking cash money to my fuckin' mama my nigga!" Justin yelled rendering a violent kick to his face causing Brian's tooth to chip.

"Oh, really?" Izaak teased.

Izaak got off on shit like this. He was the one that normally handled this for those within our squad who violated.

He walked over and retrieved his baseball bat with nails protruding from the ends of the hook on the warehouse wall.

WAP!

WAP!

WAP!

He rendered three swings to Brian's legs and he screamed like a little bitch.

"You know we were going to come for yo' ass! Why you do some dumb ass shit like this?" Izaak asked him as if he genuinely wanted an answer.

"I didn't think y'all dumb asses would figure it out to be honest." He laughed with blood streaked spittle coming from his mouth.

"This nigga high as fuck!" Izaak yelled.

He was mad that Brian wasn't feeling the full effect of the torture we were rendering.

"P, why you so quiet?" Izaak asked me.

"I'm just trying to figure out why this nigga felt he had a right to take Asha from me. I loved that woman until the death of me and he didn't care one bit that he was taking her from her kids, mother and everyone else that loved her. All because his coward ass refused to stand up and be the man he knew damn well she deserved. He would rather drag her down into his hell and watch her suffer with him. Bitch made ass nigga. Bug take the lid off one of the barrels for me."

I snatched Brian of from the floor and dragged him by the back of his shirt as we followed behind Izaak.

"Man fuck all of y'all muthafuckas! I'll see ya' in hell!" He laughed and screamed as he was being dragged.

He lifted the rusted lid and I pushed Brian's head down in the battery acid.

He kicked and tried to fight back but Justin and Izaak helped.

We held him there until he stopped moving.

When we pulled him out all of his skin was melted off of his face. His eyes were just blood filled sockets that his brain oozed from.

We let his body hit the concrete as he ceased to breathe.

"Bear chop us his body and put him back in the barrel. You know what to do after that." Izaak instructed him.

Bear nodded in understanding.

We all headed back to the car. We had our fill of revenge and didn't speak on Brian again for the remainder of the night.

It was as if it never happened but the pure satisfaction confirmed it did.

*   *   *

I arrived at Ms. Elisha' early the next morning to help with the kids. There was a peace across her face that words couldn't describe.

We all made it to the funeral where we celebrated Asha's life.

We buried her in Sunset Funeral Home out in Machesney Park.

"Ashes to ashes, dust to dust." Tears filled all of our eyes as the pastor spoke while they lowered Asha's body into her grave.

Everyone walked away once it was completed and I just stood there. I stood there with so many regrets with so many dreams unfulfilled with my love. My heart was being lowered into the ground with her body.

It just didn't seem real.

My chest was so tight I thought my heart was going to pop out on the ground like a piece of bread in a toaster.

Everything was starting to spin and I felt sick to my stomach. How was I going to live without this woman? How?

Tears poured from me like Niagara Falls and I was undone. Ripping at the very seams of my existence.

Asha was the very air I breathed. How was I to survive without her?

I felt a hand grab mine and I looked over. It was Uneek.

"I got you P. It's okay. I know she looking down on you and the kids. I know she proud of you. You were her world and her everything." She comforted me.

We both just stood there hand in hand trying to figure out how we will live without the person our hearts loved most.

Excerpt from Damage Control (Standalone)

CHAPTER ONE

KINCAIDE

I opened my eyelids but closed them in a hurry. The sun was piercing my sockets and it pained me to fight against it. I was known as the bad boy venture capitalist. Peopled loved to hate me but my money made them respect me.

My nights were spent hosting parties where booze and drugs were passed around like a collection plate on a jam-packed Sunday morning.

I would often wake up with women I didn't recognize praying that a random disease wasn't left lingering long after the night was over.

"Hey," I pushed the body next to me.

She didn't move but I felt something wet.

"I know you didn't throw up in my bed!" I

snapped.

I no longer cared about the blazing sun, I only wanted whoever this was out of my bed.

"Oh, my God!"

The wetness I touched wasn't vomit…it was blood!

"AAARRGGGHHHH!" I screamed from the top of my lungs.

I tumbled onto the floor in shock.

I could only see hair and had no idea who ended up in the bed with me.

Her caramel skin was adorned with deep lacerations. The blood had dried and her hair was beginning to stick to the cuts.

I fumbled around on the floor looking for my boxers and phone but couldn't find either. She had a whole in her head as if someone succeeded on bashing her skull in.

There was no way I did this! Did I?

I couldn't remember anything from last night. This wasn't uncommon but normally my bodyguard made sure I got to bed alright.

Sometimes I could get violent and crazy when I had the wrong combination of pills and liquor. The only way Bravon would leave when I was like that is if I were trying to fight him. Rather than having things escalate he would just leave and come and check on me first thing in the morning.

I was paying him to protect me not babysit me so it wasn't really his job to sit there and watch me all night to make sure I didn't do anything stupid.

I tripped over my own feet running out of my bedroom. I was trying to figure out if anyone else was left from the party last night.

My house was trashed but not one person was left in sight. I pulled up the security cameras and the footage in my room had been erased.

There was no evidence of what happened last night.

I picked up my house phone and called Bravon. Before I could dial the last digit, he was already walking through the front door.

The coffee in his hands would normally be just what I needed to get my day started but today it only contributed to my unsettled stomach.

"What happened last night?"

He sat the coffee on the bar

"Man, I don't know what you were on last night but you were in rare form. I had to leave before me and you came to blows."

"There's a dead girl in my bed."

"Oh, you killed that kitty cat huh," he nudged me laughing.

"No nigga, she dead dead!"

"Like in not breathing dead?"

"How else can I say this broad ain't living no more?"

"How did you kill her?"

"I ain't no killer man! I'm a nerd with swag! I ain't no killer. I'm being set-up!"

"Man, you been all on the news for domestic issues the past two months. You are fighting a lawsuit from the one girl that said you took her phone and tossed it in the street after she tried to record you leaving the club."

"Listen, I don't want to hear all that right

now. Can you just go upstairs and see who she is?"

Panic swelled up inside me, threatening to swallow me belly-first as he ascended the staircase.

"Oh my God! We need to call 911 now!" He sped by me.

"Wait hold on let's get our story together!"

"Nigga ain't no our! That girl is dead as a doorknob. I'm not going down as no accessory to murder!"

I felt helpless as I watched Bravon dial 911. He was right. I couldn't drag him further into this as he already was.

I was on the brink of a billion-dollar deal. This was the last thing I needed. It was the reason I celebrated so hard last night. I guess my celebration was a bit premature.

How was I going to prove my innocence if I couldn't remember anything?

The one person that could help me hates my guts.

I can't blame Nykee. I did what I did with the best intentions but it wasn't worth losing her now that I look back. I was overly ambitious but what I did made me the millionaire I am today.

I did what I could to make it right but once you crossed Nykee she was done with you. She doesn't forgive or forget.

My body was weighted in place by the new uncertainty of my future. My arrogance and pride have finally landed me in a place I never imagined.

I'm not built for prison. What am I going to do?

CHAPTER TWO

NYKEE

I danced around my house listening to Ciara's *Level Up*. It was my morning motivation song. I rolled my hips in my tank top and thong as I ran my hand across my magenta business suit. I swirled my black lace bodysuit around my pointer finger as I dropped it low one time.

Everything meant to destroy me in life I overcame it. I deserve the freedom this joy gave me. As I twirled in front of the window I saw my neighbors the Johnson's out exercising. She had just given birth to their son a little over a month ago.

I watched him push the stroller and he hyped his wife up, "You got this baby! Don't stop get it, get it!"

Her smile was spread from ear to ear as he encouraged her. There was so much love in their eyes for one another.

I no longer had the desire to share my life

with anyone. My empire I was building was my baby.

Nykee Isadore & Associates specialized in "fixing" the scandals of multimillionaires, CEO's, and some celebrities. I was the real-life Olivia Pope in these Houston streets.

My business allows me to cuddle up next to my seven-figure bank account under my white plush duvet.

People love to make it seem like because you're an intelligent, successful, single black woman that you're bitter. I'm not bitter though, I'm better.

It only took me to get my heart broke to drive home the realization that my time could be spent doing more productive, profitable things. In order for a man to get me to slow down he must come all the way correct.

I refuse to compromise for the sake of having someone to make my toes spread and my legs shake. I need sustenance and loyalty.

If I can't build with you or trust you while I'm working crazy hours to cover up other people's mess then I don't need you.

I've witnessed some things that will make

wonder if love really exists. The things people do to someone they claim to love baffles me. It wasn't just that. I've been on the receiving end of betrayal and I was good on that.

Success and a fat bank account was just as good as any orgasm. Besides, if I want one that bad, I can always pay for one.

My pants clung to my butt just the way I liked. The wire in my lace bodysuit had my chocolate mounds sitting up ready to get to work.

I grabbed my oversized Chanel bag I was using a briefcase and headed to the office. I loved what I did. I fixed things. It didn't matter how messy, illegal, or dangerous I was gifted to make things go away.

I had a small team that was able to dig up anything or find anyone. Situations were like the internet. Nothing goes away for good.

It was only eight o'clock in the morning, but it was already a scorching eighty degrees in Houston. My house was near the galleria which was close to downtown where my office was.

People were speeding so fast it made you think they were about to crash but just as they were, they would jump into another lane.

The thing was none of us were going anywhere because the morning traffic was always bumper to bumper.

"Hit my car if you want to!" I screamed out my window to the car behind me.

The driver flicked me off and I returned the favor.

After using every profanity in the book, I finally arrived at my office.

Chachi was at his computer. He was our computer specialist and hacker. The feds were on to him when I came to his rescue. I used one of my favors that burned a bridge when I was done.

Chachi was worth it though. I had to have him on my team. I didn't just bring anyone on. Each one of them served a purposed and meshed well with my personality. D'Mario was the muscle. He was doing what he did every morning, he was cleaning every gun we had in the infantry. Sometimes when we fixed things, we had to cross some lines.

D'Mario was facing life in prison after a double homicide. He was framed for his wife and daughter's murder and showed up instantly. They were trying to bury him because he once worked for the government as a stealth operative. D'Mario could be sitting in your kitchen waiting for you and leave without anyone ever knowing he was there. There wouldn't be a lick of evidence.

Then there was Larriel. She was bae. When you think of her think of Sunshine from *Harlem Nights*. If I could patent her, clone her, and sell her a million times over I would. She was flawless and she specializes in bending men's will. She was more than just a pretty face though. Her deep chocolate skin was mesmerizing. Her locks were neat and always styled in a way I've never seen before. Larriel's IQ is a one forty and you wouldn't be able to tell because she was so ghetto sometimes. It was all a facade.

I saw Larriel in action at an upscale strip club one night. She was a bottle girl but I watched her worked those credit cards and overcharge the entire night. The men I wasn't surprised to see her scam. It was how she even got over on the women that solidified my decision to put her on my team.

I paid them all well but most of all I loved them. Working with them over the past five years showed me how hurt all three of them were. I'm sure they have seen my pain as well.

It was our brokenness that bonded us. Our skill that strengthened us. Our loyalty that made us family. We would kill for each other without even blinking. We were all that we had.

"Hey babes!" I sang flicking D'Mario's strand of locks as I passed him.

"Stop playing," he complained.

"You know you love it," I stuck my tongue out and headed to my office. "Larriel, what's on the agenda for the day?"

"I know you don't like stuff like this, but a handler reached out to us today for a job. They've been noticeably quiet about the details of the assignment, but they want to pay you a quarter of a million dollars just to show up to a meeting today."

"Meeting where?"

"A restaurant a few blocks away."

"What time?"

"Noon."

"I want my money as soon as I sit down."

"They've already sent half."

"Really?"

I was intrigued and six figures was my weakness.

"Here's what I want you to do. Get our security firm on the phone. I need at least fifty guards all dressed in randomly colored suits. Have Chachi hack the reservation list and get all of them in. I'm not going in here blind and this sounds fishy. I don't care though for this amount of money but ain't' nobody about to play in my face today. It's money making Monday baaaby," I high-fived her.

She turned her lips up and swung her hips in agreement. Her hands were raised in the air as she snapped her fingers. There was nothing more than Larriel loved than to check a bag. That's why she was my best friend.

She was the first one I added to my team. I met her at the strip club when I was getting over Kincaide. I was in a bad place but watching everything, mainly her.

Larriel was my best friend. We hustled so hard fixing messes that we paid for the building our office was in off the muscle.

I always asked her what she wanted to do but she always replied, "I'm rocking with you until the wheels fall off friend."

She's been loyal to the core since day one and I would easily lay down my life for this woman.

I was excited about the easy money just for a meeting, but I wouldn't be me if I didn't question who would pay such a huge amount of money just for a meeting.

Fourth of July weekend had just passed so ain't no telling who did something stupid.

I've seen at least four stories pop up on my phone. I didn't recognize any of them, but they were some heavy hitters.

The few hours I had left before the meeting flew by quickly. I was buried elbows deep in fixing my next scandal when D'Mario stuck his head in the door.

"Hey, I'm coming with you, right?"

"Our security team will be there. I should be good."

"They not me Ny so stop playing with me."

"I'm not but I don't know who this is. I

don't need them to see you. You know you my secret weapon."

"Yeah, Yeah. Sounds good. I'll let you have it right now but I'm not feeling this at all. I'm going to be watching everything through your camera phone and listening in."

"Okay."

D'Mario was very protective over me. Man, I held him a lot of nights while he cried himself to sleep. You don't know heartbreak until you see a black man cry his heart out from a pain you can't fix.

We've been bonded like glue since. If anything happens to me, he's going to burn Houston to the ground.

I grabbed my blazer from the back of my chair along with my phone and headed to my meeting.

I didn't bring much else because with D'Mario listening in I would have all that I needed if I decided to take the case on.

I was arrived on time.

"Do you have a reservation?" The waitress asked.

"Yes. Isadore is the last name."

I waited until she found my name on the list.

"Your party is already waiting for you."

I followed the waitress to the back of the restaurant. It was dim but other people were still seated enjoying lunch.

I smiled as I passed them. Apart from four people all the other patrons were from the security company. I was pleasantly pleased.

I wanted to run and scream but my body became petrified stone. I drew up a shallow breath to speak but couldn't.

"Nykee," Mrs. McAllistor greeted me.

What was she doing here and why would she pay so much money to speak with me?

I didn't see Kincaide's name in any of the media hits today.

One thing I despised with a passion was being caught off-guard. How did Chachi miss this? I couldn't wait to get back to the office.

"Please, take a seat my dear."

"Mrs. McAllistor why did you bring me here?"

"Because you wouldn't help him otherwise," her head lifted as her eyes shifted to the right over my shoulder.

"Hello Nykee," Kincaide's baritone voice bellowed like a bass guitar over the perfect beat.

My stubbornness wouldn't allow me to return the greeting. I thought I was over him but seeing him within arm's reach made resentment boil deep in my bowels.

I shot him a sour look letting him know not to play with me.

I would always quickly exit out of any media coverage involving him. I was so afraid to be alone after our split. The woman I was is not the same one standing before him today.

His natural sandy colored curls were spread wildly over his head. His rose covered lips were moisturized and made me remember what they once tasted like. I despised him but fat ma' was nearly jumping out of my slacks. It be your own cat sometimes.

"Nykee, you know I wouldn't be here if it

wasn't life or death. Please hear him out for me."

"You know I would do anything for you Mrs. McAllister."

She hated what happened between us. My mother died from breast cancer when I was eighteen. She took on somewhat of a mother role while I was dating her son. It seemed fake at times, but I pushed my paranoia aside and embraced someone trying to be there for me. I still sent her something every Mother's Day and Christmas.

I hated Kincaide but I loved his mother to death. I just couldn't see her because I was too afraid of running into him. So, I called her every now and again and sent her extravagant gifts.

She also made me meet with her once a month for brunch and afterwards we got our nails done.

"Kee-"

"Don't call me that."

"Nykee. I woke up in the bed this morning with a dead girl. Mom was able to pull some strings to keep it under wraps for now and keep me out of jail but it's only a matter of time before the media get a hold of this story. You're the only one that can prove that I'm innocent."

"Are you?"

"Nykee, I'm a lot of things but I'm no killer."

"Humph."

"Please, you're the only one that can fix this. I will pay you any amount you want. You know I'm not a killer."

"I don't know anything."

"Please baby. You know he's all that I have."

I looked at the desperation in her eyes and there was no way I could say no to her.

"I know but it's going to cost him."

"He'll pay whatever you want."

"I'm only doing this for you," I stressed to her.

"I know. Thank you, baby," the tears poured from her eyes.

"I'll get my people on this. Kincaide I'll be

in touch. I'll need you to come to my office so we can go over some details."

"Just let me know when to be there."

I didn't dignify his response with an answer.

I nodded to my security team and as I stood to walk out my fifty-guards stood and walked out behind me.

It looked like scene out of a mob movie or something.

Before I could make it across the threshold, I received a notification that the remaining balance was transferred to my business account.

I loved Mrs. McAllistor but I'm not sure if I was ready to invite Nykee back into my space for any dollar amount.

CHAPTER THREE

LARRIEL

"Larriel, get your narrow behind out here neeoooww!" Nykee screamed my name from the top of her lungs.

I knew it was Kincaide's mother the entire time that wanted to meet with her but there is no way that I could tell her honoree butt that.

First, there was no way we were passing up that amount of money which she would've if she'd known it was about him. Second, she won't admit it but she still has unresolved issues with him that she needs to face head on.

"What's going on?" D'Mario asked.

He anchored his attention on me and Nykee.

"You knew the entire time that it was his mom that wanted to meet with me!"

"It was to much money to pass up and you know it Ny."

"I don't care about none of that! Now you have his mama asking me to help this fool."

"Help him what?" D'Mario interjected.

"He woke up with a dead body in the bed."

"Oh, he did that," D'Mario said matter-of-factly.

"You don't know that. Why didn't you hear any chatter about it on the net Chachi?"

"I'm not sure. If he knows the right people, they can suppress it. Had I known to look into him I could've found something before the meeting," a groan accompanied the roll of his eyes. "Let me pull the police report and 911 call. I'll let you know what I find," he informed her.

"Are we taking this case?" D'Mario asked.

He lowkey has a thing for Nykee but she's to driven to see it. She thinks he's protective of her because of all the horrible things she helped him through but it was more to him.

D'Mario is a good dude too. His chiseled bronze body didn't hurt either. His bowlegs were rippled with muscles. I tried to give him some but he rerouted me harder than a dead man's curve. He was meticulous about keeping his strong hands manicured. It was weird because he was known for beating a man within an inch of his life with those same hands.

Chachi was the opposite. His slender body was beefy but average. His hair was tapered and he prided himself on keeping it properly lubricated as if it was a vagina or something.

"So, are we taking the case?" I echoed D'Mario's question once we were in her office.

"I don't know. I know he's the only child and he know I love his mama even though he's the stuff at the bottom of a garbage bag.

"You mean garbage bag juice?"

"Yeah, exactly that," she pointed at me.

I watched her walk over and fill her diffuser with purified drinking water. The lemongrass smell filled the air immediately.

Nykee was obsessed with aromatherapy. It was one of the things she used to keep herself balanced.

She stood there staring out the window. I know she was searching for the right thing to do.

"It's okay to be nervous about being around him Ny. After what he did to you no one can blame you about being hesitant."

"All the memories are hitting me all over again. I feel like I'm reliving them all over Larriel. Finding out that negro cleaned out our bank account when I tried to pay for my wedding dress. The humiliation. The wasted money. I had to rescind my wedding invitations only to see him a week later closing on a million-dollar deal."

She stood there shaking, a low groaning sound bubbling from her mouth.

I went up behind her and wrap my arms around her in a bear hug.

"You got us now. We ain't letting nothing happen to you and you know that," I assured her.

"Ny you need this closure and tax him on the invoice with a broken heart fee," I nudged her.

The right side of her mouth pulled up at the corner into a half smile.

"Let's see what Chachi found out first," she said.

I followed her back into the conference room where Chachi was ready to brief us on what he found out.

"Let's hear head Honcho Chacho," I teased.

"That's corny but I'll proceed anyway. He didn't just kill anyone; it was renowned philanthropist Curtis Smith's daughter! The only reason they were able to keep it quiet is his family paid everyone off. She's listed as a Jane Doe as of right now. The officers on the scene are taking their sweet time with the report details. The detectives can't move forward until they have all the facts. They mislabeled some evidence but none of this is going to matter once this hits the media."

"It already has," my mouth dropped as I increased the volume on the T.V.

"Kincaide McAllister is known as the bad boy venture capitalist with his many run-ins with the law and court system. Despite his controversial social life, it hasn't stopped corporations from begging him to sit on their boards. Everything he touches in corporate America turns to gold but is the young soon to be billionaire sabotaging his career with all his recent antics? That groundbreaking business deal just may be finito. As of right

now the dead victim found in his bed is listed as Jane Doe. Her name once identified will not be released until her family has been notified."

"Okay, we still have a bit of time to try and get ahead of this. Larriel contact the McAllister's and tell them we'll take the case for and additional five-hundred thousand. Let them know the fee stand whether we can get him off or not. That's non-negotiable. I'm cutting them a deal because we're dealing with the daughter of a heavy hitter for God's sake," she sighed.

Nykee was about to burn some bridges taking this case on. She's not an attorney but once people found out she was trying to fix this it's going to be smoke in the city.

Mainly from Mr. Smith's son whom we're always having to clean up behind. He's going to see this as the ultimate betrayal and try to take us down with Kincaide.

Maybe I didn't think this all the way through.

ABOUT THE AUTHOR

"There is no greater agony than bearing an untold story inside."
Maya Angelou

This holds true for Shaunessy as she has always had a passion for writing. Shaunessy has always had a passion for writing.

As a little girl she would make paper handwritten books out of notebook paper and crayons. She even copied some of her favorite books word for word just for fun. Her seventh-grade teacher told her she had a way with words and that she would one day be famous for her words.

Shaunessy is new on the urban fiction scene. She is determined to make her mark among the greats; while giving her readers a twist on common situations some of us have dealt with.

She believes that everything around us is a possible story to share with the world.

Shaunessy lives in Houston, TX with her husband.

If you have any questions or would like to interact please add her on:

Facebook: Author Shaunessy or follow her on

Instagram: @Author_Shaunessy.

Website: www.shaunessyb.com

Also, via email info@shaunessyb.com.

www.ingramcontent.com/pod-product-compliance
Lightning Source LLC
Chambersburg PA
CBHW071635260626
47170CB00001B/107